Praise for *Fiona and Jane*

A *Time*, NPR, and *Vulture* Best Book of the Year
A Belletrist Book Club Pick

"Over the course of the book Fiona and Jane become real and electric and precious people. The stories move through intimate, cinematic scenes. . . . The world Ho creates between the two women feels like one friend reading the other's story, wishing she were there. . . . Even to those not from Los Angeles, Ho's debut collection feels like a shared experience."
    —Tammy Tarng, *The New York Times Book Review*

"*Fiona and Jane* captures the textures of female friendship and all the intensity, loyalty, and occasional torment of it."
    —Ailsa Chang, NPR's *All Things Considered*

"Ho's debut work is the perfect modern example of great American fiction. It's a brilliant series of stories about the lives of two Taiwanese American women and their friendship over twenty years as they explore identity, sexuality, heartbreak, and family secrets. . . . What a great read! I feel like Fiona and Jane are friends of mine. I cannot wait to see what Ho writes next. *Fiona and Jane* brings you into the lives of these women in a relatable, authentic way. You will love it."   —Jake Tapper

"Jean Chen Ho's debut collection . . . evokes a distinctive multiethnic Asian American experience coming of age in Los Angeles in the late twentieth century: R&B mixtapes, Cool Water cologne, red faces drunk on soju. . . . Through shifting perspectives and evocative milieus (from night markets to seedy Korean bars and exclusive clubs), the assemblage comes as close to a primer on modern L.A. Asian American rites of passage as anything in recent memory."   —Lisa Wong Macabasco, *Vogue*

"Ho's strong debut follows two Taiwanese American besties from grade school through their thirties, flipping through decades to highlight key relationships, crises, nights of drinking, and sex. Other people, the world, and the girls themselves change, but the friendship between beautiful Fiona and sturdy Jane endures."

—*People*

"A refreshingly honest treatment of long-term friendships—particularly their inexorable ebb and flow. Story by story, the book captures the way friendships negotiate their own boundaries, at times dissolving unexpectedly and at others flourishing into something more, even if just fleetingly."

—Meena Venkataramanan, *Los Angeles Times*

"A confidently nonlinear debut collection that sluices through the interiority of its protagonists without diminishing the passion and powerfully mysterious intimacy of female friendship."

—*Vulture* ("The Best Books of the Year [So Far]")

"Intricately rendered . . . *Fiona and Jane* celebrates a woman's ability to be late, to show up in their own lives when and where they want to, to change their minds, to be lonely and to be in love, and to be respected regardless."

—Rosa Boshier, *The Washington Post*

"Ho renders both women so real that they begin to feel like people you've encountered and hung out with. . . . It's precisely the fact that the women's trials and tribulations feel refreshingly life-sized that makes the book ring so beautifully, sometimes terribly, true." —Ilana Masad, NPR.org

"This debut collection navigates the intimate contours of female friendship through the eponymous women, Fiona and Jane, who grow up together in Los Angeles and drift apart when Fiona moves to New York."

—*Oprah Daily* ("The 50 Most Anticipated Books of 2022")

"Judging by the cover alone, you can tell *Fiona and Jane* is probably going to be one of the hot girl subway books in 2022."
—*W Magazine* ("The Most Anticipated Books of 2022")

"Jean Chen Ho's *Fiona and Jane* follows the eponymous Taiwanese American duo over the course of twenty years. After growing up together in California, the two best friends are separated when Fiona lights out for New York—a move that leaves Jane to deal with her father's untimely death without her BFF by her side."   —*Bustle*

"While an intimate portrait of friendship, *Fiona and Jane* also tackles themes around sexuality, social class, immigration, family secrets, mental health, and Asian American identity."
—*Fortune*

"Chen Ho is a masterful storyteller. . . . In a world that is increasingly defined by social media connections, the waxing and waning of Fiona and Jane's bond reaffirms that close, in-person friendships still have a chance."
—Susan Blumberg-Kason, *Asian Review of Books*

"[An] astounding [book] about adult friendships and two remarkable women who aren't quite sure if they still fit together like they did when they were children."   —*POPSUGAR*

"Compelling . . . Fiona and Jane—both earnest, curious and heart-full—epitomize the realities of growing up in America as young women, as immigrants, as Asian Americans. . . . By the [book's] end, readers will feel as though they carry some part of these women with them, as if Fiona and Jane are our friends, as if their stories might yet overlap with our own."
—*BookPage* (starred review)

"I have long maintained that there aren't nearly enough books centered on the intricate, fascinating complexities of close female friendship, and I'm so glad to learn that Ho's novel *Fiona and Jane* follows a deep friendship between two Taiwanese American women. I must read this book. Publishers, please give us more books about friendship."

—R. O. Kwon, *Electric Literature* ("61 Books by Women of Color to Read in 2022")

"These linked stories lovingly and unflinchingly explore the complications of familial relationships, shifting notions of home, and how friendship can be both a wound and a balm."

—Tiffany Babb, *Observer*

"Brutally honest, tender, funny, and . . . with characters that will stay with you long after reading."

—Erica Ezeifedi, *Book Riot*

"With *Fiona and Jane*, Jean Ho announces herself as a bold and provocative new talent to watch out for. In this sexy and stylish set of stories about friendship, love, loyalty, and betrayal, she fearlessly delves into the intimacies between women and delivers a knockout of a book."

—Viet Thanh Nguyen, Pulitzer Prize–winning author of *The Sympathizer* and *The Committed*

"Unsentimental, subtly subversive, and always surprising, Jean Chen Ho's beautiful debut *Fiona and Jane* glides me into revelations about the ambiguities of friendship, queer sexuality, and love. I rarely read portraits of friendships like that of Fiona and Jane, two flawed women who are each other's constants throughout the crossroad in their lives. Jean Chen Ho is not afraid to give us a funny, unresolved, and very *real* portrait of Asian Americans just getting by in L.A. and New York. I love this book."

—Cathy Park Hong, author of Pulitzer Prize finalist *Minor Feelings*

"If you're looking for a book about female friendship, look no further than Jean Chen Ho's *Fiona and Jane*."   —*Marie Claire*

"*Fiona and Jane* is a high-wire act of a collection, the stories born of the experiments in daring you feel around the friend you are sure will always be there. Amid the intricate fretwork of ad hoc desires, missing family, and rehearsals for adulthood, a cool-handed nerve shapes it all—Jean Chen Ho's brilliant debut is as assured as what must surely follow."
    —Alexander Chee, author of national bestseller *The Queen of the Night* and *How to Write an Autobiographical Novel*

"Loving and fierce, sharp and emotionally resonant, *Fiona and Jane* is not only the story of two best friends as they grow into adulthood—it's a love letter to Asian American women's friendship, in all of its most beautiful and heartbreaking iterations."
    —Lisa Ko, author of National Book Award finalist *The Leavers*

"A brilliant examination into young life and told in a brilliant fashion. Jean Chen Ho has created two of the most memorable characters in recent fiction."   —*Debutiful*

"I loved every one of these vibrant, sharply observed stories that explore the complexities of friendship, love, lust, youth, and identity. Jean Chen Ho's writing is spiky, surprising, and funny, suffused with wit and sadness. On top of all that, she writes about Southern California with specificity and insight, mapping corners of it that I haven't seen before in fiction. A striking debut from a very talented writer."
    —Charles Yu, National Book Award–winning author of *Interior Chinatown*

"*Fiona and Jane* is the book I did not know I was waiting to be written—one that brilliantly examines what it feels like to be young and woman and hungry for a meaningful life right now. Via language that is tender, shot through with humor and undergirded with lyricism, Jean Chen Ho has created a universe of mothers, daughters, lovers, and, vitally, friends who become sisters. Read this remarkable work of fiction and feel the world open up around you."

—Angela Flournoy, author of National Book Award finalist
The Turner House

"Wondrous . . . I loved how the stories were told from alternating perspectives and how we got a fuller portrait of both women through each new tale."   —*Alma*

"Told in each of their voices, this debut centers on the intensity, resentment, and love of female friendships."

—Sarah Stiefvater, *PureWow*

"In this tender and timeless debut, Chen Ho explores the intimate facets of female friendship, Asian American immigrant experiences in Los Angeles and New York, and the debilitating power of family traumas."   —*Booklist*

"Jean Chen Ho has created an iconic pair of friends who are messy and sexy and so thoroughly alive that I'm pretty sure we once snuck into a club together. Joyously specific and true, *Fiona and Jane* is my new favorite book."

—Jade Chang, author of *The Wangs vs. the World*

"Intimate . . . Ho excels at creating characters whose struggles feel deeply human. This packs in plenty of insights about love and friendship."   —*Publishers Weekly*

"Ho's adept captures of childhood confusion, teenage angst, and adult malaise lend the stories a universality that is not undermined by her equally precise dissections of racial and sexual issues facing Fiona and Jane. . . . Readers will wish for a Fiona or Jane in their own lives."   —*Kirkus Reviews*

PENGUIN BOOKS

FIONA AND JANE

Jean Chen Ho has a PhD in literature and creative writing from the University of Southern California, and an MFA from the University of Nevada, Las Vegas. Her writing has been published in *The New York Times Magazine*, *The Cut*, *Electric Literature*, *Los Angeles Times*, *Georgia Review*, and elsewhere. She is the 2023 Mary Routt Endowed Chair of Writing at Scripps College. Born in Taiwan and raised in Southern California, she currently lives in Los Angeles.

You can visit the author's website at jean-chen-ho.com.

Look for the Penguin Readers Guide in the back of this book.
To access Penguin Readers Guides online,
visit penguinrandomhouse.com.

FIONA
and
JANE

Jean Chen Ho

PENGUIN BOOKS

PENGUIN BOOKS
An imprint of Penguin Random House LLC
penguinrandomhouse.com

First published in the United States of America by Viking,
an imprint of Penguin Random House LLC, 2022
Published in Penguin Books 2023

The following stories were published previously in
different form: "Doppelgängers" in *Guernica*; "Korean Boys
I've Loved" in *Apogee*; "The Movers" in *The Offing*; and
"The Night Market" in *The Georgia Review*.

ISBN 9780593296066 (paperback)

THE LIBRARY OF CONGRESS HAS CATALOGED THE
HARDCOVER EDITION AS FOLLOWS:
Names: Ho, Jean Chen, author.
Title: Fiona and Jane / Jean Chen Ho.
Description: New York : Viking, [2022]
Identifiers: LCCN 2021011938 (print) | LCCN 2021011939 (ebook) |
ISBN 9780593296042 (hardcover) | ISBN 9780593296059 (ebook)
Subjects: LCSH: Taiwanese Americans—Fiction. | LCGFT: Short stories.
Classification: LCC PS3608.O14 F56 2021 (print) |
LCC PS3608.O14 (ebook) | DDC 813/.6—dc23
LC record available at https://lccn.loc.gov/2021011938
LC ebook record available at https://lccn.loc.gov/2021011939

Printed in the United States of America
1st Printing

Designed by Alexis Farabaugh

For my family, near and far

In memory of Sarah Trueway Lin

"I have always felt that a human being could only be saved by another human being. I am aware that we do not save each other very often. But I am also aware that we save each other some of the time."

—James Baldwin, *Nothing Personal*

CONTENTS

FIONA
and
JANE

The Night Market

My last evening in Taiwan, my father wanted to show me Shilin Night Market. We rode the subway, transferring at Taipei Main Station for the northbound red line. Saturday night, the market was jammed with people strolling up and down the arteries of the main thoroughfare. Baba and I dragged along with the crowd, pausing here and there to browse the wares. We'd made up from the fight in the car driving down Yangmingshan yesterday, at least for now. He'd promised to rethink the new university contract and seriously consider coming back to the States for good.

The air was saturated by the scent of grilled meat, custard pudding and red bean pies, propane fumes and human sweat. Deep house music pumped out of every other storefront speaker, as vendors shouted into megaphones pointed at the passing hordes: *Two-for-one ladies cotton underwear! Genuine leather sandals for men! Motorola flip phones unlocked here! DVDs! CDs! Come take a look!*

At the food section in the back of the market, Baba stood in line to order us bowls of oyster vermicelli while I staked out seats at the communal tables set up in the center of the stalls. We dipped into the noodles. The oysters floated on top, fat and glistening like polished jewels.

"Listen, mei. There's one more person who wanted to see you before you leave," Baba said, between bites.

I asked if it was another relative. If Baba sensed my irritation, he didn't show it.

Before this trip, I hadn't seen my father in two and a half years, since he took this job. In the last week—my spring break—I'd barely spent any time with him alone. Every day, another banquet dinner with dozens of cousins, uncles and aunties, family friends who asked if I remembered them from the last time I visited the island, when I was just a kid.

"You can call him Uncle Lee," he said. One of his college buddies, my father explained. For a second, he looked like he had more to add. "He's been a good friend to me," he said finally.

"That's him over there now." Baba lifted a hand and waved.

The man waved back and made his way to our table. He moved with the compressed energy of a wrestler, his chin slightly down, arms swinging deliberately, as if ready to grapple at a moment's notice. Lee wore a red tank top with a cartoon duck printed on the chest, the hem tucked into a pair of tight black jeans, an FOB outfit that would've caught stares back home, but here he looked cool, I thought.

"My baby daughter," Baba said.

"Uncle Lee," I said in Mandarin. "Pleased to meet you."

"Sit down, sit down!" He offered his hand to me, and I shook it. "A big lady, tall like Old Shen here."

"She takes after her mother more than me—"

"I should hope so, with your teeth," said Lee, and they both laughed. He extracted a blue handkerchief from the nylon fanny pack around his waist and wiped down his face, which gleamed with sweat. "Much hotter here than LA, right? And it's only March." He gestured toward the empty Styrofoam bowls on the table. "You like Taiwanese food? Even the broiled intestines in the vermicelli?"

"My daughter eats very well."

"Wah! Like you, then." Lee jabbed a finger into my father's side.

"Uncle Lee, have you eaten yet?"

Lee smiled. "She's quite mature. Good manners." He glanced at my father approvingly. "All foreign-born girls, not this way. Sometimes you hear stories about overseas children."

I felt my cheeks warm under Lee's scrutiny.

"And your Mandarin isn't bad," he said. "I thought your father was exaggerating, going on about 'My daughter Jane doing this and that, memorized the periodic table when she was only twelve, super number one classical piano.'"

"My mother stuck me in Saturday Chinese school for years," I said. "Baba bribed me with McDonald's."

"Lee and I used to compete in the university badminton courts," Baba said. I was glad for the subject change. "When I moved back here, I went looking for a game at those same courts, and I saw him there, believe it or not."

"In our college days, the girls crowded the bleachers," Lee said. "Just to catch a glimpse of your father in those white athletic shorts."

"Lee! Don't make up stories."

"Sometimes he even played bare chest," Lee said, grinning. He pantomimed pulling off his shirt with a flourish of his arms. "Quite a scene you created, brother."

"You, Baba?"

"Not me," he replied. "You must be remembering someone else, Lee."

"Don't be so modest," said Lee. "Your father was the school prince."

Baba shook his head.

"We all knew he'd be the one to go to America."

"I was lucky, that's all," said my father.

"Luck!" Lee exclaimed. "You're brilliant. You worked hard—"

"I made certain choices," Baba said. "Left or right—"

"Like deciding to move back here," I said, with more force than I intended. "And stay here," I added. "Or was that luck?"

A silence. Then Lee laughed lightly, a sound almost as if he were clearing his throat. He exchanged a look with my father, and I saw something pass between them, the wordless language adults believe only they know how to speak. My father was silently apologizing to Lee: My daughter is a moody, sensitive girl prone to bursts of emotion, and something about these old stories puts her in a sour mood. She's in her last year of high school but still a child. Still childish. I'd better get her home.

"The university students your father helps are the lucky ones now." Lee's eyes fell on me, and I forced a smile to my lips. I nodded, pretending to agree. But the way he spoke about my father in the old days gave me the creeps. I couldn't imagine Baba like that at all—someone the girls swooned for? Who was that person?

The job in Taiwan was only supposed to be for one year. And sure, there'd been emails, and phone calls when the hours aligned. But why hadn't he come home to visit?

He left the summer after my freshman year. Before that, Baba had been out of work for I didn't know how long; at some point when I was still in junior high, he'd been laid off from his job at Boeing out in Long Beach. Mah was selling houses, out every weekend at showings, wooing clients over dim sum, managing contractors in every suburb in LA County where Chinese-speaking families lived: Alhambra, West Covina, Torrance, Cerritos. All I remember Baba doing during that time? He stayed in bed and read comic books. He'd dug them out of a cardboard box in the garage. Sometimes I sat next to him with my own reading, a novel assigned for English class, or an issue of *Sassy* borrowed from Fiona, my best friend. The pillow smelled like Mah's face cream, even though she'd started sleeping in the guest room. "Because Baba snores," she'd complained.

Weekdays, he didn't get dressed or ever leave the house. No more badminton at the park on Saturday afternoons with the other church dads, and he stopped accompanying Mah to Sunday service at First Chinese Calvary over on South Street. He wasn't acting like a normal father anymore. I was in the ninth grade and embarrassed about everything, including this.

One Sunday afternoon, the church dads showed up unannounced. They dragged Baba out of bed and forced him into the shower, chanting, "Jesus loves you! He will provide! Praise Him!" Crowded outside the bathroom door, they sang a rousing hymnal while Baba cleaned up, their voices ringing through the house. They came the Sunday after that, and again on the third Sunday. They wanted Baba to get back to himself, and this was how they thought they could help, with earnest harmonizing, shouts of Hallelujah, wreathing my father in God's holy spirit.

It didn't work. After they left each week, Baba crawled back into bed, surrounded by his comic books. There were volumes stacked on the nightstand, a few tossed on the ground. One time, I flipped through a copy. All those hours of Chinese school homework, that dreaded calligraphy notebook with pages of black grids, and I could only understand about half the text in the comics. The illustrations filled in the rest. A teenage boy wakes up on a Taiwanese fishing boat with amnesia; he'd survived the typhoon but remembers nothing about his past.

What finally helped, I guess, was finding another job. He and Mah told me together in July that year: Baba was moving to Taiwan for a position at his alma mater, working to secure overseas internships for their engineering grads. I can't remember who packed the suitcases or if I rode along in the car to LAX. Just that one day he was gone, like nothing.

Sophomore year, I picked up smoking menthols from Fiona. I turned sixteen. Failed my driving test a bunch of times before I gave up. Baba didn't come home that summer like he'd said he would. Mah explained that he'd signed on for another academic year. I asked if they were getting a divorce. "We need his salary for your college," she said. "Don't be ridiculous."

As if to make up for his absence at church, Mah threw herself into her devotionals even more vigorously than before. She hosted Friday night Bible study at our house once a month. Not long after Baba left, she bought a huge Jesus painting and hung it on the living room wall, above the black leather sofa with the rip in the arm. A crown of thorns rested on His head, and rivulets of blood flowed down His temples. Jesus's soft blue eyes gazed over the furniture—the matching leather love seat to the side, the walnut-and-glass coffee table decorated with a white doily at its center—and landed on the upright Yamaha against the opposite wall, where I took my weekly piano lessons.

Junior year, I learned to drink soju and beer with my friends. Another school year passed, and then it was summer again. I was seventeen. I asked Mah if Baba was coming home. Instead of answering, she said she was switching me to a new piano teacher.

Ping was a grad student in music composition and performance at CalArts up in Valencia. Mah had heard about her because another girl under Ping's tutelage kept winning first place at piano competitions and junior talent shows all over LA, South Bay, Orange County. Mah wanted Ping to work her magic on me, too.

Last August: the first time Ping came over to give me a lesson, I caught a look of horror in her eyes when she saw Mah's huge painting of Jesus. I was caught off guard—He'd been hanging there for so long I sort of forgot about it—but when Ping's eyes met mine, she gave a bighearted, booming laugh. I laughed, too. She looked back at Jesus, then again at me. She wiped tears from the corners of her eyes and shook her head. It was the first time an adult (Ping was twenty-four, she told me later, when I asked) had ever used that secret language with me, telling a joke without words. We sat down at the piano, me at the bench, Ping in the chair beside it. She wore a plain black sweatshirt over green cargo pants, and black ankle socks on her feet. Large, docile eyes set wide apart on her round face gave Ping the appearance of a curious goldfish. When she pushed up her sleeves, I saw that her arms were covered in tattoos. I'd never imagined someone from China like that, the doomed way Mah talked about the Communist mainland: starvation, corruption, pollution.

Senior year now. I turned eighteen in March; only sixty-four days until graduation. Two years, seven months, since the last time I saw my father. I had to come here to find him. Nine days together in Taipei, finally. To invite him home.

I shifted in my seat, peeling sweaty thighs off the molded plastic chair. Lee's presence irritated me. It was my last night in Taiwan—couldn't Baba and I have spent it alone, just the two of us? There were things I wanted to talk to him about, like when exactly he was planning to return to LA, to Mah, and to me.

I wondered if Mah had been one of those girls watching my father at the badminton court. Neither of my parents had ever been forthcoming about the early days of their romance. I'd tried to ask about it, but they only ever gave me desultory answers, claiming there'd been nothing extraordinary about their courtship.

I asked Lee if he knew my mother back then, too. Before he could answer, Baba's cell phone jingled. "Her ears must be itching," Baba said, flipping the phone open.

Lee took out the blue handkerchief again, shaking it in the air a few times before refolding it into a neat rectangle. He turned away from us and blew his nose violently, his eyes squeezed shut.

On the phone, Baba repeated my flight info to Mah. He promised to follow Taoyuan regulations and get me there three hours ahead of the scheduled departure time.

"What we're doing now?" For an instant, his eyes slid toward Lee. "You want to talk to her?" He handed me the phone.

"Hi, Mah." She asked what foods we'd eaten today, and I listed them for her, everything at breakfast, lunch, dinner, the night market. After a pause, she asked if I'd had a good time. I said yes.

"You still want to come back, right?" She gave a soft laugh. "Fiona called yesterday for you. I tell her you're not home yet." What time was it in LA? Fifteen hours behind, so it was Friday morning there. My mother must have been getting ready to leave for work.

"Did you cancel Ping for this week, too?" I said. My lessons were on Friday afternoons.

"Oh!" Mah cried. "I forget. I have to call her—"

I promised one last time to get to the airport early, and then we hung up.

"Heavens," Lee said. "Don't be late for this, don't forget that—I bet you can't wait to go off to college and get away from all the nagging."

He was right, but I didn't want to give him the satisfaction by agreeing.

"You look so much like her." Lee's unwavering gaze made me uncomfortable. "It's almost like being back there again, twenty years ago."

So he did know my mother, before.

"You're going to have to find a new badminton partner, Uncle Lee," I said.

"I see," he said. "Of course. You miss him."

"He's coming back to the US soon."

"But in six months, you're leaving home, too. Correct?" Lee's eyes hardened, as if he'd been assessing me this whole time and had just now decided something. "Isn't this American tradition? You move out of your parents' house after high school. Different from Taiwan—"

"He doesn't belong here," I said. My voice was unsteady. I took a breath. "He belongs with my mother—me—"

"Did you ask him if that's what he wants?"

"I don't have to ask him." *He's my father. I know him. He's mine.*

"She's our only child," Baba said. He put a hand on Lee's arm. "Let's go home so you can finish packing." His voice was gentle, but firm.

I shook Lee's hand when we said goodbye. He exclaimed at my long fingers, how wide my palms were. I could span an octave easy with my right hand. The left needed practice, but I was getting there.

Baba and I strolled in the direction of the subway station. As we walked, I clenched my left hand in a fist, then spread my fingers wide, as far apart as possible. Ping had taught me this exercise to loosen up my reach. Imagine fire shooting out, she'd said. *Energy! Power! Add gasoline!* I tightened and relaxed my left hand at my side, over and over again.

It was past eleven, but the night market still thronged with people at this hour. Baba and I picked our way through the crowd, both of us silent. We passed into an alley that led to a turnout to the main road; neon signs lit up the storefronts along the boulevard. We paused at the corner, waiting for the traffic light to change. Now that we were a ways off from the night market din, the sound of cicadas chirping filled the air all around us, teeming thousands nested in the camphor trees.

I thought about Mah. Was she missing me? Baba? Or was she glad to be free of us? Her way of loving was sharp, never tender. She needled us about every little thing, blamed us for every strand of gray hair on her head, every frown line that settled on her face. I missed her all of a sudden. I realized I'd barely thought of her at all, my whole time here.

As if reading my thoughts, Baba began to tell a story about her.

"After college," he said, "Mah worked as a clerk at the department store. They only hired the most beautiful, elegant girls. Ones who knew how to dress, how to talk to customers. Everyone—I mean everyone—admired her. She could have picked any young man to marry." He paused for a moment. "But she chose me."

I thought of the photos I'd seen of them from those days, preserved behind vellum in an album back home. They'd looked like actors in a movie to me: Baba all Bruce Lee bravado in yellow aviators and polyester button-down shirts with huge collars, Mah rocking bell-bottom jeans and platform sandals, her waist tiny, hair curled into lustrous ringlets.

Mah had always blamed the pregnancy for ruining her trim

shape. One time, in a moment of rage when I was a kid, Mah unzipped her pants and let her gut hang out, the loose flesh puckered with purple stretch marks. She'd grabbed me by the neck and smashed my face against her belly. "You did this to me. You! Are you happy?"

"Before I left Taiwan," Baba said, "she made me promise not to meet any American girls. I gave her my word." He smiled. "That was our engagement."

"No ring?"

"It was a secret between us," he said. "And then I went to the US for graduate school."

The traffic signal flashed green. Baba reached for my hand and tucked it into the crook of his arm. We crossed the street linked together that way. Past the median, a dozen scooters flew within inches of us, mufflers rattling as the riders sawed through the night.

"I want to talk to you about Lee," he said. We were on the other side of the street now.

"Tell me more about you and Mah," I said. "You never—"

"She's a part of this story."

"Lee had a problem with me," I said. "He was trying to pick a fight."

"Twenty years ago, we were inseparable," Baba said. "Best friends, like brothers. But we lost touch after I moved overseas." He paused a moment before continuing. "When I came back here, I asked around. I found him, through old friends."

"I thought you said— The badminton court—"

"I went looking for him," Baba said. "When I saw him again"—he stopped, as if to catch his breath—"I realized something about myself."

His words hung in the air between us. I looked at him carefully. Baba wore his hair longer than he used to, or maybe it was that he was overdue for a cut. He'd gained back the weight he lost before, the year he stayed in bed. I studied his golden-brown skin, his dark amber eyes.

We'd reached the entrance to the subway station. Under the fluorescent bulbs, my father looked exhausted, as if all the talking had worn him out.

"What did you realize?" I asked. A block of ice had settled in my stomach. I knew what my father was trying to tell me but I couldn't hear it. There was no room for it inside of me.

"Jane," he said. "My daughter. My dear daughter."

"You're staying here for good," I said. "That's what you're saying to me."

"I didn't know this would happen," he said. "Lee and I—"

"Does Mah know you're not coming back?"

"We'll always be a family," he said. "Nothing can change that." Then he said, haltingly: "I'm in love—with . . ."

"No." I met his gaze and held it for a long time. "No," I said again. "You're supposed to— You can't just—"

"I care for him. Very much." He was quiet for a moment, before adding, "And he cares for me."

"What about Mah?" I said. "What about me?" I shook my

head. "So you don't care about us, then? You haven't been thinking about anyone except yourself." The words left my mouth before I knew what I was saying. "You're selfish—"

"I wanted to tell you the truth," he said. "You're eighteen years old."

"We don't need you," I said. "*I* don't need you."

"You're angry," he said. "Let's talk when we get home."

"You're right, Baba. I'm not a little kid anymore," I said.

"Jane."

I fumbled for my subway card and held it out against the sensor. The gate glided open with a pneumatic hiss. I walked ahead. He kept his distance, five or six paces between us. I rode the escalator down and stood on the platform, my eyes on the white line painted on the ground. A gust of wind announced the train's arrival, followed by two short whistles as the leading car thundered toward the station.

The train's door opened, and I stepped inside. From the corner of my eye I saw Baba follow me in. He didn't try to sit next to me. The AC blasted cold air. I clutched my stomach. The ice cube was melting, ice water draining down my legs, into my shoes, but I didn't feel any warmth replace it. The train's movement hid my trembling.

That night, trying unsuccessfully to fall asleep in Baba's bed—he'd insisted on taking the sofa while I was visiting—I thought about Ping.

It happened four piano lessons ago.

I'd kissed a few guys before, spin the bottle in junior high, seven minutes in heaven at some dim basement party, a date to the movies where we made out the whole time in the back row. The only girl I'd ever kissed was Fiona, and that was just for practice, we'd said. What friends did to help each other prepare for the real thing.

Ping and I were in the middle of a lesson, me on the bench and her in the chair next to me. We had just started a new piece, Chopin's Scherzo No. 2 in B-flat minor. The first step was sight-reading. I was doing terribly.

"Your fingering here," she said, pointing to a bar on the sheet. "Try this." She slid onto the bench. Our thighs were touching. I didn't move my leg away.

She showed me the correct finger passage, and I wrote down notes on the sheet. At the end of our forty-five minutes, she made me promise I would practice every night that week.

"I promise."

"One hundred times." She held out a fist with her pinky finger extended.

"One hundred?"

"Every time, you write it down in the notebook. Twenty times per day. Easy," she said.

I rolled my eyes, but I hooked my pinky against hers anyway.

And then—I couldn't tell you how it happened or who made the first move—our hands opened up, and we were touching palms. Ping smiled and drew her hand away. I held her gaze. We tilted toward each other, and then. It happened.

We sat on the piano bench like that, just exploring each other with our lips. I felt a rushing in my ears. I held my breath. My eyes were shut, and I wondered if hers were, too. I was too afraid to peek. *We're kissing*, I thought. *Me and Ping. We're kissing!* Was that allowed? I didn't care. I was kissing Ping, and she was kissing me back.

Mah picked me up at LAX on Sunday afternoon. She gave me a hug, then held me at arm's length, studying my face for a moment. I braced myself for criticism, but she didn't say anything mean. We picked up my luggage at the carousel and crossed to the parking structure.

She had a cassette playing in the car, a live recording of Mandarin praise songs, acoustic guitars, tambourines. I was too tired to object. Soon enough I was falling asleep in the seat. One minute I was staring at the gray concrete freeway stretching out in front of us, the next minute, I was out. Then we were home, pulling into the driveway, the white garage door scrolling up. I slept through dinner, woke up at three in the morning. Mah let me stay home the next day to recover.

Back in school on Tuesday, I felt as if I was walking through the halls asleep on my feet. I couldn't pay attention in class at all; at lunchtime, Fiona caught me staring into space while she was in the middle of a story. "Helloooo? Why do you look like you're concentrating really hard?" she said. "Holding in a fart or something?"

I claimed jet lag, but that wasn't it. I couldn't stop thinking about my father and Lee. I thought about talking to Fi about it. I couldn't. It was too strange. If there was anyone I could tell, I realized, it was Ping.

Friday, three o'clock: my weekly piano lesson.

Ping had shaved her head again while I was gone. "Because I was bored," she said. "I missed to see the real shape of my head." She took one of my hands in hers and placed it on her crown. The skin on top of her skull felt soft, pliable.

"Your head shape is beautiful," I said.

She accused me of trying to flatter her because I knew I was in trouble. "Did you practice Chopin this week since you come back from Taiwan?" Yes, I said. "Prove." She nodded in the direction of the keyboard. "Jesus is watching," she added.

Ping twisted the knob on the electric metronome and set it on top of the piano. The digital pulse clicked on. I held my hands over the keys for a moment. My face felt warm all of a sudden.

At first, I was intensely aware of Ping's gaze, her attention switching back and forth between the sheet music leaning against the rack and down toward my fingers, curled, then reaching. When I landed at the wrong chord progression, muddling through the middle, she made a sound with her mouth, lips kissing teeth. I relaxed into the second half anyway; the piece ended with a series of seventh inversions and I leaned into them, ignoring the metronome. My foot on the damper, I dragged the harmony out sweet and long. I knew she hated this kind of sentimental performance, but I didn't care. I was enjoying myself, sweating a little under my arms. When I finished, I realized I was smiling. An imperfect rendition, but I was pleased.

I snuck a look at Ping, nervous to hear her verdict. "Not bad," she said.

"Really?"

"Will you still study the piano in college?" she asked.

"No way," I said. "No offense."

"You have a talent for music," Ping said. "But you're so lazy."

"Ping!" I said, laughing. "That's so mean."

She said it was true. Then she laughed a little, too. "Is that mean to say?"

"I'm your favorite student," I said. "Admit it."

This made her laugh harder. I liked it when Ping laughed at something I said. Her whole face changed; it opened right up and became something else. When Ping smiled, she looked pleasant and kind, but you noticed right away that she was carefully hiding her teeth. Only when she laughed would you ever catch Ping's mouth stretched wide, unguarded and lovely.

"Jane," she said, "I will really miss you." She pretended to wipe tears away from her eyes.

"We still have the summer," I said. "Plus, I don't know where

I'm going, if I'm even going anywhere. I haven't heard back from colleges yet." I looked down at my hands. I thought of my father, and Lee, again. "Ping, can I ask your opinion about something?"

"I have some news to tell you," Ping said. "Actually, I am going back to China."

"What? When?"

She said her mother was ill, so she wanted to go home to Xian sooner rather than later. Once she was there, she'd decide if her mother's case would require her to stay through the rest of the year. "It's hard to know the truth, over phone calls," Ping said. "Even if she is much worse than she tells me, I know my mother will never ask me to give up my life here." Ping shook her head. "Until it's too late," she added. "I'm sorry. It's very sudden—"

"So then this is—our last lesson?"

"I already told your mom," she said. "Everything happened last week." She paused a moment. "What did you want to ask me? My opinion about . . . ?"

"Nothing," I said. "Never mind."

Mah had wanted me to learn from Ping, to grow into a new and improved girl, the kind of daughter who placed in piano competitions and brought home trophies. My transformation hadn't happened in the last eight months with Ping as my piano teacher. I kept losing. The judges never called my name. I was a loser, and there was nothing I could do to change that.

"Jane. What's wrong?"

"What about—well, you know. What happened—"

"I'll always be your friend. We'll stay in touch." She reached into the cloth tote bag at her feet. "I brought you a present." It was a CD, obviously, wrapped in silver paper. I took it from her. "Aren't you going to open it?" she asked.

After she left I threw the CD in the trash. I didn't want her stupid goodbye present.

Adults were all the same. Even Ping. They were always feeding you some line, expecting you to eat it up without any questions. I'd thought she was different, like a friend's cool older sister, someone who listened. Though of course she was more than that to me, or could have been, anyway. The trip to Taiwan had taken everything away.

When Mah got home later, I asked if she wanted my help setting up the chairs for her Bible study, but it wasn't her turn to host. She was going to a fundraising dinner that Calvary was throwing for Auntie Ruby's son, who was taking a leave of absence from Stanford to go on mission next year.

"Evan flunked out of freshman chemistry, calculus, everything. That's really why," Mah said. "Everyone knows, but no one will say that. Too shame." A pleased expression glimmered in her eyes. "If Baba was here," she added, "he could tutor that dummy boy."

"Ba? I don't think he's ever coming back," I muttered.

"What you say? Don't talk crazy," Mah said. "Of course he

is." Then she asked me about my piano lesson. "Ping told you about her mother?"

I started to say I was fine, but my voice choked up. I tried to swallow down my tears, but they turned into hiccups. Finally I just buried my face in my hands.

Mah sat down on the sofa next to me. For once she didn't tell me to dry up the tears. "I know you really liked Ping," she said. She stroked the back of my head gently. Her tenderness was a surprise.

"You didn't say anything all week about Baba," she said. "Until now." I looked at her through my fingers, lost for a response. "I miss him, too," she said softly.

The phone rang, and she got up to answer it. I heard Mah telling whoever was on the line that she would be late to the church dinner. Then she came back in and sat down next to me again.

"I'll tell you something," she said. "Listen to me. A real secret." She hesitated for a few seconds, then said, "I was pregnant with you, before I marry your father."

I glanced up into her face. Mah's cheeks were slightly flushed. A light was in her eyes, like lamps turned on in a house at dusk.

"By the time I realized you were growing in my belly, he was gone to the US. I had to tell my parents." Mah shook her head, almost as if she were still embarrassed. I'd never seen her so girlish. "They wanted him to move back right away, take his responsibility!"

"What happened?" I was mesmerized.

"He flew in for one week only, we married, and he flew back. Few months later, after the visa cleared, I came over. Everything fast." She snapped her fingers three times quickly. "Just like that."

"That's why you got married?" I said. "Because your parents forced him?"

"We loved each other," she said sternly. "Then God stepped in to help."

"In Taiwan," I said, "Baba told me you could've married anyone you wanted."

"Good, that turkey remembers," Mah said. "Anyway, everyone agreed we made one perfect match." Then, her expression darkened. "All except for one of Baba's friends. Think of it now, he showed up at my job, I remember." Mah shook her head. "What a lunatic!"

My throat tightened. I knew she was talking about Lee.

"Remember when Baba was in bed all day? Reading those comic books?" Mah said. I nodded. The boy at sea who lost all his memories. She went on: "Baba was sick like that, before. When he was young, after college." She peered into my eyes, as if deciding whether she should go on.

"We all thought it was because he studied too hard," she said. "You don't know this about your father. I never told you." She paused for a moment. "He hurt himself—he tried to do it—too much pressure. He couldn't handle." The light in her

eyes had changed. They were dimmer now, like embers glowing at the end of a beach bonfire. "He almost died. Before you
came."

"He was alone? By himself, in the US . . ."

"Only after I told him I was going to have a baby, then he
was able to walk out of the dark that time," Mah said after a
moment.

"Do you still love him?"

"I never loved anyone else." Mah smiled. I hardly recognized
her like this. "I'm telling you this story," she said, "because you
have to know your father loves you. From the beginning to
now. You are his reason—"

"No," I said bitterly. "I'm not."

Then I did something regrettable.

I told my mother about meeting Lee at the night market in
Taipei with Baba. "You called while we were all sitting there,"
I said. "He and Baba—they're—they're together now."

As soon as the words left my mouth, I was sorry to have said
them out loud.

I had no way of knowing then that I'd regret everything that
followed, for the next twenty years of my life.

Mah pressed her fingers to her brow and kneaded her forehead. The phone rang again, but neither one of us moved. The
answering machine picked up; in a cheerful tone, a man left a
message saying he hoped to see my mother at the dinner soon.
I thought I recognized the voice as one of the church dads who
had shown up years ago to sing my father out of his depression.

"His friend named Lee," Mah said. "He was the one at the department store. He scolded me—he said I should let your father go free, start over in America—"

"They're in love," I said.

"Baba said that? That's what he told you?"

"He said I'm old enough to know the truth—"

"The truth!" Mah said. She gave a hard little laugh. "In love?"

"You told me he was going there for a job. But now—"

"Mah knows everything, you understand?" she said. "You think it's so easy to hold this family together?" Her voice was suddenly quiet, and cold as a knife. This was the mother I recognized, not the one who'd shown me kindness earlier. "For years, that man writes letters to Baba." Her eyes were black now, no light in their depths at all. "I read them. I know your father better than anyone. I know him better than he knows himself." Her words chilled me. "All those comic books—*he* sent those to your father. Presents. Each time a letter inside."

Mah stood abruptly and walked out of the living room, and I heard her unhook the cordless roughly from its cradle in the kitchen. She strolled back in, the phone in her hands. As she punched the keypad, Mah began chanting for Jesus.

"We're all here," Mah shouted when Baba answered. She always shouted when we had him on speaker, even though he told her, every time, that he could hear us just fine.

In Taipei, it was ten o'clock in the morning, Saturday. Baba was in the future. I imagined him in the midmorning light, gripping a battered badminton racquet, bouncing on his feet. He wore a pair of scuffed white Reeboks, the bottoms squeaking on the green rubber court as he chased the shuttlecock. Lee on the other side of the net, returning the volleys.

Or maybe they were in my father's apartment, having breakfast. Did they spend nights together? Lee in my father's bed, where I'd slept. I wondered if Lee had a family; I hadn't thought to ask.

"Is Jane okay?" Baba asked. "What's wrong?"

Who do you belong to? I wanted to ask him. *Who do you belong to, Baba?*

"You tell her, Shen. Tell your daughter it's lies. She's confused."

There was a silence.

I thought of a call with Baba from last summer, before Mah hired Ping. On the phone, Baba had dismissed her prejudices and said that Mah was being paranoid. China wasn't the mess it used to be, he said. That afternoon, he'd reminded her that we were all Chinese, separated only by geography, politics, civil war.

"Dog fart," Mah had replied.

"You think something will happen to Jane? She will fall for mainland propaganda and run away with her piano teacher? The revolution is over," he said.

Mah had laughed, and I was relieved, though I didn't totally understand what they were talking about. "Your daughter is one hundred percent American, like it or not," Mah said, which made Baba laugh, too. I'd felt like I was being insulted, but another part of me enjoyed being the punch line to their jokes. I hadn't heard my parents laugh like that in a long time.

"Baba," I said. My voice was caught in my throat. "I'm— sorry. I . . ."

My heart was beating fast in my chest. It wasn't my secret to tell, but I'd told it anyway. All I wanted—all I'd ever wanted— was the possibility of my father's safe return to us. I thought revealing the truth about Lee, the reason he was growing more and more distant from Mah and me, would bust the problem wide-open. Call him back to his life—his real life—with us. But I was wrong. In the silence before he said anything, I realized: Baba was already living his real life.

"Jane," he said. "It's okay. It's okay, my daughter. My baby daughter." He kept saying it was okay, over and over again, as if that might make it true.

The Inheritance

Fiona Lin was twenty-two, in her final semester at UC Berkeley, when her grandfather passed away from a stroke. He'd had two of them already, since turning eighty. The first was a warning, the second a threat, promising imminent death, said his doctors at National Taiwan University Hospital. Even then, he refused to give up smoking, according to Fiona's eldest uncle, and there was nothing anyone could do to change his mind. The family was lousy with heart conditions and respiratory troubles; two aunts had undergone chemo for breast cancer in the same year, a cousin diagnosed with a degenerative autoimmune disease who was being treated simultaneously with Western medicine and Chinese herbs. The Lins always survived. Fiona had heard this mantra her entire life. The power of this belief held such sway that his third stroke, the one that took her grandfather's life, managed to catch everyone by surprise, including the patriarch himself.

Fiona hadn't seen her grandfather in years. In high school, there'd been occasional phone calls her mother monitored, and red envelopes in the mail for Chinese New Year. Fiona was the only daughter of her grandfather's youngest child. At times, her mother lamented the curse of being his favorite, the surprise baby after six older siblings and the only one born on the island after the family fled the mainland in 1949. His favorite, and his biggest disappointment: her mother's way of explaining the long periods of estrangement between them, the reason why Fiona didn't meet her grandparents until she was six years old. Back then—back in Taiwan—her name was Ona. No one called her that anymore, except her mother.

Fiona's mother flew to Taiwan for the funeral the following week. When she got back, her mother called to relay the news that Fiona's grandfather had left behind money for all of his grandchildren. Today, a banker's check arrived in the mail to Fiona's apartment on Blake Street, addressed to her name in Chinese, accompanied by a short letter she couldn't read, signed and stamped by a notary. She walked down to the B of A on Telegraph and deposited the check.

Ten thousand two hundred fifty-seven dollars and thirteen cents, minus the international conversion fee, credited to her account, just like that.

Fiona knew work; she'd held part-time jobs since she was thirteen, when she knocked on the doors of their apartment building to ask if anyone needed a responsible babysitter (she was in charge of her younger brother, Conrad, all afternoon anyway—what was another kid to watch?). In high school, Fiona was highly sought after as a peer tutor for almost every subject, and she'd worked during all four years of undergrad, supplementing her Pell Grant and work-study maximum with the money she earned pouring coffee and bussing tables at Caffè Strada on College and Bancroft. She knew how to save, seeing the figures add up month after month. She set a goal and reached it: like how she bought Shamu, her first car, not long after she turned sixteen. What she didn't know was how to deal with money like the unexpected inheritance check, all those zeros suddenly in her bank account she hadn't earned.

In a month, Fiona was graduating with a bachelor's in political science. Her boyfriend, Jasper Chang, was an English major whose greatest desire was to move to New York and write the twenty-first century's Great American Novel. Only people who grew up with money thought this way, casting about life without a realistic plan, an inherent trust in things falling into place, Fiona thought. Everyone else begged, borrowed, and stole— Fiona had done all three.

Two years ago, she'd let herself be talked into taking an envelope of cash out of the pastor's office at Jane's mother's church, while her best friend stood watch outside the door. Her hands tingled and her stomach lurched at the memory of it.

The money was meant for a team of volunteers going on mission. Jane hated that church, how her mother had been transformed into an evangelical fanatic by those people. She felt none of the guilt Fiona did, only the thrill of subterfuge. In Jane's eyes, it was a game, something to get away with. What they did wasn't exactly right, Jane reasoned, but on the plus side, they were definitely sparing some innocent African people from cultish Jesus rhetoric spewed by a traveling band of Christian crazies. Fiona needed the money. There was nearly three thousand dollars in cash donations stuffed inside the envelope. The opportunity presented itself, and Fiona had seized it, with Jane's help.

She hadn't told Jasper or anyone else about the inheritance money. Only her mother knew. She could draw from the sudden windfall and pay back the church. Figure out a way to do it anonymously. What about New York? another voice inside her asked. Moving costs, a security deposit, and first month's rent on a new apartment?

When Jasper asked last week if she would move with him, Fiona couldn't help but be swept up by the romance of it: a new city, a new start. Her impractical sweetheart. She loved Jasper. And so she'd agreed to go with him. She said yes to New York, yes to living with him. Today, when the inheritance check arrived, Fiona felt like she'd been given a sign. She was suddenly one of those people for whom things magically fell into place. She'd yet to break the news about her decision to her mother,

who, Fiona knew, expected her to return to LA after graduation. Nor to Jane, who Fiona assumed felt the same.

When her mother was twenty-two—the age *she* was now—
Fiona was six years old. That was the year she took ballet lessons with Miss Fang. Her last year in Taipei, before she and her
mother moved to California, sponsored by her mother's older
brother. She was still Ona then. She thought of what she'd
learned as a child about the mystery of her father's absence—
how her grandfather had once promised to make the missing
man appear at her dance recital, on Father's Day, no less. Memories passed through her mind as she left the bank and strolled
down Telegraph Avenue. What did she recall of that time? Her
mother was her whole world. And Shulin, the downstairs neighbor, who died in the earthquake. Fiona shook her head, as if
to clear it. It felt as though she were tunneling down into some
secret theater, the air slightly damp there, pictures tinged in
nostalgic sepia tones. She burrowed deeper—she let herself remember being a girl called Ona, inhabiting a time when she
answered only to that name.

Ona's mother used to watch her ballet class every week through
a large window cut into the wall separating the studio from
the front office. Chairs were lined up for this purpose, and
other mothers sat there, too, observing the girls as they went
through the exercises at the barre and took turns moving across

the floor while Miss Fang counted the beats out loud. After class, Ona and her mother would stroll down the street for steaming bowls of soup noodles. Her mother liked the Cantonese-style with red roasted beef, and Ona always ordered the thin Taiwanese vermicelli in clear onion broth.

The dance studio and the noodle shop were located in a part of Taipei bustling with college students. They traveled in groups, with their backpacks full of books, eyes bright and darting behind glasses, their conversations filled with words like "project objectives" and "oral presentations." Even then, Ona knew those students had something her mother wanted, from the way her mother's eyes followed them down the street. Something else Ona knew: her mother was a "widow." She'd heard one of the other mothers at after-school pickup whisper that unfamiliar word, then cast a pitying glance in Ona's direction.

On Sundays, Ona and her mother visited her grandparents at their apartment on Kwang Shin East Road. They rode two buses then walked several blocks, cutting through a large green park with a long soccer field. They'd started this routine only recently, soon after Ona began her ballet lessons with Miss Fang. Before these audiences, her mother fussed over Ona's hair, inspected her fingernails, made sure she wore clean white socks and underwear without any holes.

Her grandparents lived in a tall building with more buttons in the elevator than Ona could count. Nearby, there was a private elementary school, and more than once Ona's grandmother had badgered her mother about transferring the child there. She was at it again this Sunday.

"I'm telling you, I know the woman who works in admissions," Grandmother said. "There's an impossible wait list, but she owes me a favor."

"Ona's happy at her school now," her mother replied.

"The son of Chiang Kai-shek's first cousin goes to that school. What does that tell you?"

"She adores her teacher." Ona's mother glanced down at her. "Don't you, bao bei?" The girl nodded. Her mother smiled, and Ona smiled back.

Grandmother sucked her teeth. "How easy it would be for me to pick her up from school, and in the afternoons, we can keep her here while you're at work." She cast her gaze toward Ona, then back up at the girl's mother. "Maybe you can go back to school, too. You're always carrying on about how you want to finish your courses, get your degree." Her expression softened, and she reached out and put a hand on her daughter's arm. "There's still time for that, Wen."

Ona stared up at her grandmother, waiting for her mother's reply. She studied her grandmother's eyebrows with fascination, the two arched lines tattooed underneath the brow hairs, a few of which were gray at the outer corners. The ink was fading from black to dark blue. The same color rimmed Grandmother's eyes, under her lashes.

"Where's Ba?" Ona's mother asked. "He's out?"

"Why are you so stubborn? I'm trying to help you! The best thing for the little girl, and for you—"

"Ona," her mother said. "Do you see him hiding somewhere?"

The glass door leading to the balcony slid open, and Ona's grandfather poked his head into the living room, as if he heard himself summoned. He motioned with his hands for Ona to come outside.

Still a little shy around him, Ona shrank against her mother's leg. "Go on," her mother said. She gave Ona's shoulders a gentle push.

Grandfather beckoned with his hands again. "Hurry—I want to show you something exciting—you really have to see this," he said, making his eyes wide.

She left her mother's side slowly.

Her grandmother kept on about Ona's schooling, asking where the teacher earned her credentials. Ona heard her mother sigh as her grandfather pulled the glass door shut after them. Then she couldn't hear her grandmother's voice anymore.

"Look down there."

Ona peered over the gray concrete ledge of the balcony. A large unmarked truck was being unloaded in the gated park in front of her grandparents' apartment building. The trailer had windows on its sides with vertical bars running across them, the bed much longer than the squat delivery trucks that skirted the streets and alleys of the night markets Ona was used to seeing. Three men stood at the truck's rear. A wide mechanical ramp slowly unfolded before them.

Her grandfather lit up a cigarette and asked Ona what she thought the men might retrieve from the truck.

"Carnival games," she said. "Basketball hoops and pachinko, things like that." The girl answered with confidence. She was one of the top students in her class, bringing home penmanship worksheets with "100" written across the top, math quizzes with all check marks. She thrived under the attention of adults who wanted to probe the contents of her mind, those who didn't condescend to children.

Grandfather smiled. "You think so, eh? What makes you so sure?"

He was retired now, but Ona's mother had told her that he'd been a professor in Beijing, a highly respected scholar of classical Chinese literature. This was before the Maoists won control of the mainland, before the family escaped to Taiwan during the civil war. There was still an air of the stern professor about Ona's grandfather, that wild head of hair still entirely black despite his age. After more than three decades in exile, Ona's grandparents had long ago let go of believing in Generalissimo Chiang Kai-shek's promise to reclaim the mainland from the Communists. Though the Beijing they knew no longer existed, they still hoped to return one day, if political relations between the two regimes improved. In the meantime, they'd managed to send all their children abroad for Western educations, to get their college or graduate degrees in the US or Canada. All except Ona's mother.

"Mama and me, we passed by a carnival before," Ona said.

"Next to the train station and the Family Mart where a fat orange cat lives in the alley." She remembered the row of trucks, like the one below, parked behind the grounds. She recalled the children clutching cones of bright pink cotton candy, others with clear plastic bags filled with water, minnows darting inside like pieces of glinting silver. "We didn't go in, though."

"Why not?"

Ona looked down over the balcony's ledge. She remembered the laughing man wearing a floppy hat, the long strips of red paper tickets coiled around his neck. How her mother had held Ona's hand tight and said they couldn't afford to throw away money on silly games that were rigged anyway.

"We had to catch the train," Ona said finally.

At the top of the ramp now, one of the men held a length of rope looped around the neck of a massive black stallion. The animal towered powerfully over the man, who was trying, unsuccessfully it seemed, to lead it down.

"It's not a carnival," Ona said. "It must be . . ." She searched her mind for another possibility. "A pony ride," she decided.

"If you're right, we'll go down there and you can ride one."

Ona wasn't sure if she wanted a pony ride, but she nodded anyway. Below them, the man in the park coaxed the horse step by step down the incline, at turns pulling gently on the rope, then halting to stroke its mane, whispering into its ears. Ona had never seen a real horse before, only pictures of them in books. Even from her perch on the balcony ten stories up she saw clearly the wet smoothness of the eyes each time the animal blinked, the musculature in its flanks rippling under the glossy black hide. Something inside her trembled, watching the scene below.

Her grandfather asked about her ballet lessons, and Ona told him she was going to have a recital soon.

"When is it?" He spoke with a proper Beijing accent, a curl to his pronunciation, which only added to his serious demeanor in Ona's eyes.

"The eighth of August," she answered.

"Father's Day?"

"There's going to be a special routine for the finale." Ona showed him her pirouette, followed by a deep bow with her arms held in third position. "And after that, all the fathers are invited onstage."

Her grandfather drew on his cigarette.

"Mama said *she* would go up there for me. But that's not right, is it?" Ona's chin dropped to her chest, and she stared at her feet. "All the other girls—"

"Look at me," Grandfather said. She lifted her gaze up to meet his and saw kindness there. "This is what we're going to do, my dear. I'll go up there with you."

"Did you know my father when he was alive?" Ona asked.

Her grandfather was silent for a moment. "Yes," he said. "I knew him."

"What was my father like?"

Just then, a loud squealing rose from the park. Two men hunched over a silver cage on the ramp. They hurried to guide the cage down. On solid ground, the men unlatched the door and released the animal—a large spotted pig—into an enclosed pen surrounded by bales of hay they'd set up in the grass. The pig trotted in circles, still raising a frenzied racket.

"Something you should know, Ona." Grandfather's voice was a whisper. She leaned in closer, smelled the tobacco on his breath. He paused for a long moment, then said: "Your father isn't dead. He's alive, as alive as that pig shrieking down there."

Ona frowned, shaking her head. "No he's not. Mama said—"

"We can't tell your mother," Grandfather said. "You want him to come to your recital?"

Still frowning, Ona nodded vigorously.

"Then I'll invite him. On your behalf."

"Will he really be there?"

"You understand, he'll have to hide himself. No one can know about him. I'll be onstage with you, representing him. But you'll know that he's in the audience, watching you dance."

"What about Mama? Why can't we tell her?"

"Not a word," Grandfather said. "Part of the deal." He touched an index finger to his mouth. "Understood?"

Ona bit her bottom lip, unsure of what to say. Finally she nodded.

Grandfather lit up another cigarette. They watched the men in silence a few minutes more, then went back inside the apartment after he'd only smoked half of it.

Ona's mother and grandmother had gone out. Grandfather turned the knob on the television set and landed on a Sunday variety show. He adjusted the antennae before sinking down on the sofa next to Ona. They sat together, watching the comedians onstage banter with a panel of pop starlets and soap actresses. The secret he'd floated out on the balcony hung between them, but she knew that there would be no more talk of it. She glanced nervously from the TV to her grandfather in profile and felt like a balloon filled to its capacity, ready to burst. It seemed as if she had to breathe very carefully or the secret would tumble out.

Ona heard her mother's and grandmother's voices in the hallway outside. The front door swung open.

"Mama!" Ona cried.

Knotted plastic bags hung from her mother's wrists. "Stinky tofu," she said. "I had a craving."

Grandfather straightened up and cleared his throat. "Little girl's excited from seeing the animals outside."

"What did you see, bao?" her mother asked.

"Yes, we saw them too," said Grandmother. "It's a production of the Monkey King chronicles, and they're setting up a petting zoo for the children." She kicked off her brown leather flats and nudged them to the side. "I told you it's a special school," she said to Ona's mother. "Does Miss What's-her-name show them real farm animals?"

"A petting zoo?" Ona said, looking from her grandmother, to her grandfather, and, finally, to her mother. "You're allowed to touch them?"

"Seems a little unsanitary to have a pig running around," her mother said. "A monkey, too?" She shook her head.

"Of course you can touch them," Grandmother said. "We should go back down and see if—it's only for the school, but maybe they would make an exception—"

"You know the woman in admissions," said Ona's mother. "So we've heard."

"Of all the farm animals, pigs are actually quite clean," Grandfather put in.

"See? You think you know everything," said Grandmother. "But you don't," she added.

Ona's mother crossed the room to the round dining table and began to open up the bags of food. She told Ona to go wash her hands for dinner.

The auntie who cooked and cleaned for Ona's grandparents had the week off to visit her family in the southern part of the island, so rather than eating a home-cooked meal, they picked from the night market foods Ona's mother and grandmother had brought back from their walk. Grandfather complained about indigestion, but he ate everything in his bowl and cleaned up what remained in each of the Styrofoam boxes, down to the last pieces of deep-fried fish cakes drenched in sweet chili sauce.

After dinner, while her mother and grandfather retreated to the balcony for their cigarettes, Ona's grandmother led her to the bedroom at the end of the hallway, past the kitchen. Ona smelled mothballs when Grandmother pushed the bedroom door open.

"Try it," she said, and gestured toward the child's bed, which was set up next to the far wall. A pink-and-white-checkered blanket lay over the mattress, a pillow with a white scalloped case at the top. "What do you think?"

Her grandmother took Ona by the hand, and they sat down on the bed's edge. Next to it stood a white bookshelf. Ona noticed a few familiar titles, books she'd been allowed to borrow from her school's library for a week at a time. She longed to run her finger along their spines but did not dare to do so. Who did they belong to? Some lucky boy or girl, Ona thought.

"Isn't this a nice room?" Grandmother said. "I ordered a little desk, and a chair that's just your size. It's being delivered next week."

"My size?"

"All you have to do now is tell your mama you want to stay here, and this room is all yours."

"Me?" Ona said. "Here in this room?"

She imagined a desk and chair tucked into the corner, under the rectangular window with the frosted glass, like her grandmother proposed. At home, Ona finished her homework on a Formica table in the front room, the same place where she and her mother shared their meals.

"Can Shulin visit? She lives downstairs from Mama and me."

"Of course." Grandmother paused a moment before adding, "But you know, you'll make friends at your new school, too."

Ona bounced softly on the bed a few times. This bedroom was smaller than the one she shared with her mother, but it would be her very own. She'd never slept in her own bed before, all by herself. What would happen during an earthquake? In her own bed, there would be no holding hands, no curling toward Mama, waiting together for the rocking to subside.

"Things will be different from now on," Grandmother said. "The ballet lessons are just the beginning of things your mother can't—"

"What did you say? What are you doing!"

Ona jumped at the sound of her mother's voice.

"Respectable women don't smoke cigarettes," Grandmother said coolly. She stood and crossed her arms, putting herself between the girl and her mother. "You're going to end up with a mouth full of brown teeth."

"I can't turn my back on you for one second," said Ona's mother. "What are you showing her this room for?"

"Just once, why don't you think about your daughter instead of yourself?"

"Go get your shoes on." Her mother's mouth was set into a thin straight line. Ona moved toward the door but slowed when she felt her grandmother's hand squeezing her shoulder.

"Let the girl stay." Her grandmother's voice was soft. "One night. Just to see how she likes it."

"Time to go, bao. Come on," said Ona's mother. The child

squirmed out of her grandmother's grasp and ran to her mother's side. She felt her mother's hand on the top of her head, a warm shield.

"Please, Wen." Grandmother lifted her hands in the air, surrender in her voice. "I've already prepared this room. She would be comfortable."

Ona felt heat radiating from all over her mother's body. Wrapping her arms around her mother's leg, Ona felt sleepy all of a sudden.

"She's *my* daughter," her mother said. "I take care of her."

"And she's our granddaughter."

"After everything, you should be grateful I even—"

"You're too proud," Grandmother said. "That's always been your flaw, since you were a child."

"I bring her here and you—you—"

"You made a mistake. A huge mistake!" Grandmother cried. "And now, when I'm just trying to help you, this is the thanks I get? You were always spoiled—"

Ona burst into tears. She felt as if her mother and grandmother had forgotten she was still standing there while they argued.

Her mother bent down and picked her up. Ona buried her face in her mother's neck and let herself be soothed by her mother's voice calling her tender baby names: sugarcane sister, sweet mosquito bite, my red sour plum.

When Ona's sobs subsided into soft hiccups, her mother brought her into the bathroom and wiped her face with a moist hand towel. Mama asked if she was ready to go home. Ona thought briefly of the bed in the room at the end of the corridor. She wondered if both she and her mother could fit in it together, and she decided no, it was too small.

She clasped her mother's face in both of her hands. "I don't want to live here, Mama. Don't make me live here." She felt tears rising in her throat again.

"You live with me," her mother said. "Wherever I am, that's your home."

Ona nodded. There were still things she didn't understand, but her mother's answer was all she needed to be sure of for now.

Downstairs, Mama was silent on the walk to the bus stop and on the entire way back home. Ona watched her mother in the darkened bus, head leaned against the thick pane of glass, eyes shut. Every once in a while a sweep of neon light from outside the bus passed over her mother's face, illuminating its sharp planes.

When they got home, her mother fetched Ona's school uniform from the clothesline outside. She hung the white collar shirt over the back of a dining chair and placed the blue pleated skirt on the seat cushion, then told the girl to go wash up before bed.

Because she was still unaccustomed to bathing alone, Ona

left the door open while she undressed. The bathroom was a small rectangular room with a squatting toilet on one side, white tiles on the floors and walls. A set of spigot knobs protruded from the wall opposite the door, and two rubber hoses had been attached to the taps, each one curling down into a pink plastic pan that rested on the floor, next to a short wooden stool with three legs. Ona turned on the water and sat on the stool while she waited for the pan to fill. She looked toward the open door. Her mother pushed a broom across the floor in the front room.

She missed the days when her mother bathed with her, how her mother soaped the back of her neck and rubbed her shoulders. She recalled the feeling of her mother's fingers massaging her scalp, the careful way her mother rinsed the shampoo from Ona's hair, cupping a hand over her forehead to prevent water from dripping into her eyes. Ever since Ona started first grade, however, her mother said she was old enough now, she had to get used to washing on her own.

After, Ona wrapped a towel around herself and slipped from the bathroom to the bedroom. She changed into the pajamas her mother had laid out on the bed and climbed under the covers, while her mother took her turn to wash. She wanted to stay awake until her mother finished, to feel her mother's body next to her in bed, to hear her mother's voice whisper in her ear: Goodnight, my oyster pearl, my pirate's treasure. Goodnight, my little daughter.

———

The Father's Day ballet recital was held in the auditorium of a nearby middle school, which was also its gymnasium. Appropriate for the occasion, the father of the Republic gazed benevolently over the audience: a large oil painting of Sun Yat-sen hung on one wall, facing opposite a basketball hoop that had been retracted to lie flat against the whitewashed cinder blocks. The girls had been practicing their routines for weeks, including a dress rehearsal the previous Saturday. Ona peered down into the audience from a gap in the curtains. Was her father already among them? Or would he slip into one of the few remaining chairs at the last minute?

After that Sunday afternoon out on the balcony more than a month earlier, her grandfather hadn't mentioned his promise to invite Ona's father again. She and her mother had continued their weekly visits, but the door to the room at the end of the hallway had remained shut thereafter, and her grandmother hadn't raised the question of Ona transferring schools again.

Ona spied her mother in the second row, next to her grandparents. Her gaze passed over the men in the crowd once more. She'd never seen a single photo of her father; her mother had said that she got rid of them all, because they hurt her heart too much.

"Move over," said Shulin from behind her. "I want a look." Ona gave up her spot at the curtain. "Oh, there's my baba!"

Shulin giggled and turned around. "He said he's nervous about his part onstage. We practiced it again this morning. Three times!"

Ona liked Mr. Wang very much. Whenever she skipped downstairs to play with Shulin, he always offered the girls something to eat, a sleeve of shrimp crackers, bright yellow egg tarts from the bakery across the street, black sesame cookies for dunking into a bowl of warm soy milk.

"My grandfather isn't worried," Ona said. "We practiced, too."

"Grandfather?" said another girl, crowding the gap between the curtains. "It's Father's Day, not Grandparents' Day."

Shulin told her to be quiet. She said, "Grandfathers are fathers, too, stupid."

The girl turned up her nose and stalked off.

Shulin took up her spot at the curtain again. Ona crowded next to her and peeked out, too. Almost every seat was filled now, a dozen or so rows of metal folding chairs set up across the gymnasium floor. The space buzzed with chatter underneath the ceiling fans swishing round and round overhead.

"Girls! Girls!" Miss Fang clapped her hands to get everyone's attention backstage. "One minute to curtain. Dancers, take your places now, please."

Shulin grabbed Ona's hand and squeezed it. They ran to their spots next to each other on the stage marked by two pieces of blue electric tape, the distance between them measured by the span of Miss Fang's hands touching, fingers spread. Shulin wore a plastered-on smile, her parted lips painted a pearlescent fuchsia. Miss Fang had come around backstage ten minutes earlier with a tube of lipstick in a slick gold case, applying the bright color to the girls' mouths in decisive strokes. Ona had offered up her face readily. Some of the other girls' mothers had darkened their daughters' brows with black pencil, rouged their cheeks, washed their eyelids shades of blue; not Ona's mother, who owned not a single lipstick or eye shadow palette, whose only beauty regimen was a swipe of Vaseline over her lips.

Ona struck her pose, one arm raised over her head and the other curved in front of her chest. She waited for the curtains to part, the music to crank on. The first number was a harvest dance; she listened for her cue, the sound of a rooster crowing.

Then: the ground beneath her feet moved. Ona glanced over at Shulin—the pink had smudged a bit at the corner of her smile—and in the next instant, Shulin crumpled to her knees, then fell forward flat on her face. A heavy globe light thudded onto the stage next to her, just beyond the reach of her out-stretched fingers.

"Take cover! Earthquake! Earthquake!"

"Run for the doors!"

"The children!"

The adults in the auditorium cried out in panic, and some of them rushed the stage, crashing through the curtains. The bright lights all around Ona flickered once, twice, then went out completely, sending up shrieks. In the darkness she crouched down where she'd been standing on her mark and crawled on her hands and knees toward Shulin. She felt shoes and knees in her back as bodies stumbled and fell over her; panicked voices cried out the names of the girls in her dance class: *Juju! Where are you? Xiao Ming? Mama is here! Where? Where?*

Ona lay down beside her friend to protect her from the stampede. She whispered Shulin's name, urged her to get up. The ground had finally stopped rolling. Ona lay a hand on Shulin's back and shook her gently. No response.

Then Ona was lifted up in the air, being slung over someone's shoulders. She realized it was her mother by the pungent spearmint scent at her throat.

"Wait! Shulin's hurt," Ona cried. But her voice wasn't coming out right. She tried again to speak, but her words didn't make any sense and it sounded as if she were only sobbing "Mama, Mama" over and over again.

Outside, sirens screamed. Ona's mother gently laid her down on a patch of grass. "Tell me if this hurts," she said, examining every part of her daughter urgently. "And this?" Ona was still crying, but she shook her head. "No? And here? Do you feel this?"

Grandfather's face appeared above. "Is she bleeding?" he asked.

"Doesn't seem so—must be someone else—"

"I'm bleeding?"

Ona's grandfather put a warm hand on her cheek. "You're safe, my girl," he said in a steady voice.

"Did he come?" Ona searched her grandfather's eyes. "Was he here?"

"Who, baby?" her mother asked. "What did you say?"

Ona's mother was still kneeling beside her. She was so beautiful, Ona thought. A fine dust covered her head, a gray-white seam where she parted her hair. Earlier that day she'd wrapped a length of pink ribbon around the ponytail at the nape of her neck before they left the apartment, a piece left over from the spool she'd bought at the crafting shop to plait into Ona's braid, special for the recital. "We're twins," the girl had said, very much pleased, and a broad smile spread over her mother's face. When Grandmother spotted them in the vestibule of the auditorium, however, she'd said Ona's mother was too old to wear ribbons in her hair: "You look ridiculous!" she'd scolded. Ona had watched her mother yank off the bow without a word. She didn't understand why her grandmother was so unkind. What had her mother done to warrant her disdain?

A thing her mother often said: You're my own heart, walking outside of my body. Ona knew this meant she wasn't ever supposed to stray too far from her mother, because a person needs her heart to live. In the minutes after the earthquake, amid the panic and mayhem, the accounting for little girls in tutus, Ona wasn't sure if she was dreaming or awake. What was real, and what was make-believe? Had her father been there? A chilling premonition passed over the girl. One day, she would have to leave her mother. Ona shivered all of a sudden. She shook her head vigorously, said "No!" into the air. In the next moment, she passed into weary sleep, her head in her mother's lap. By the time she woke up, the premonition had gone, like sand through a sieve.

All these years later, did the money from her grandfather change anything? How she felt about her mother's parents, her missing father? Did the money alleviate the loneliness she'd sustained all these years?

She'd become Fiona in the second grade, shortly after she and her mother arrived in the States. A white boy in Miss King's class had declared that *Ona* wasn't a real name. She was new, and the boy spoke with authority, so she'd believed him. She needed a new name. A proper American name. In the back of the dictionary, her mother found a list of girls' names. They landed on Fiona, adding a syllable in front of the name she already had. If she said it fast, "Fiona" sounded like the Mandarin word for "wind." When she pointed that out, her mother had laughed and added that "wind" was also a homonym for "insane."

"My crazy, windy girl," her mother teased. "Don't fly away from me!"

"I won't leave you," Fiona had promised. "Never."

Her mother had met a man and married him a year after they landed in California. Fiona, eight years old and already in glasses, wore a canary-yellow dress with a white Peter Pan collar in the photos on the courthouse steps. Her stepfather was a regular at the Commerce casino where Mom dealt blackjack, generous enough to his wife's daughter, until his own child from the union arrived. Fiona's brother: a baby boy named Conrad, born when she was ten. From then on, Fiona escaped her stepfather's notice completely—and she changed in her mother's eyes, too, it seemed. She was a big sister now, no longer her mother's little girl.

If not for Jane, she thought, her loneliness might have been unbearable. Her parents were from Taiwan, too, but Jane was born here, in California. She spoke crooked Mandarin, a bad student at weekend Chinese school. Jane's tonal accents were often mixed up and off-key, a funny song that made Fiona giggle, though she found comfort in the fact that they both had to grope for words. Jane was a wonder: Fiona's first friend in this foreign place, an American Taiwanese girl. What was most astonishing to Fiona was Jane's house. Two stories, full of hallways and doors that led to more rooms than there were people to fill them, and a swimming pool shaped like a kidney bean in the backyard. Jane had her own bedroom, a bunk bed even though she was an only child. There was a beautiful black piano in the living room—Fiona had never seen one, up close, and couldn't believe how Jane treated it as if it were another piece of furniture, no more extraordinary than a desk lamp or armchair. On top of all this, Jane had a doting, sentimental father, and a mother who doled out cash for the girls' ice-cream cones without launching into a lecture.

Before today, the most money Fiona had ever had at the same time was when she and Jane stole from the church. She had ten thousand dollars in her bank account, the first time her savings balance had ever held five digits. Did she feel more free? Was she changed? The receipt for the bank deposit was folded in half, tucked inside Fiona's jeans pocket. Headed back to her apartment, she resisted the urge to take it out, read the printed numbers again.

She hadn't been allowed to attend Shulin's funeral; her mother said it wasn't appropriate for children. Ona wailed and protested, but her mother stood her ground. The girl whipped herself into a frenzy, shrieking into the ceiling, throwing herself back against the flattened cushions of the love seat. Her mother allowed this to go on for a few minutes, watching Ona quietly while she howled.

"It's not fair, Mama." Ona sniffed away the last of her tears.

"Listen to me." Her mother stood from where she sat at the Formica table. The chair made a scraping sound against the linoleum floor.

Kneeling down next to her daughter, she said: "One day, bao bei, you'll be grown up. You'll be able to do anything you want, go anywhere you please." She pulled a white handkerchief from her pocket and held it to Ona's nose. The girl blew into it and waited for her mother to go on.

"For now, and for just a bit longer—you're my little daughter. Sometimes you won't understand why I say this way, or that way, but it's always for your best. Understand?"

Her mother's eyes were a deep, dark brown, nearly black. The whites were slightly pink and the skin under her eyes was puffed up, and so Ona knew her mother had been crying for Shulin, too.

What would happen to Shulin's uniforms? And what would Mr. Wang do with all her toys, like her favorite doll with the curly brown hair and freckles dotting her cheeks? All of the colorful rayon scarves and bits of scrap fabric Mama Wang saved for the girls to play dress-up with? What about Shulin's pink leotard? Her black ballet slippers?

"Where did they put her?" Ona asked. "Where is Shulin now?"

Her mother paused a moment before answering. "She was in the emergency room, remember? And now—well, I suppose she's still there—in the—" She turned her face toward the wall and tented her fingers over her eyes, slowly shaking her head. "Do you remember what happened to the Monkey King at the end of his long journey?" she said finally.

Ona nodded. "The monk removed the gold ring around his head, and Monkey got his freedom."

"He got to go to a special place," her mother said. "Some people believe that's where people go after this life. You meet all of your loved ones again, all your ancestors and friends, after you pass on."

Ona thought about what her mother said. "That's where Shulin is now?" she asked. "Will she get to grow up there?"

The question made her mother smile. "I don't know," she replied honestly.

"And who will take care of her?"

"Maybe you get to choose," her mother said. "Maybe if you want to grow up, you can. Or you can stay the same if you want, and never change at all."

She thought of the lines on the doorframe of their bedroom, her mother marking Ona's new height every year with a stub of pencil. She thought, too, of all the pairs of shoes her feet outgrew each year. It occurred to her then that at some point, people stopped growing. Her mother owned only one pair of shoes, for example. Before the ones she wore now, she had a nearly identical pair of black shoes, which she had thrown out and replaced with the current pair right before the Lunar New Year, not because her feet grew too large but because the soles had been worn out and cracked. As for her grandparents, they weren't growing, either. Though they were changing in a different way, Ona realized—Grandmother's constant complaining about her lower back, Grandfather's false teeth, which had frightened her to tears the first time she saw them resting in a jar of water in the bathroom—what was that sort of changing called?

Shulin had died all of a sudden, a terrible accident. The circumstances were a "tragedy," a new word she gleaned from the whispers of adults the same way she'd learned her mother was a "widow."

"Mama," Ona said suddenly. "What if someone you loved wasn't really gone? What if you only thought they were, but they were still here?"

Her mother rubbed the back of Ona's neck, her tiny shoulders, bony as anything.

"Wouldn't you want to know, Mama?"

"Know what, baby?"

Ona chewed her lip, scared to say what was on her mind. She'd never lied to her mother before—but she'd also made a promise to Grandfather. Which was right? To tell or not to tell?

"My b-b-baba," Ona stuttered. "He's—he's—alive—"

"Who told you that?" Her mother's voice was quiet, but there was something in it that made Ona lift her gaze to her mother's face. She saw anger flashing in her mother's eyes. "Who talked nonsense to you? Your grandmother?"

"You knew it!" She twisted away from her mother on the love seat, squirmed out from under her mother's arm. "How did you know?"

Her mother was silent.

Ona blinked. Another realization dawned: The secret she'd promised to keep from her mother wasn't the one she thought she'd been guarding at all. She understood now that her grandfather had wanted Ona to stay quiet because the girl wasn't supposed to know. Her mother had deliberately kept her in the dark.

"Oh, Ona . . ." Her mother pressed her fingers to her temples. "I wanted to tell you when you were older. When you could understand better . . ."

"Why doesn't he live with us?" Ona said. "Where is he, Mama?" In a small voice—the smallest voice—the girl finally asked the question that had been plaguing her since that afternoon out on the balcony: "Doesn't he love us?"

"Love?" her mother said. She paused a moment. "No, my dear. He does not."

Ona recalled her grandmother's criticisms: That her mother was too proud. That her mother had made a huge mistake. She thought of the bedroom her grandmother had offered, a bed of her own next to a bookshelf filled with picture books. Her mother had refused it, and the girl didn't understand why.

"What did you say to him?" Ona asked. "You made him go away?"

"That's not what happened," her mother said. "He left on his own."

Ona stood from the sofa, apart from her mother. "Why?"

"A father is not a necessity," her mother said. "It's nice to have one—even better, a grandfather—"

Ona shifted from one leg to the other. She scratched a mosquito bite on her left arm, above the elbow.

"Love is a condition suffered by fools," her mother said at last, under her breath bitterly, but Ona caught the words, and they stayed with her, whether her mother meant them to or not.

She was six years old, turning seven in September. That Sunday afternoon, Ona made a choice to put away any questions she'd had about her father: who he was, and why he didn't come around. More importantly, she resolved that one day, when she herself became a mother, she'd never tell her own daughter any lies. Still, she forgave her mother almost instantly. She would always be the kind of daughter who did so, with ease. In this respect, Ona and her mother differed greatly.

Back in her apartment, Fiona called her mother. She told her about receiving the check in the mail, depositing it at the bank.

"You're rich," her mother said. Fiona laughed. "Don't tell anyone," her mother added, becoming serious. "You don't need to say—"

"I know, Mom." Fiona paused. "Did you book your plane ticket yet?" The hotel room, the rental car—Fiona wondered if she was supposed to reimburse her mother for these expenses for attending her commencement, now that she had the cash. Jane was coming up for the ceremony, too. Fiona hadn't talked to her yet about moving to New York. She was afraid of what Jane might say to ruin it for her.

"Ona," her mother said. "I'm so proud of you," she said. "When you walk across the stage—"

"I'm not coming back to LA after graduation," Fiona blurted out. "I'm moving to New York." Her mother didn't answer. Fiona hesitated. "I'm going with Jasper," she said finally.

On the other end of the line, she heard the sound of a lighter clicking, then her mother's sharp inhale.

"We haven't found an apartment yet," she said. "Jasper has a friend there, Kenji—he's going to help us look—he graduated a couple years ago. I want to work for a couple years then apply to law school. I already talked to my professors about it, for letters of recommendation. I still need time to study for LSATs. I—" Fiona broke off her rambling. Her mother still hadn't replied. "Mom? Aren't you going to say something?"

"What should I say?"

"Are you mad?"

"You love this boy?" her mother said. "You want to marry him?"

"I—Mom—yes," Fiona stammered. "I think so. Maybe. Not right now. In the future—"

"You told him?"

Fiona was silent.

Her mother sighed. Or maybe she was only exhaling her cigarette smoke. "Remember your ballet classes in Taiwan?"

Fiona pressed the phone against her ear.

"Remember that big earthquake? You had a friend—she lived downstairs?"

"Shulin."

"Shulin. That's right." Her mother paused a moment. "We didn't have anything back then, did we?" Another pause. Fiona imagined her mother lifting the cigarette to her mouth, the ember glowing orange between her mother's fingers. "We had each other."

"You wouldn't let me go to her funeral," said Fiona.

"The money for ballet—your slippers and costumes—I just couldn't afford them."

Fiona said aloud what she'd long ago figured out. "My grandparents paid." She recalled suddenly the neat little bedroom in her grandparents' apartment, the smell of mothballs, her grandmother's gentle voice inviting her to test the bed. She'd passed away six years ago—another funeral Fiona had missed.

A long silence.

"Mom?"

"Did you eat dinner yet?" her mother asked, as if Fiona had just walked into her house.

"You were so young, Mom."

"I told you a long time ago," her mother said. "Your father—he wasn't someone who could take care of us."

"I remember," said Fiona. Her chest felt tight.

"You never asked about him again." Fiona heard her mother clicking the lighter again. She didn't know where this conversation was headed. She felt nervous, her hands suddenly ice-cold. Her stomach rumbled; she hadn't eaten since lunch, a turkey sandwich on white bread she ate standing up in the kitchen, before going down to the bank.

"He was your grandfather's student," her mother said. "Your grandfather adored him. He was often invited to our house for dinner." Then her mother explained that Fiona's grandfather opposed the relationship because of the age difference—the boy was in college, after all, when her mother was still in her secondary-school uniform, her hair cut short in the compulsory style, just below the ears.

"So we ran away together," her mother said.

"That's not what I'm doing," Fiona protested. "Jasper and me—"

"Your grandfather tracked us down. I had to come back home. The boy was expelled from the university."

"We have a plan. I'm not going to— Just because you—"

"He never knew about you," her mother said quietly. "Your grandfather decided that was for the best. I never saw him again."

Fiona sat down at her desk, one hand touching the laminate surface, the other holding the phone up to her left ear. Her gaze moved across the apartment. It didn't have very far to go.

"I'm not sorry it happened that way, Ona," her mother said. "I'm sorry for your father. He missed out—he didn't get the chance to see you grow up."

"Mommy—"

"I'm not mad, okay? I understand." She paused for a moment. "Ona," she said. "Are you happy?"

Tears sprang to Fiona's eyelids. She hesitated before answering. "I am," she said. Then she heard herself saying that she wanted to give half the inheritance money to her mother. "A graduation gift from me—"

"No, no," her mother said. "I'm supposed to give *you* a gift—that's backwards."

Fiona laughed, growing more certain as she insisted that her mother accept this gift. "I'm the one graduating college," she said. "But, Mom, it's all—it's only possible—because of you."

"Me?" said her mother. "Me?"

"Mom," said Fiona. She remembered something her mother used to say to her, when she was a child. "You're my own heart, walking outside my body. I have to take care of you."

"Oh, Ona," her mother said softly. "My crazy, windy girl."

Fiona would have to pay back the church money another day, another year. She'd give half of what she had to her mother now and keep the other half for her move to New York. None of this made any sense, given her usual system for making decisions: collecting data points, setting budget constraints, a lengthy Pros vs. Cons list. She realized she'd never considered the question her mother had posed today: Are you happy?

Fiona sat in her mortarboard and black polyester gown in the orchestra section at the Greek Theatre, waiting for her row to be called up. It was an especially hot Friday morning in the middle of May, and Fiona fanned herself with the paper program for the poli-sci ceremony.

She thought of that Father's Day ballet recital years earlier, when she'd believed the yarn her grandfather had spun about inviting her father to watch her dance, if only she could keep it a secret. She'd been caught under her grandfather's spell. After the earthquake, she found out her mother was in on the lie; she wasn't a widow, and Fiona's father wasn't dead. The last piece of the story, as her mother told it finally; all this time, her father never knew he had a daughter. Fiona didn't exist to him. Was it cruel of her grandfather to stir up her imagination, fuel a false hope to glimpse her father's face in that darkened auditorium? She chose to believe that he did it because he loved her. And she forgave him for what he did to her mother, too, making her father leave. Her mother had no choice but to accept the boy's disappearance, but then she did the one thing no one expected: she left the family. For six years, she lived on her own. Her mother had survived, day by day. She was a Lin, after all.

She thought of Shulin, who died in the earthquake that day. Fiona remembered afternoons watching cartoons on the television in Shulin's living room—Astro Boy soaring through the sky, a magical robot cat with a bottomless pouch of toys, the colony of blue forest creatures who lived in mushroom cottages (she'd learned they were called "Smurfs" after she came to the US, amazed that they were suddenly speaking English on this side of the world)—the sun streaming in through the windows, casting patches of light and shadow on the parquet floors. She imagined her grandfather and her childhood friend meeting in the mythic afterlife, the place where the Monkey King was finally allowed to rest, after passing the monk's tests. Shulin was still a little girl there, and Fiona's grandfather held her hand. The picture made Fiona smile, impossible and tender. Suddenly the little girl was Fiona herself, looking up at her grandfather. Then she changed again, and became her mother. She wore Fiona's commencement gown. Or was it a black funeral robe now?

After the ceremony, her mother would spring for the additional service the university offered for shipping official diplomas, which included professional matting and framing. When it arrives at the apartment a month later, she would hang it up proudly in the living room. Anyone who came over would be sure to hear about it: Ona, my daughter, the college graduate.

Fiona crossed the stage and shook hands with the dean. Squinting against the sun, she found her mother in the audience. She waved, and her mother beamed and waved back. Her stepfather and Conrad sat to her mother's left, and on her right side, Jasper held a bouquet of sunflowers. Jane, up on her feet and clapping wildly, next to Won—their old friend; he and Jane had driven up from LA together. Fiona felt a thrill, seeing them all together in a row, cheering for her.

She remembered the admiring gaze her mother had cast toward those college students in Taipei, when they slurped down hot noodle bowls after her ballet class. Fiona had thought her mother wanted to be like those young men and women, free to fill up her life with books and learning, if only she wasn't saddled with a small child. She realized she'd been wrong about her mother's eyes trailing after those college students in Taipei; her mother's gaze had always returned to her. Fiona could finally feel the power of her mother's eyes on her. She turned a silly little pirouette and bowed, surprising herself, then walked down the stairs to exit the stage.

Go Slow

The year we turned sixteen, Fiona decided it was time we learned to drink. We drove to the Norwalk swap meet and laid out fifty bucks each for fake IDs from a passport photo, faxing, and color copy stall. A Gujarati family owned the business, and the girl we paid off had graduated from our high school a few years back. When she handed us the finished IDs, we knew right away we'd been scammed. They were flimsy laminated jobs no better than Blockbuster membership cards, overexposed photos of our unsmiling faces glued onto a rectangle of white paper with CALIFORNIA IDENTIFICATION CARD typed across the top, our names and birthdays below, minus those crucial five years to age us up to twenty-one. We were too embarrassed to demand our money back. Still, we were eager to test them out. That was when we called Won. He said he knew a place, and the three of us set out one Saturday night in Shamu, Fiona's hatchback she named after the Sea World killer whale because of the corroding white patches all over the black paint.

The freeway glowed with stop-and-go brake lights. We barely moved: no more than ten, twelve, fifteen miles an hour. Seven thirty at night, the sky was a washed-out indigo, a few dirty gray wisps hanging low. No doubt Shamu was a hoopty, but she was ours. Well, she was Fiona's. Which meant she was mine, too. We were best friends; we shared everything.

Won leaned forward from the back seat. "Lucky this place doesn't card," he said. "You guys are dumb if you think those janky IDs will get you anywhere."

"Put on your seat belt before I get a ticket," Fiona said.

Won told her the name of the exit, somewhere off the 5 in Garden Grove. He was taking us to a "sooljip," he called it.

"Trust me," Won said. "It's gonna work out. Just be cool. You hear that, Jane?"

"Shut up," I said. "I can be cool—"

"Behind there—it's that place in the corner."

I looked out the windshield to where Won was pointing.

Fiona steered into the parking lot of a strip mall. She hesitated. "Should I— Right in front?"

Between a brightly lit twenty-four-hour donut shop and a dry cleaners with its pleated metal shutter pulled down for the night, there stood an unmarked storefront with a row of large windows, the glass tinted black. You couldn't see inside at all.

A neon sign buzzed red in one of the darkened panes, something spelled out in Korean characters.

I exchanged a quick glance with Fiona before we climbed out of Shamu. I could see the excitement in her eyes, and that she was trying to hide it.

We trailed in behind Won and sat down at a booth. The place looked nothing like the bars I'd seen on TV. First of all, there was no bar to speak of, no bartender standing behind a long countertop lined with stools. There were tables and chairs and booths, just like at a restaurant, except the lights were dimmed. I smelled fry oil and garlic in the air, and some cleaning agent, a chemical scent like a chlorine, but covered by citrus. The walls were papered in newsprint comic strips and glossy magazine ads that people had tagged over with black Sharpie markers in English and Korean.

When the waiter approached, Won did all the talking. His voice sounded different in Korean. Harder, somehow, like stone striking stone. The waiter, unsmiling, tipped his head toward Fiona and me. The name tag pinned to his black button-down shirt read SUNG. A raised pink scar stretched from his left ear to his chin, where a thin patch of short black hairs sprouted. I noticed Fiona watching him. Won answered him, and the waiter nodded, then backed away.

"What'd he say?" I asked.

"It's cool," said Won.

"Should we show him our IDs?"

Won just shook his head and laughed. A minute later, the waiter materialized with a tall pitcher of beer and three frosted mugs on a tray. We fell into a nervous silence as he placed everything on the table. Soon as he walked off, Fiona and I looked at each other and busted up laughing.

Won poured out three glasses. My first taste of beer nearly made me gag. I sipped slowly, trying to get used to the bitter taste, the bubbles burning down my throat. Half a glass in, I felt heady, my face warm to the touch.

"You like it?" Won said. "This is nice, right?"

A loud burp escaped Fiona's throat, and she clapped a hand over her mouth.

"I don't know how I feel," I replied honestly. "Is this drunk? Am I?" Won refilled my glass.

"Won, I love you," Fiona said. He grunted. "No, really," she said earnestly. "I love you." She turned to me. "And, Jane, I love you, too. I love you the most."

"This one turns into a happy ass." Won looked as pleased as I'd ever seen him. "What about you?"

"Jane," said Fiona from across the table. "Girl, you okay?"

"I love you, too," I said.

"Oh shit," Won said. "You're one of those depressed drunks."

"What?" I said. "No I'm not."

"Two types," Won said knowingly. "You're not going to start crying, are you?"

"The waiter," Fiona said. "He's kind of cute."

"Him?" Won said. "You got on beer goggles."

"I do?" Fiona said. "What's that?" Then she laughed again.

Fiona, Won, and I have been friends since second grade, Miss King's class. Same junior high and same high school, too, until Won got tossed last year, when we were sophomores. He was already on probation for ditching, a couple of fights, some other stuff. Then one day last April this football player, a big Samoan dude, decided to punk him for no good reason.

Won had the kind of face that summoned bullies like flies to dog shit. They thought he was stuck up because of the Boyz II Men–inspired cable-knit sweaters; preppy button-down shirts; and cuffed chinos he wore when everyone else sported white tube socks with Adidas slides, size forty waist jeans, and XXL Fruit of the Loom tees. People called him "Pretty Boy" and "Richie Rich," and they didn't mean it like a compliment, either.

Fetu toed up at lunchtime and said he heard Won was talking trash about his girl. Not only did Won suffer the humiliation of getting his ass beat in front of everyone in the quad, our evil vice principal decided it was the last straw for Won's disciplinary offenses and kicked him out (nothing happened to Fetu; he was a senior with two months left and was untouchable anyway because of his rushing yards average). Won got sent down to the continuation school with the druggies, pregnant girls, and gangbangers. Last stop before dropping out, juvie, or deportation.

Won wasn't who people thought he was, though. He wasn't some spoiled fuck-up with a dad who owned a chain of liquor stores or gas stations or SAT cram schools. We knew other Koreans like that, sure. But Won ganked all his fancy clothes. Shoplifting came easy to him, Won said, because mall security was always too busy hassling the Black kids to notice a skinny Asian redeeming his five-finger discount. For years he'd used a fake address to go to school with us, a better district than the one in his zip code.

Most of the boys we knew from school were Neanderthals with pimples, drenched in Cool Water cologne. Won wasn't like them. He was different. We felt safe with him. Fiona and I would never actually tell him to his face, but Won was all right by us.

We finished the pitcher. I felt a weight in my shoulders, a strange muscle ache.

"I can't go home like this," Fiona said.

Won asked what she wanted to do. It was a little after ten o'clock.

"The beach?" I ventured.

Won claimed he was sober enough to drive Shamu, even though he was as bright red in the face as Fiona. "Trust me," he said. "I've done this before."

We paid the bill, each of us contributing what we could—me with my allowance and some leftover lunch money, Fiona and her tutoring-job funds, and Won with cash from who knew where, probably a side hustle reselling the stuff he stole from the mall.

Fiona asked the waiter about his name when he picked up the black plastic tray.

"Sung?" Her voice was dreamy. "The past participle for 'sing.'"

The waiter held a blank expression in his eyes. But when Fiona smiled at him, he smiled back. His fingers flew to the scar on his face, as if to hide it.

"Let's bounce." When Won stood from the table, Sung's gaze shifted to him and back to Fiona again.

I made Won promise to drive slow. On the way to Huntington Beach, we passed by an Albertaco's, and Won pulled into the drive-through. Fiona, slumped in the passenger seat, perked up and leaned over Won to shout into the crackling box.

"Carne asada taquitos," she cried. "Con salsa roja. Por favor! Gracias!" To Won and me, she said, slurring, "I'm taking AP Spanish, okay? I'm getting a five on that bitch."

We cackled and hooted, called her a nerd.

Everyone at school knew Fiona was smart and respected her giant brain, but she wasn't considered a geek. She had those big doe eyes with real double-eyelids that other girls tried to approximate with bits of glue or tiny strips of Scotch tape. Her lashes went out to there, and her skin hardly ever broke out.

And because she had her tutoring gigs, with more clients all the time from positive recommendations, Fiona always had dough to spend on new clothes and kicks. She worked extra hard the last six months to save up cash and buy Shamu.

"This is so weird," Fiona said. "I've never sat here before." She turned her head to look at me. "It's like—I'm you!"

Ever since Fiona got Shamu, my butt has been a permanent fixture in shotgun. A new level of freedom had suddenly opened up. No more running to catch the bus, no more begging our parents for rides. Sometimes we cruised down PCH to Seal Beach and tried to sneak into one of the fancy hotel pools, parking blocks off so no one would suspect us of trespassing. At night we drove up to Signal Hill, where the rich white families lived, to steal their views of the Long Beach basin glittering all the way to the *Queen Mary*, that old haunted ship. When it was especially clear, you could see lights from Catalina Island winking out of the ink-black water.

And now, here we were, drunk for the first time. I'd wanted to give up after the swap-meet debacle, but she pressed on, insisted we call up Won. Fiona always knew what to do.

"You ever gonna learn to drive?" Won said.

I found his eyes in the rearview mirror and stuck out my tongue. So what if I'd failed the driving test a couple times? I just needed a little more practice.

"Tell the truth. I heard you hit a hydrant—"

"The DMV's racist," I said. "They didn't even make Tim Lockwood parallel park, and that other wrestler guy, what's-his-name? I heard he ran a stop sign but they passed him anyway."

"Naw," said Won. "You just suck at driving."

I kicked the back of his seat. "I hate you so much. Shut up!" But I was laughing, too.

"You love me. Been in love since Miss King," he sang. "Give it up, Jane. Never gonna happen!"

"You think Miss King ever misses us?" Fiona said. "You guys, I have the best idea!" Her voice was breathless, full of ardor. "We should go visit her—"

"Quit hogging the taquitos," I said.

We passed the Albertaco's sack between us all the way to the beach. Fiona had a mixtape playing, a cassette one of her admirers had made: Whitney Houston, Tony! Toni! Toné!, Salt-N-Pepa. Slouched in the back of Shamu, I crunched on those thick greasy sticks, the wind brushing my cheeks and the bass thrumming through my back. The air started smelling of salt. I took it in in big gulps. Won pulled into a parking lot, empty of cars at this time of night. Fiona turned the music off. We sat there, cradled inside Shamu, listening to the waves beat against the sand and roll back out. We couldn't see anything out there at all. For a while, no one said a word.

I recalled a Bible story from years back, when I used to go to church with my parents, before Baba moved back to Taiwan. Jonah trapped inside the whale, waiting for God to rescue him. The moral was something about betrayal and repentance, forgiveness and second chances. Here with Fiona and Won, I didn't want to be saved. I made a silent wish to stay like this forever, the three of us, perfect.

A shiver went through me. The weight in my shoulders disappeared. Won was wrong about me and what he'd said earlier, the two drunk personalities: I was happy.

After that first time, the three of us started posting up every Saturday. Won taught Fiona and me a few phrases: "Go-mahp-soom-nida" when Sung brought our order, and to add "oppa" after Sung's name as a sign of respect. Won tried to get us to call him "oppa," too, but we said no way. He sneered back and said he heard Taiwanese girls had stanky pussies. "Wouldn't you like to find out," I retorted. "Stop coming on to me," Won said. "I don't like you like that, Jane!"

We chased soju shots with frothy glasses of Hite; sucked down Marlboro Lights one after the next, filling the plastic ashtray on the table with a pack's worth of butts. Buzzing was a place to get to, and we were constantly asking each other if we were there yet.

"Do you feel it?"

"How about now?"

"After this one, for sure."

"You buzzing yet? You good?"

"I love you—I love you guys so much—"

When we drank, we felt wild. Here, there were no parents,

no teachers to tell us to sit down, be quiet, listen up. We stepped through the tinted-glass door of that sooljip as if crossing a portal, becoming new and more ourselves, simultaneously. "Sixteen was the best of times, and the worst of times," Fiona said one Saturday night. "The age of wisdom, the age of foolishness." I didn't figure out she was quoting from a book until way later. She was taking AP English, and I was in regular. When she said that, anyway, I'd thought it was just another typical Fiona thing: dramatic, beautiful, and true.

Another shot of lemon soju. More beer. Clink glasses. Cheers! Ganbei! Jjan! Which led to: Shit, I gotta puke.

Together, we'd sway out to the parking lot behind the bar. The one who needed to purge squatted next to the green dumpster while the other two chanted encouragements until we heard a splash hitting the pavement. A ritual we repeated, week after week; if it wasn't so gross, you might've called it religious, transcendent.

Sung learned our names, and when the bar wasn't too busy he sat down with us. He was twenty-two, we found out. When he wasn't working as a waiter, he held down shifts as a security guard at the Arirang Supermarket nearby. We shared our cigarettes with him, which he accepted readily, pinching them out of the pack two at a time: one to smoke now and another he'd tuck behind his ear for later.

Fiona began to nurse a crush. She thought his scar made him sexy and invented stories about how he got it, knife brawls and flying daggers shit.

"You think Sung would say yes if I asked him to our prom?" she said one night at the bar.

"You want him to find out we're in high school?" I said.

"Not like there's anyone else to go with," she muttered.

Won blew out smoke in rings, one after another. Fiona reached up and broke them in the air.

"My turn," I said. "I gotta puke."

They got up to follow me outside to the dumpster. Fiona squatted next to me and patted my back a few times. Behind me Won's steady voice murmured something reassuring. After, I headed for the bathroom alone to rinse out my mouth. I checked my reflection in the mirror above the sinks. Bloodshot, watery eyes, but my inch-thick black eyeliner was somehow still in place. My cheeks were a ghostly, almost bluish white.

Fiona was the pretty one, that much I accepted. She got her period first and went up a bra size from seventh to eighth grade. Freshman year she started growing her hair out, and now it was almost down to her waist. Her features were pronounced and striking—more than once, some old weirdo on Third Street Promenade had approached to ask if she was interested in modeling—but maybe my face could be considered pleasing, too. My eyes, though small, were very symmetrical. My nose didn't come right out and announce itself, but it was a fine enough nose, straight and unassuming. All those times

Mah reminded me to pinch on the bridge while I was watching TV—who knew if it made a difference. Whereas Fiona was outgoing and friendly to almost everyone, I cultivated mystery. It was hard to stay invisible, though, after I grew three inches last year. I knew people called me Fiona's bodyguard, behind my back. Whatever, I didn't care.

I dried my hands and shuffled back to the table.

"We're going to a party," Fiona said. She had the same excited look in her eyes as the first time we rolled up to the bar, except now she wasn't trying to hide it.

Sung stood by our table. "It's nothing big, just kicking back with a few homies," he said. "You down?"

"What about your curfew?" I said to Fiona. "What time is it?"

She laughed, too loud, and turned her face up at Sung. "Where did you say it was again?"

He wrote down the directions and address on a napkin. Fiona tucked it inside her red nylon "Kate Spade" bag, a purchase from another vendor stall at the swap meet.

Sung said he was on the clock for another hour. "I'll page my boy and tell him you're coming."

"Sweet of you," Fiona replied. She wore a broad, eager grin on her face. Sung rapped on the table with his knuckles a couple times and walked away. Her eyes followed him, then swiveled dramatically back to me. "Oh, my God," she whispered. "We're going to a college party."

"You coming?" I asked Won.

"Sorry, Won. I don't think it's like that—"

"Hang on," I said. "So we're just showing up to some party? Who are these people?"

Fiona rolled her eyes. "Come on, Jane. Don't be such a B-A-B—"

"I'm not being— I'm just asking—"

"He thinks we're eighteen," Fiona whispered. "College freshmen."

"So you didn't bring up the prom idea," I said.

"She told him we go to UCLA," Won said.

"Doesn't matter," Fiona said. She fixed me with her gaze. "You have to come, Jane. I need you."

"I don't think you know how dudes—if you two—"

"You stay out of it. Jane can make up her own mind."

I felt the weight of their eyes on me.

"Fine," I said finally. "But I have to be home by midnight."

"Midnight. I promise," Fiona said. "This is going to be so much fun," she added.

I tried to exchange another look with Won, but he wouldn't meet my eyes.

The car ride to drop off Won was completely silent, charged by anticipation. I felt bad, but I followed Fiona's lead. In front of his apartment complex, I got out and folded the seat down. He didn't say bye to Fiona or me. But when I got back into Shamu and shut the door, Won walked around the front and tapped the glass on Fiona's side. She rolled her window down.

He pulled his wallet out of his jeans pocket and opened it. From one of its inner folds, he removed a square of light blue plastic. "If you're going to hoe around, you should at least be prepared."

Fiona stared at the condom wrapper. I grabbed it and threw it back at Won. It bounced off his chest and landed somewhere on the ground.

"What do you think is going to happen at the party?" he said.

"Fiona, drive. Let's go."

We peeled off, nearly hitting Won when Fiona angled Shamu away from the sloped driveway. I watched him grow smaller in my side mirror. After we'd passed at least four or five lights in silence, I asked Fiona if she was okay.

Her hands gripped the steering wheel. I waited for her to blink, say something.

"He shouldn't have done all that," I said. "But maybe we're wrong, too," I added slowly. "We only knew about the bar because of him—"

"I don't care," Fiona said suddenly. "He's such a—just a boy. I'm over high school guys, you know?" She ran her fingers through her hair, raking a tangle that didn't exist. "I knew he liked me," she said. "But there was no way I—" Fiona shook her head and sighed. "I didn't tell you before. But we've like, I don't know. We made out."

"You what?" I said. "With Won? When?"

She nodded almost imperceptibly, her eyes fixed on the road.

I stayed silent while she signaled left and swung back onto the freeway.

"You're not mad, are you, Jane?" she said. "It's seriously not a big deal."

I didn't know what to think. I told myself it was no big deal, just like she said.

"It just happened." She glanced over at me quickly. "I was going to tell you, but—"

"Do you like him?"

"No. It's Won." She frowned. "Oh, Janie. You didn't—you don't—"

"What? Me?" I laughed a little. "Him? No way. Gross."

"Right," Fiona said. I was waiting for her to laugh, too, but she didn't. "Well, he's not—completely gross. Actually he does this thing with his tongue—"

"Ew," I cried. "I really don't need to know."

Now she was laughing. "Sorry."

It was no big deal, I repeated to myself. They kissed. Fiona and Won kissed each other. I realized I'd been clenching my fists. I let go of them softly. A strange feeling throttled me.

We passed by a sign on the side of the freeway announcing Cal State Long Beach, next exit. Fiona signaled, then moved into the right-hand lane. All of a sudden I felt nervous about what would come next.

"Do I look okay?" I considered my outfit: an oversized T-shirt with maroon and green horizontal stripes across the chest, a pair of dark blue jeans, black socks, and black Vans with black laces.

"Use the lipstick in my purse," Fiona said. She was wearing a white scoop-neck baby tee tucked into tight black jeans that flared at the ankles. "Can you check the directions?"

At the next stop sign, Fiona reached over and put a hand on my arm. "This is going to be fun, okay? Let's just relax and have a good time." She sounded so confident. Fiona always sounded confident. "You look great," she added. "I mean it. You really do, Jane."

I squinted at Sung's handwriting on the napkin.

"You look like one of those people in the CK One ads. Cool 'cause you're not trying so hard to be something."

I flipped the visor down and studied my face in the tiny rectangle mirror. My eyes weren't bloodshot anymore. I found Fiona's Toast of New York in her purse. I opened my mouth just a little bit and applied the brown color with soft strokes. The girl in the mirror pressed her lips together into a thin straight line, then puckered them in a kiss. I slapped the visor shut. Did they make out here, in Shamu? *Just be cool. You hear that, Jane?* No big deal, I said to myself. It was no big deal.

Sung's directions led us to a motel near the Long Beach Airport, a two-story stucco building painted salmon pink, with ocean-blue window trims and doors to suggest a seaside resort theme. A large black satellite dish rested on top of the roof, which was missing more than a few of its terra-cotta tiles.

Fiona maneuvered Shamu into an open parking spot. We sat buckled into our seat belts for a moment after she shut off the engine.

"Should we have a plan?" Fiona said. "A signal. If we want help from each other, or—"

"We don't have to go up there," I said.

"How about this?" She held up two fingers in a V and pressed them to her chin.

"We can turn around right now, and go home. You can sleep over—"

"If either one of us gets in trouble, just do this," she said. "And we'll leave right away."

I mirrored her, held my fingers up to my chin. The digital clock on Shamu's dashboard read 9:45.

"Ready?" Fiona unlatched her seat belt.

"Remember, I have to be home by midnight," I said.

"Home by midnight," she said. "I won't forget."

The white boy who opened the door to 205 wore a black Raiders beanie. Tiny silver hoops dangled from both his earlobes.

"Sung's UCLA friends? Come in, come in." He stepped aside for us. "What's your names? I'm Koala," he said.

"Koala," Fiona repeated. "Like, the marsupial?"

"Damn, girl," he said with a laugh. "What'd you call me?" Koala threw an arm out and gestured at the guys who sat on one of the beds. "That's Johnny, and the butt-ugly one over there's Viet."

There were two queens in the room, each covered by a pink comforter patterned with white conch shells. Pink ruffle skirts grazed the tan carpet, which still bore vacuum lines. A McDonald's bag rested on the nightstand between the beds, the bottom stained by oil blots. A few crumpled napkins and balls of yellow wax paper lay scattered next to the bag.

"Got anything to drink?" Fiona's voice brightened the room. "Should we take off our shoes?"

"We got vodka, tequila, pineapple rum," said Viet. "We got ice. We got juice and mixers, whatever you need," he added. "None of that nasty soju stuff."

"Sure," Fiona said cheerfully. "That's why we came." She elbowed me and whispered, "Smile, Jane. Why do you look like that?"

"Make them your specialty," Johnny called out. "You never had Jungle Juice like Viet makes," he added excitedly. "You're in for a treat. Because this mofo straight up from the jungle!" Johnny cracked up at his own joke, slapping his knees.

"You so stupid, man," Viet said, shaking his head. He turned his finger in circles next to his temple. "This guy did too many drugs in high school. He's a walking billboard for Just Say No."

Johnny was still laughing by himself, red with joy. "Did Sung tell you we're related?" he said. "Cousins. He got the looks in the family, but I'm the smart one."

Viet walked over to the kitchenette and opened the door to the mini fridge under the sink. He wore a tight white tank, and underneath the thin, ribbed fabric his nipples were visible, two dark coins on his chest. His black athletic pants rustled whenever he moved.

Of the three, Viet was the best-looking, with his hollow cheeks and brooding eyes. He had a thin, morose face, sculpted with hard planes like a marble bust. His entire head was shaved, except for a thin fringe of long bangs, which he wore combed back. One strand on the left side was bleached a dark orange color. Then Johnny, who wasn't outright fine, but pretty cute, in a goofy way. I wondered if he really was Sung's cousin, or if he'd said it as a joke. They looked nothing alike. The skin on his cheeks was riddled with tiny scars like the rind on an overripe orange, and he had a set of dark eyebrows that arched up dramatically, lending his face an amused, almost crazed expression.

Koala's nickname was cruel in its accuracy, his beady brown eyes set too close together and that long, bulbous nose, which indeed seemed a shade darker than the rest of his face, just like the snout on a koala bear. Being the white boy of the group, though, Koala held a certain exotic appeal.

A thought came to me, unbidden: When Sung arrived, there would be four of them and two of us. And what would happen then?

"Are there more people coming?" I asked.

"You're bored already?" Koala said.

"Sung said it was a party—"

"Oh we're just getting started. Don't you worry, baby girl."

While Viet mixed our drinks, Koala invited us to make our-selves comfortable. "Get up, fool," he said to Johnny. "Make room for the ladies." Johnny moved to sit on one of the dinette stools, where Viet stood at the bistro table pouring from differ-ent bottles into five red cups. "I gotta get me a pair of break-aways like these," Johnny said. He stretched out one of his legs and rubbed his foot on the side of Viet's pants, along the row of white buttons that ran from waist to cuff. "Easy access, man. Snap! Bam! There it is!" He finished with a playful kick to Viet's butt.

"Quit that!"

Koala leaned forward in the rolling chair next to the door, using his heels to scoot closer to the bed where Fiona and I sat. The wheels on the chair erased the vacuum lines in the carpet.

We accepted cups from Viet, filled nearly to the top with brown liquid and ice cubes.

"What's in this?" I sniffed at the rim.

Fiona took a tiny sip, and then another. "It's not bad," she said.

Koala edged closer, watching her lick her lips. I pretended to sip from my own cup.

"Bo-rinnnnnggggg," Johnny said. "Down that shit," he cried. "One shot!" He drank from his cup, tilting the entire contents down his throat. His Adam's apple jumped each time he swallowed. Ice cubes fell on his face, a wet glaze on his nose and under his eyes. He jerked around and shook himself, invigorated. "One shot," he chanted, pumping alternating fists in the air. "One shot, one shot!"

"Come on, Fiona." Koala smiled at me. He held his cup out. "You got this, girl."

"I'm not Fiona," I said.

"Dumbass," Viet said. "That's Jane."

"Can we drink yet?" Koala raised the cup to his mouth.

"You think Sung's coming soon?" Fiona asked.

"Sung?" Koala wiped his mouth with the back of his hand. "Fuck that guy." Viet and Johnny broke out laughing. "That fool owes me twenty bones."

"He owes me forty," Johnny added. His eyes tilted toward the ceiling. "No, wait. I owe *him* forty—"

"Why's my dude always talking about, 'I got three jobs.'" Koala used a whining voice to imitate Sung. "'I'm working graveyard this weekend, I gotta put in hours at the grocery store,'" he added. "And Sung is still the brokest motherfucker I know?" The guys laughed again. He slid his eyes toward Fiona. "The girlies like him though."

"Looking like one of those K-pop boy bands," Viet said. "Homie's about to get a perm next."

"Does he have a girlfriend?" Fiona asked.

"Who's asking?" said Koala. This made Viet and Johnny roar.

"Hey," I said to Fiona in a low voice. "Slow down with that." I nodded toward her cup, which was half-empty.

She smiled but shot me a look that meant I was being a buzzkill.

"Remember our sign?" I held up two fingers and wiggled them in the air, down by my lap.

She turned away from me and took another sip from her cup. "So where do you guys go to school?"

"School?" said Koala. "We don't do that."

"We got bigger dreams," Johnny added. Then he repeated himself, fading out like an echo: "Bigger dreams . . . dreams . . . dreams . . ."

"Says the genius who failed his GED," Viet said, shaking his head again.

"But see, I only failed it twice," Johnny explained. "Third time's the charm, though."

"I'm taking a couple business classes at LBCC," Viet said. "What you ladies study?"

"I'm undeclared," Fiona said. "But I'll probably do political science, pre-law."

How did she know those words?

Viet looked at me expectantly.

"Um—writing?" It was the first thing that popped into my head.

"That's a major?" he said. "I hate writing."

"Me and Koala are starting a business. You'll be seeing us up in *Forbes* in a few years." Johnny began shadowboxing, bouncing on his toes, throwing hooks and jabs in the air. "Right, Koala Bear? Tell 'em about it."

"It's a secret," Koala said. He held up a finger to his lips. "If I tell you I'll have to kill you."

"And don't worry, we'll do it nice and slow," Johnny said. His face broke into a maniacal grin. "First I'll tie you up with rope. Then I'll use the pliers." He fixed his gaze on me. "You got nice teeth—you had braces, huh?"

"Shut up, asshole," Koala said. "He's just messing around."

"You still wear retainers at night?" Johnny said.

"We're not scared." Fiona nudged me with her elbow. "Right, Jane?"

I glanced over and saw that her cup was empty.

"I've never had braces before," I said evenly. "These are just my teeth."

Someone pounded hard on the door. "Open up! It's the cops! We got you surrounded!"

I froze, but the guys started laughing. "Always the same corny BS," said Koala. He walked to the door and opened it. "Get you some new jokes, homie," he said.

Sung strode in grinning. "The party's here," he said. He sat down next to Fiona at the foot of the bed. "My friends treat you okay?" She nodded, smiling. "Yo, we got the other room, right?"

"Yeah, 201. Down that way." Koala threw him a set of keys.

"Let's go for a walk," Sung said to Fiona. He plucked at her elbow. "Come with me for a sec, will you?"

"Where?" Fiona said.

"I want to talk to you," Sung said softly. He stood and held out a hand.

Fiona stood from the bed. She was wobbly on her feet and reached toward Sung to steady herself. He threw an arm around her waist. "There we go," he said. "Nice and easy, gorgeous."

"This mother . . ." Koala muttered. "Mr. Smooth Operator."

Viet and Johnny were sitting up on the other bed. Someone had turned the TV on. Koala stood by, waiting for Sung and Fiona to make it to the door so he could open it for them, like some sort of butler.

"Hang on." I stood up and grabbed Fiona's arm. "She's— You can't just take her—"

"Chill," Sung said. He lowered his mouth to Fiona's ear and whispered something. "See?" he said with a triumphant smirk. "She wants to come with me."

"Come on, Jane. You don't want to hang with us?" Koala said. "I thought we were getting to know each other here."

"Janie," Fiona mumbled. "It's okay. I'm okay." She shook me off. "I'll be right back. We're just going to talk."

"You heard her," Sung said.

I pressed two fingers into my chin. "Fiona. You see this?"

"What's all the commotion?" Johnny called out. His voice was a song. "We're trying to watch porn over here."

Now Koala was pulling on my arm—I stumbled a few steps. Fiona turned back to glance at me over her shoulder. I tried the signal again. She smiled and shook her head, then looked away. Her hair was a cascade down her back. I watched them walk through the door. Koala shut it softly behind them, and then my best friend was gone.

"Another drink?" Koala said brightly. He parted his lips in a grin. His teeth were stained dark yellow along the gums.

I glanced over at Viet and Johnny on the far bed. A synthetic melody played from the TV speakers. Viet rubbed an open hand across his crotch, roving in slow circles. His athletic pants gave off a crackling silky sound, as if static electricity sparked when he touched himself.

Johnny's face was nestled in the space between Viet's neck and shoulder. He raised a loosened fist softly toward Viet's moving hand, but it was batted away. Johnny sighed: a mournful sound. He buried his head deeper inside the crook of Viet's neck, then started to kiss his collarbones, his chest. He licked at the two dark coins through Viet's white tank.

If any of what Johnny was doing to him had any effect, Viet didn't show it. His eyes were pinned to the TV screen, where two naked bodies, a man on top of a woman, writhed on a bed with red satin sheets. As if he suddenly remembered I was still standing there, Viet turned his head in my direction. He looked at me through half-closed eyes.

"I'm not gay," he said. "Just so you know." His eyes drifted back to the TV. "Cut the lights, Koala. Too bright in this bitch."

Then the room was dark, except for the glow of the TV. I couldn't look at it. I turned around and caught Koala staring at me from his chair, bathed in a weird green light. He opened his mouth, dragged the tip of his tongue over his chapped lips.

"You get down like this, College?" He slid his eyes over the empty bed and back to me. "I know your type. You act mean at first, but once you get a couple drinks in, you're down to party." He stood and took a step toward me, a crooked grin painted on his face. The hoops in his ears shook and glinted. Before he could get any closer I crossed to the door. I slid the chain off, and then I was outside.

I ran down to Shamu—luckily, Fiona had left the doors unlocked. I sat in the passenger seat, shivering. Room 201 was only a few doors down from where I'd just escaped. Five minutes, I told myself. If Fiona didn't come out, I'd go knock on the door.

Five minutes turned into ten, then fifteen.

On the ground level, I spotted a pay phone box stuck to the wall. There was only one person to call. I punched in Won's pager, left the pay phone's number, my code, and 9-1-1.

He rang back almost immediately.

"I need help," I said. "I don't know what to do— Fiona disappeared and I'm waiting out here by myself—"

"You have to go get her," Won said after I told him what happened. "Then come over here. Can you drive?"

I said I didn't know where we were or how to get home. Then I remembered we were by the airport. He gave me directions and made me repeat them back, twice.

"Go slow," Won said before we hung up. "You'll make it, Jane."

"Won," I said. "I'm scared—"

"You can do it," he said. "I'll be here waiting."

I pounded on the door marked 201. Sung answered—I pushed him out of the way.

"Fiona?" The room was decorated the same as the other one, except with a king-size bed. There was a lump under the comforter. I sat down and pulled back the blanket. Fiona's eyes fluttered open.

"We were just talking." Sung's voice behind me. I glanced back and saw that he was holding up the waist of his jeans with one hand. A braided leather belt hung loose off the loops.

"Are you okay?" I asked Fiona. Her hair lay fanned out underneath her head on the white pillow. Her top was still on.

"I barfed." When she said it, I smelled the rancid odor in the air.

"You can't stay here," I said. "We have to go."

"I don't feel so good," she moaned. She screwed her eyes shut against the light.

Sung stepped next to me. "She just needs to sleep," he said. "I'll take care of her—"

"We're in high school," I blurted out. "We don't go to UCLA. We're sixteen."

"Oh fuck. What?" Sung threw a hand up and backed away slowly, the other hand still clutching the waistband of his jeans. "I never touched her," he said. "I swear I didn't. Nothing happened." He stroked nervously at the scar on his face.

"Help me—"

"Her shoes are here somewhere . . ." Sung got down on his hands and knees to search under the dust ruffle.

After he found Fiona's black wedges—one kicked under the bed, the other in the shower, somehow—Sung helped carry her down the stairs to Shamu.

"I knew you were lying," he said. "I thought you were hoodrats pretending to be college girls, but damn. You're sixteen?"

Although it would've been faster on the freeway, I drove Shamu along the side streets all the way to Won's. The last time I took my driving test, I forgot to turn and look over my shoulder while trying to merge onto the freeway. There was no one cruising in my blind spot, but still, it was a critical mistake. An automatic fail.

When I finally pulled up to his complex almost an hour later, Won was standing outside, waiting. Fiona woke up, disoriented, groaning, when Won threw her over his shoulder. He carried her like that up the stairs to his apartment. I followed, afraid he might lose his grip and drop her.

Won laid her down in his bed. His room was dark. We'd been here, the three of us, a million times before.

"Jane," she murmured.

"I'm here." I sank to my knees on the floor beside the bed. "We're at Won's house."

"Won?" she said softly. "What happened . . ."

"You're drunk," I said. "You're safe now."

"Me?" she said. Her voice dropped to a whisper. "Jane— don't tell Won what happened— I don't want him to know—"

"Know what?" I said.

"I love him," she said.

"You're drunk—"

"I have to tell you something important," she said urgently. "He loves you. Did you know that?" She sighed happily. "And I love you, Jane. We're all in love."

Won shifted behind me. I heard him breathing softly in the dark.

"Don't tell him what happened," Fiona said again. "Promise me. It'll ruin everything."

When I looked behind me again, Won had left the room.

"Jane," she said. "Sung told me how he got the scar on his face." I waited for her to go on. "His mom threw a plate at him. He's blind in one eye." She spoke breathlessly. "He's twenty-six, not twenty-two."

"What?"

Fiona kept talking. Sung told her that he used to be smart,

like she was, before his mom threw the plate—he'd won the spelling bee one year, in junior high. He met Koala a couple years back at an Herbalife recruitment event, and they launched a campaign targeting LBCC students until they got banned from campus. Koala's family owned the motel. Sometimes Sung lived there, or else he slept on the floor in Johnny's room, at his aunt's place. He had plans to save money and open up a bar of his own one day—Viet was going to help him, with his business degree and all.

"Was he mad when we left?" she asked.

"I told him our real age—"

"Why'd you do that?" she said. "Now he won't ever call me. Thanks a lot, Jane . . ."

I found Won sitting downstairs, on the bottom step, smoking a cigarette. It was way past midnight, and Mah must be frantic by now. I knew I should get home as fast as I could, but one look at Won's face, and I felt like crying. By the time I reached the bottom the tears were spilling out. I hiccupped, gasping for breath. Won wrapped his arms around me, and I leaned against his shoulder, letting my snot drip into his sweater like a slob.

He said he regretted taking us to the bar, meeting Sung. "None of this would've happened," he said. "You all right?"

"She told me you guys—you know," I said. "Not that I care—"

"Told you what?"

"The kiss," I said. "Whatever."

Won didn't answer.

"You're in love with her," I said.

He made a sound with his mouth, forcing air out between his lips. "In love with Fiona?"

"It's okay," I said. "I get it."

"I'm trying to tell you," he said. "I— We kissed because—" Won hesitated. "I had to test something out."

"You're not the only one," I said. "Everyone's in love with her."

"Not me." Won stared at the ground. After a moment he glanced up and held my gaze. "I don't like Fiona. Not like that."

"That's why you got so pissed off earlier."

"I don't like any girls, like that—"

I thought of the motel room earlier. The sound of Johnny sighing, his face buried in Viet's neck. Then, Viet turning to say, *I'm not gay.*

"You mean . . ."

Won nodded.

"Since when?" I said slowly. "Are you sure? How do you know?"

Won didn't reply.

"Fiona thinks you—the kiss—"

"Jane," he said quietly. "You won't tell anyone, will you? You can't tell Fiona. No one—"

"I won't," I said.

I asked him why he was telling me this now. I asked him again if he was sure of it.

"I trust you," Won said. "You pay attention to shit other people don't." He hesitated a moment. "I thought maybe you knew it already." He hesitated again, longer this time. "When that football player—Fetu—he kicked my ass—"

"Fuck him," I said.

"I used to meet him in the park," Won said. His voice was pinched in his throat. "Under the freeway, off Shoemaker." He busied his hands, lighting up another cigarette.

"For what?"

"What you think?" he said. "I gave him football advice. We rode the swings." Won jerked his fist back and forth in the air, a motion like shaking dice.

"Fetu?"

"Until his little cheerleader girlfriend followed him one night."

"You and him?" I said. "Won, I didn't know."

"Now you do," he said.

We were both silent for a while.

"You know that guy Sung's, like, really, really old," I said. "He's twenty-six."

Then we were quiet again, each in our own thoughts.

"You ever think about what's going to happen after next year?" he said finally. "After bullshit high school."

"I know she's going away," I said. "Some fancy college on the East Coast. Shit with ivy climbing up the brick walls."

"And we'll still be here, doing whatever we're doing."

The way he said it sounded depressing as hell. But when I caught his glance we both busted up laughing at how we were feeling sorry for ourselves, our pitiful futures, while Fiona—our Fiona, the destined one—was laid upstairs in Won's room, passed out drunk in his bed.

Oh, it felt good to laugh.

It seemed I hadn't laughed all night, not since before I was puking in the parking lot behind the bar with Fiona and Won, their murmuring voices reassuring me that I'd be feeling fine soon enough. I felt soft for Fiona suddenly. And then, something else, for myself. I felt strong, more sure on my feet than I'd ever been, before tonight.

Years later, I'd think back and remember this night, this moment, standing at the foot of the stairs outside Won's apartment. The night-blooming jasmine giving off its sweet, heady scent, carried through the air on a gentle breeze. A dog barked somewhere down the street, twice. Then it was silent again, except for the steady thrum of midnight freeway traffic, the sound of fast cars cutting through the dark. A fake ID in my back pocket that would've fooled no one. Fiona's idea. Always Fiona's ideas, and me, saying yes. My best friend. We shared everything, I believed. Still, she was the one in the driver's seat. I rode shotgun. And Won, cruising in her blind spot. Not mine, though. He told me about himself that night. I listened.

The strange feeling I'd had earlier—the one I couldn't place, when Fiona said she and Won had kissed—came over me again.

My throat tightened. I'd thought it was jealousy before, and I'd crushed it down inside of me, ashamed. I didn't want to be jealous of Fiona. Sure, there was plenty to envy about her, but I'd never felt anything close to competition between us. Until tonight. Until I learned she'd kept a secret from me.

But it wasn't jealousy. It was the shock of grief, that we didn't share everything, no matter how much I wanted to believe we could. And now I held my own secret with Won, with Fiona on the outside of it.

Then something drained out of me and suddenly, I felt dead tired.

"My ass is grass," I said. "Give me a ride home?"

Won ran upstairs to grab the keys to Shamu. The rushing freeway traffic from beyond the concrete divider wall sounded just like the ocean at night, if you closed your eyes. I waited for him to come back down, for what felt like a long time. I wished he'd hurry up.

Korean Boys I've Loved

There was Dr. Park, my dentist. When he put his fingers in my mouth the smell of the latex turned me on, and I made super intense eye contact with him while he scraped the plaque off my teeth. You're a smoker, he said. Uh-huh, I replied, which made drool drip from the side of my mouth. When he unclipped the bib afterward, the back of his hand grazed my left nipple and I knew it was on.

What do you write? he asked me once. I answered, but he wasn't listening.

This bitch is bleeding me dry, he said, his eyes watching the phone screen. Men, Korean and otherwise, were always asking *What do you write?* then forgetting to wait for the answer. Dr. Park was separated from his wife, and every other Saturday he picked up his twin boys from the house in Larchmont where he used to live with them, and her. He never asked if I wanted to meet his sons, and I never expressed interest. Sometimes he showed me pictures of them in his phone, two pumpkin-headed toddlers grinning. They had his mouth, his ears. Little assholes, Dr. Park called them. They don't really like me, he said bitterly. They're mama's boys.

The writing wasn't going well. I felt it coming, but it still hurt when my manager dropped me after another flopped pilot season. I needed cash, so I pinched Dr. Park's Rolex one night. Snuck out, hit the road, I-15 toward Vegas. He knew I needed the money, and if he'd just given it to me, it would've been easy, but he wanted to prove our affair wasn't dirty, when in fact. Well. Let's just say I was alternating antibiotics—Cipro, Amoxil, whatever—every other week, urinary tract infections and tonsillitis and even pinkeye, one time. Always begging to fuck me in the ass—he said his wife would never let him, and that was why Taiwanese girls were better than Korean ones. That was supposed to be a compliment. Ha.

I pawned the watch, doubled it in an hour at the craps table at El Cortez, then somehow lost it all again. Every last chip. Nothing left to do but call him and confess. He said he understood, told me to come home and he'd give me the money I needed. When I got there he was waiting in my apartment, smoking a cigarette in the dark. Don't know how he got in. Dr. Park had his ways. He stood up and slapped me a couple times. Guess I deserved that. Then he shoved me against the wall and really started hitting me—not in the face, you understand. Never in the face. I took it. He was crying. I felt so tired. You probably won't believe me, but we really did love one another. Anyway, he went back to his wife. Said it was because he didn't want to lose half his money if they divorced for real, and I had to respect that. Plus they had the kids to think about. What could I do?

Kyung, he used to be my writing partner. I met him back in my first-ever screenwriting class at Santa Monica College. We only did it a handful times, in his dank little room, that narrow apartment off Olympic and Alvarado. Outside his bedroom window you could hear MacArthur Park. The ghosts moaning. I was drunk off Chamisul, as usual. The Decemberists singing something, something. We knew it was a bad idea to touch, all the things they say about sex ruining friendship and so on, but it was the week between Christmas and New Year's, and we were both so lonely.

We blamed the soju the first time but had no excuses the next couple times. His mouth tasted like menthols burned to the filter, and the whole time I was thinking, *He'll never leave this apartment, this neighborhood. This is where he'll die.* Inhaling the asbestos, slow and steady, or else shot or stabbed. He'd already been mugged twice and started carrying a knife around, but I knew he wouldn't ever use it.

I was wrong, though. Years later, after all the drafts of our suburban vampire romantic comedy went nowhere, he chose law school over the Asian American Studies program at UCLA. A few years back he got married to a German woman. On Facebook

I see their camping trips to Yosemite, Zion, places even farther than that. He seems happy.

My first real boyfriend, Danny Chung, I met when I was twenty-two. His friends called him Casper because he was so pale. After his parents died of cancer, one after the other, he and his addict brother went their separate ways. He didn't ever want to do anything fun. Couldn't sleep for shit. Couldn't talk about the sadness. That was fine by me; it was the year my dad died and I didn't have much to say, either. He got stoned twenty-four-seven and stuffed his face with junk. King Taco carne asada fries, Shin ramen with ripped-up Kraft singles, Sourdough Jacks and jalapeño poppers picked up from the drive-through. Not that he was in great shape before, but he really blew up after that. He still had those dark mean eyes that got me, a softness in his face. I was with him the night he got arrested. He insisted he was fine to drive. Idiot. When the blue and red lights flared behind us, he pulled over to the shoulder and turned down the music. Drew out a cigarette from the pack resting in the cup-holder. We were almost home, just one more stop on the 91. He told the cops it was my fault. *She was hitting me—she made me swerve!*

If you really want to know the truth, Won Kim was the only Korean boy I'd ever really loved, just don't tell him I said so.

Back in high school we were both closeted as hell, but maybe some part inside each of us sensed it in the other and that was why we clung together. We watched out for one another. He came out first, then me, a few years later. No, we never kissed, had sex, nothing like that. He'd kissed Fiona one time, though, back in high school—the only blemish on his Gold Star status. I'd kissed her a few times back then, too; *practice*, we called it. The three of us used to be in love with one another. We were so innocent—its own kind of power—before you got to be so scared of things, labeled it *growing up*. We thought we knew it all, didn't we?

And then there was Paul, the pastor's son. We were both twelve. He said he wanted to show me something behind the church, and I followed. In the stairwell of the parking structure, he unzipped his Levi's and pulled his dick out—swollen, purple, lifted. I stared at it. The stiffness seemed almost mechanical. He asked me to touch it, and I said no. Just a little, he said. Please?

His dad scared the shit out of everyone, talking about the rapture. Gnashing teeth, fire and brimstone. Koreans worshipped with a fervor far and beyond Mah and the First Chinese Calvary. I believed it all. Thought for sure I was going to hell. I was sure Paul was going to hell, too. I don't care, Paul said. I love you, he said.

The next week, he told everyone at school about my mouth,

my tight wet pussy. One of my older cousins, who claimed Wah Ching, got wind and kicked his ass. Paul shut up after that.

Later on, my cousin was caught in the cross fire at a pool hall shoot-out in El Monte. Seemed he was in and out of jail for years after that. Eventually, they hit him with the third-strike rule, locked him up in Calipatria, middle of nowhere. He would've hated Dr. Park. He would've said: I told you to stay away from Koreans. I know, I'd say back. I know, I know.

Doppelgängers

Over brunch at Clinton Street Baking Company on Sunday, Fiona debriefed Tish on what happened after they parted ways last night. His name was Gabriel, she said. They scarfed down cheese slices from Ray's, and then she'd climbed the stairs to his place in Alphabet City, swishing her hips in his face up the three flights. About his penis: average length, but thick enough so that her thumb didn't touch her fingers when she wrapped a fist around its base. A notorious size queen, Tish made a gesture kissing her fingers, then opened her hand in the air like flower petals blooming.

"The sisterhood of hoes welcomes you back," she said. "Congratulations, you slut!" Fiona laughed. "Now that you got laid," Tish added, "watch. They'll start circling."

"You're reinstating my membership?"

"Men are like sharks—"

"He was cute, right?" said Fiona.

"They can smell another dick on you like blood in the water."

"I liked that little gap when he smiles."

Tish made a noise, sucking her teeth. "You always do this."

"Do what?"

"You don't know nothing about him, babe. Trying to fall in love with his teeth?"

"I think he said he was a teacher." Fiona struggled to remember, but the hangover had her in a haze. "Something with high school kids."

"In other words, he's brokety-broke." Tish drained the rest of her bloody mary and raised a finger to get the waiter's attention. "The sisterhood has you on probation." She lifted an eyebrow, making Fiona laugh again.

Her Motorola chimed, an unknown number flashing across its little window. Fiona instinctively rejected the call. She swirled the last dregs of the mimosa in the flute and tilted the glass to her mouth. The phone beeped, alerting her to a new voicemail. Fiona knew what they wanted. She'd missed the last three payments on her Mastercard, four months past due to Sallie Mae. Envelopes appeared in her mailbox, late fees and overdraft notices, ballooning interest rates, letters from the collections department threatening Serious Further Action. She ripped up the letters and threw them in the trash, sometimes without even reading them. Then the phone calls started.

Tish asked if she was free Wednesday. "My brother and his little friends are throwing some rooftop party."

"Where?"

"It might be dumb. I mean, it's Malik." Tish rolled her eyes. "But whatever, he said it's open bar." She pulled out her Black-Berry and tapped on the keys. "At that new hotel on Riving-ton," she said, then rattled off the names of some DJs Fiona had never heard of. "End of summer, yadda yadda . . ." Tish looked up from her phone and frowned. "Is it really Labor Day next weekend?"

"Shit," said Fiona. September came too soon. The woman she was subletting the apartment from was due back in the city November 1. "What have we been doing with our lives?" There was a joke in her voice.

Tish smiled. "The first rule of the sisterhood—"

"Wait, you said Wednesday?" Fiona said. "I'm supposed to be going on a date."

"Oh come on," Tish said. "You can just change it."

Fiona hesitated.

"Girl. You need options in this life," Tish said. "Blood in the water, remember?"

Fiona nodded slowly. Willy, her ex, had disappeared in May. What had she been doing since? Besides think about him, con-stantly. Besides imagine that he might show up at her door, sorry in his eyes. She wouldn't forgive him. Not right away.

"Blood in the water," Fiona repeated.

"And also," Tish said, "you gotta quit with these artist types, love."

Tish was a product manager for a biotech firm—Fiona didn't

know exactly what the job entailed, only that Tish hated her boss but made a huge salary. She only dated hedge fund managers, I-bankers, the occasional corporate lawyer. Her boyfriends were often older, and white.

The waiter stopped by the table, finally. "Anything else I can get you ladies?" He was a Lower East Side hipster with a Sailor Moon tattoo on the inside of his left forearm.

"We've been waiting for refills," Tish said. The waiter apologized, murmured something about being short staffed today. She interrupted him and said they might as well take the check.

He drew the slim black folder from the back pocket of his jeans and laid it down on the table. "You probably get this all the time," he said, his eyes still on Tish. "People ever tell you that you look just like Tyra Banks?"

Tish exchanged a glance with Fiona before she answered him. "I don't see it," she said. "But okay." She reached for the check.

"She was in here couple weeks ago," he said breathlessly, as if divulging a secret. "Wasn't my table, but when you walked in, I thought—"

"What's the damage?" Fiona asked.

"I got this." Tish tucked her card inside the vinyl folder and slapped it shut. "You take Amex, yeah?"

"You have her eyes," he said, soldiering on. "The same skin color, too." The black folder with Tish's card sticking out of it sat on the edge of the table. Fiona wondered if she should offer to cover the tip at least. In her pocket there was a ten and a few singles, change from the bodega where she bought a pack of Camels yesterday.

All of a sudden the waiter's hand shot out, and Fiona watched in horror—time slowed, everything jelly—as his fingers reached for Tish's hair, which hung in long twists over her shoulders and down her back.

"Boy, I swear to God," Tish said, her voice cutting through the sludge.

The waiter dropped his hand in midair. Fiona realized she was holding her breath. She picked up the black folder from the table and shoved it toward the waiter. "Be right back with this," he said, and walked away.

"Fuck out of here," Tish muttered under her breath. She leaned back into the booth.

Fiona touched her shoulder. "You okay?"

Tish didn't answer.

"Hey. You want to talk to the manager?"

"I'm fine." She fiddled with a bra strap that had slipped down her arm.

Fiona didn't know what to say. "I thought he was hitting on you," she blurted out.

"I'm fine," Tish said. "Girl." She shook her head, screwed up her face in a quizzical expression. "He was so gay, hello?"

A few minutes later the waiter sailed by to return the check with Tish's card. "Hey, so I didn't charge you for the drinks."

"Oh," Fiona said. "Thanks," she added after a second.

"You're welcome." He gave a quick bright smile and left to fill another table's water glasses.

"You're still in the running," Tish said to his back, "to become America's next top waiter."

Fiona fell out laughing. "Don't leave him any tip."

"Then you know he'll be like, 'Black people—'"

"But he tried—oh God." Fiona shook her head.

"Listen," Tish said. "Back to this Gabriel person. Whatever you do, don't let Rico Suave wife you up. Have fun with him . . ."

Fiona braced herself.

". . . I just don't want to see you getting caught up like last time—with Willy—"

"Let's not get into all that, please? I just can't—not right now." Fiona dragged herself out of the booth. Slipped the shades that were resting on her head over her eyes. Tish knew a little bit of what had gone down. She didn't know all of it, though.

"You're still getting your money back from him, right?" Tish asked. "When's that motherfucker going to pay you?"

Fiona wanted to go home, sleep off the rest of her hangover. Her phone rang again. Another unknown number, an unfamiliar area code. There were times when she thought it might be Willy, calling from his new phone. He'd have an explanation that would make sense of everything, turn her life right side up again. In those few seconds before her embarrassment flooded in at how stupid this seemed, Fiona felt her heart beating hope, hope, hope. She said goodbye to Tish outside the restaurant, and they walked in opposite directions down the sidewalk.

Last night at the club, Fiona had figured that the gorgeous brown-skinned man on the edge of the dance floor, a hungry grin on his face, meant to approach Tish. He wore a gray tweed newsboy cap, the brim tilted to the side. Soft dark eyes with heavy lids, a closely cropped beard with meticulous edges. Fiona was surprised when Gabriel had sidled up and placed a hand on the small of her back, gently, and asked her her name. His voice had air in it, like wind caressing leaves, coaxing them to fall. Later, when the rest of the girls said they were dipping out to another bar, Fiona stayed behind. "Use a condom!" Tish had whispered in her ear before giving her a slap on the butt, a coach sending a player out on the field.

At brunch, Fiona didn't let slip how nervous she'd felt, going home with Gabriel. It had been three, four months since Fiona slept with someone. The first, since Willy. In the dark, Gabriel removed her clothes first, then his own, like it was the most natural thing in the world. Fiona kept anticipating some unpleasant feeling to arise—shame, or disappointment, or even just plain boredom. She felt none of those things, but unexpectedly, a tentative freedom. His mouth tasted like scotch and the waxy spearmint of his lip balm. They fell into the unmade bed that took up nearly all the space in his room, Gabriel muttering between bites of her neck and collarbone about how she was beautiful, so damn sexy. Fiona remembered something she once knew but had misplaced and then forgotten she'd wanted to find again: her body was a thing that belonged to her, and no one else.

The afternoon sun beamed from high overhead. Fiona strolled uptown, buzzing softly from the mimosas. Her phone vibrated with an incoming call. She picked it up this time.

"Ona?" Her mother sounded a little out of breath. "Why didn't you call me back yesterday?"

"Sorry, Mom," Fiona said. She reached for a lie. "I was just about to—"

"I need your help." Fiona tensed. "I need to borrow five thousand dollars."

"What?"

"Vitamins," her mother said. "Business opportunity. I have a chance to get in at this level, but only this week—"

"What vitamins?" Fiona said. "I don't have the money," she added. She shook a cigarette out of her soft pack.

"It's a good investment, Ona. Guaranteed return. I have five thousand saved, I need the other half. Vitamin supplements, everything organic. Collagen, fish oil, top-of-the-line best. A big Chinese investor is backing, and there's only a limited chance for smaller angels. And we get free samples to try, every month." Her mother went on, describing the starter kit of dis- counted products that she could use herself or sell at a profit, how she planned to host living room parties to recruit more investors to her team.

"Ona?" her mother said. "I was thinking, maybe it's a good time for you to move back. We can be partners. You and Mommy."

"It sounds like a scam," Fiona said. "Who told you about this?"

"They have a website, you can go look at the videos. Very professional!" her mother insisted. "I researched everything already. No scam."

"Mom, it's a pyramid scheme," Fiona said. "The people at the top get all the money, and they keep adding more and more people at the bottom. Don't do it, okay? Promise me you won't do it."

"How much do you have in savings?"

Fiona stayed silent. She could hear her mother breathing into the receiver, waiting for an answer.

"How is Willy?" her mother said finally.

"Willy? He's fine." Fiona tossed her cigarette on the ground and stamped it out. "I have to go, Mom. I'm catching the bus."

"Are you still smoking?"

"Mom," she said, exasperated. "I'll look at the website when I get home."

"You promised you were going to quit. Why do you lie?"

"I really have to go, Mom."

"Tell me before Wednesday night, or else I lose my place in line. I'll FedEx some samples for you to try this week." Her mother cleared her throat, and it led into a phlegmy cough.

Fiona held the phone away from her ear while her mother hacked. When the spell ended, her mother said, "You're still young, you can make a change, just like that. Think about it. We'll call it Lin and Daughter!"

More often lately, her mother needled her about moving back to Los Angeles. Conrad had left home when he turned eighteen, two years ago. His dad, Fiona's stepfather, long gone. Maybe her mother was feeling lonely. Fiona was turning thirty this year, but she knew her mother didn't see a problem with her grown daughter moving back in. Did the vitamin capsules home business stand in her mother's mind as a real proposal? Or was it a farfetched tactic to get Fiona packing her bags, shabbily disguised as a cry for help?

Her mother cut a supremely unlikely figure for pushing healthy dietary supplements. She was overweight and prediabetic; last year, an episode of gout forced her into a wheelchair for two months. After she got her legs back, Mom switched from Newports to Mild Seven menthols. She cut down to three cigarettes a day, the best she could manage, despite her doctor's warnings. Still, her mother nagged Fiona all the time about quitting herself.

She kept walking, drifting east toward Gramercy. Eight years in New York City. Her mother had never visited, not even once. And what did she want to show her mother, anyway? Fiona imagined her life through her mother's eyes, wreathed in disappointment. The law degree left unfinished, though she was still

paying down the loans; a string of attorney-adjacent jobs that
didn't add up to a career. Unmarried, childless. The mess with
her ex, Willy. At least her mother didn't know about that.

Last Christmas, she'd brought Willy home to meet her family.
Her mother had read Willy's face and declared him blessed, five
seconds into the introductions. Oh, just look at that intelligent
forehead, she'd said, and such big, beautiful earlobes. Fiona translated loosely: Mom likes your face. Willy was fourth-generation
and didn't speak a syllable of Mandarin, Cantonese, Toisan, nothing. Her mother added, in English, "Lucky. Rich!" Fiona had
snorted out a laugh, then recovered by hiding it as a cough. Willy's business cards, which he had designed himself and printed
up at Kinko's, said he was a documentary filmmaker. He was
twenty-eight, a year out of Tisch. He scraped together a living on
thin royalty checks from downloads of his MFA thesis, a short
doc on Coney Island sideshow performers; the occasional DP gig
on shoots that paid in IMDb credits, MetroCards, and catered
food. Willy's only consistent cash flow came from delivering
laundry bundles for his uncle's fluff-n-fold on Henry Street. She
had laughed at her mother's read on Willy's face, but Fiona also
wanted to believe that her mother knew something she didn't,
some greater future for Willy, and for herself. Willy was a hus-
tler, one of the things she had liked most about him. She'd just
never imagined that she could be one of his marks. And after
all these years in New York, where she'd learned how to live as
if always on guard.

This most recent Christmas in LA, she'd invited Jane over one night. She'd introduced her to Willy as "my best friend," though in truth they'd hardly kept in touch. A distance between them Fiona felt acutely, marked by unspoken things, added up. She knew the contours of Jane's life, not its interior. If Fiona moved back to LA, what would their friendship be like—no longer held aloft by the nostalgia for their high school years, the romance of their present distance?

A fire truck blasted its urgent sirens a few blocks up. It was moving away, not closer. Everywhere she looked people walked in pairs, holding hands, filling the street with their smiles and knowing, intimate glances. Where the sun touched her face, her body, Fiona seemed to feel more and more alone. Cars passed up and down the streets she crossed. Every once in a while a yellow cab stopped on the corner and someone got out, and another passenger waited to slide in, then slammed the door shut. Her eyes followed a bike messenger riding up Broadway, weaving through the traffic, until she lost him to the distant horizon.

She thought of Gabriel. How might her mother read his features? The prominent curve of the Cupid's bow on his upper lip, those high cheekbones, his laughing brown eyes. Did color matter? What fortunes might her mother glean from Gabriel's burnished-copper complexion? Then she shook her head, remembering Tish's warning about her tendency to settle into relationships, careening from one man to the next. *You don't know nothing about him, babe. Trying to fall in love with his teeth?* It occurred to her that she didn't even know Gabriel's last name.

Fiona forgot about her mother's vitamin business proposal until she lay down to sleep that night. She breathed in the dark. Her mother wanted five thousand dollars. She thought of the money she gave her mother, the night before she boarded the plane to New York. Fiona had kept the other half of the inheritance from her grandfather for herself. Of course she didn't have it anymore; that money had been spent long ago, many times over. And now, Fiona didn't even have five dollars to spare.

Wednesday night, Fiona texted Tish she might meet up later, depending on how her date went. Gabriel had suggested a Cuban place on First Ave. When she was out of the subway and above ground again, her phone beeped with a new voicemail message. She listened to it, walking toward the restaurant.

"Ona," her mother's voice rasped. "Call me, okay, honey?" A pause. "Don't forget, tonight is the deadline." Another pause. "This is Mommy."

Fiona stuffed the phone back into her purse and made her way down the block. She saw him first, before he noticed her approaching. Gabriel leaned against the wall next to the restaurant's entrance. He had on the same newsboy hat. There was a slight chill in the air, but it wasn't cold enough for a proper coat—he wore a black puffy vest over a long-sleeve button-down. They hugged, and Fiona smelled something woodsy and citrus on his neck. Gabriel was taller than she remembered, or maybe the heels she wore on Saturday had cut their height difference.

"Glasses," she said. "Are those for real?" She lifted her hand to his eyes, index finger extended, as if she meant to tap on the lenses.

"I'm blind as a motherfucker," he said. "Astigmatism and everything."

"Reading by candlelight?"

"Damn, how old you think I am?" he said, laughing. "Watching TV like this." He held up his palms an inch in front of his nose. "Only reason I'm not a NASA astronaut, you know. Otherwise I'd be up there, discovering aliens and whatnot."

"I thought maybe you wouldn't recognize me . . ."

"You look nice. Did I say that already?"

She smiled. "We were a little bit not sober the other night."

"I don't black out when I drink," he said. "I always remember everything." The way he said it made her blush.

They went in and followed the hostess to the middle of the dining room. The walls in the restaurant were painted dark red, and votives on the tables cast dots of light through the room, little fires reflected in the mirrors that hung on the walls. They sat down with the menus.

"My kids are reading *Love in the Time of Cholera* right now," he said after a moment. "You know the part when he begs the restaurant owner to sell him the mirror?"

Fiona looked up and shook her head.

"Oh, never mind."

"Tell me," she said. "Please."

"I can see the side of your face in there," he said. Fiona turned to the beam next to the table, where an oval hand mirror with an ivory handle hung from a nail. "So brother is mad in love with this woman, Fermina. She's married to a rich doctor, he's doing his thing with other girls, whatever. But he spots her at a restaurant and after she leaves, get this." He paused for effect. There was that gap in his smile. "He buys the mirror off the wall because her reflection was in it."

"Can I ask you something?" said Fiona.

"Don't say you thought that story was corny."

"What's your last name?"

"Rivera," he said. "What's yours?"

"That story wasn't corny," she said. "It's romantic."

"Colombianos, man." He struck his chest with a fist, as if stabbing a knife into his heart.

The waitress came by, and they ordered. Fiona asked him if he was from New York, and Gabriel told her his parents still lived in the Bronx, same apartment where he grew up. "Same old sofa, too. Cushions smashed, but Mami would kill you if you try to take the plastic covers off."

Fiona smiled, thinking of her own mother, how she used to shrink-wrap everything, too. The TV remote, the cream-colored lampshade that hung in the living room, the dining room chair cushions. Every time you sat down to eat you risked plastic burn. One time Mom had tried to wrap up the Nintendo controllers, but Conrad protested, and for once, she'd relented, let him mash away on the buttons with his greasy thumbs.

"You been out here long?" Gabriel asked.

She told him she was thinking of moving back to LA, even though it wasn't true. Not really.

"For what?" he said. "Earthquakes to split your building in half. Sitting in traffic for hours?"

"Don't you ever get tired of New York?" she said. "It's so humid in the summer, and in the winter you're walking around wearing a sleeping bag. For months, just miserable."

"I like the seasons," he said. "We need markers, you know? But worse, no Boricua out there."

"What about—what's his name?—on the Dodgers?"

"That don't count. I'm talking regular folks," Gabriel said. "Plus I heard people fake as hell in LA."

"Oh, right. Like there's no one fake in New York."

Gabriel forked a slice of plantain from his plate into his mouth and chewed. "True, true," he said after a moment. "But, girl, you can't leave now. You just met me!"

Fiona shook her head.

"Why you laughing?" He feigned a hurt expression.

"My mom wants to go into business with me," she said. "But it sounds like a total scam."

"What is it?" he asked. "Nigerian prince with a frozen bank account hit her up?"

"Chinese people," she said vehemently, "are way more shady than any Nigerians."

"Word?" Gabriel raised his eyebrows. "You're Chinese? Do I need to watch my wallet?"

"My ex," she started to say, but her phone interrupted, bleating its robotic jingle. "Sorry," she said, unzipping her clutch to reach inside. "Thought I had it on vibrate— Oh, actually—" Fiona pressed a button to silence the ringing. "I'm sorry, it's my mom. I actually do need to talk to her, for just a minute."

"Don't apologize. I get it," he said.

She stood and made her way toward the entrance, the phone pressed to her ear. Her mother's voice on the line was asking Fiona for money—demanding it, then pleading. Another deadline, for the next level of investors: "Better deal, guaranteed to make our money back in three months, if we follow all the right steps . . ."

When she sat back down at the table across from Gabriel, Fiona was shaking.

"Is everything all right?" he asked tentatively.

"Want to get out of here?" she said. "I have this bottle of rum at my place I've been saving. My coworker gave it to me from her trip to Barbados."

He gazed around the restaurant, searching for the waitress. When he got her attention, he motioned for the check.

Fiona straightened her back. She arranged her mouth into a smile. "You gonna come back later to buy this mirror off the wall?"

"Oh yeah," he said. "I already asked them to wrap it up for me. With the flan."

The rum was all gone. Fiona felt loose, giddy. Gabriel stood from the couch and moved toward the bed. He sat down on the foot of it, his knees spread open.

"Get over here," he said.

Fiona crossed the room. She stood between his legs.

Gabriel's hands rested on her hips. "Come here," he said.

"I am."

"Closer."

Fiona wrapped her arms around his neck and sat down on his lap. He was still wearing his hat. They kissed a few times, then he pulled back. He looked at her. "You're lovely," he said. "You know that?"

She laughed softly. His face didn't change from its serious expression.

"I'm going to be hungover at work tomorrow," she said with a sigh.

"Your face," Gabriel said. "Reminds me of this student I had."

Fiona stiffened. "What do you mean?"

"Vanessa Chang was her name. She died. My first year teaching." Gabriel shook his head. "It was so weird. She was a senior, solid B student, headed to a SUNY on a swimming scholarship. She had her group of friends, involved in a couple clubs after school," he said. "Out of nowhere, she jumped off the roof of her building, into the elevator shaft."

Fiona couldn't help but imagine it, glancing toward the window, a dark shadow flicking past, falling too fast to register a face, a body. Seconds later, a sickening crunch far below.

Gabriel was going on about the memorial service they held at the school, grief counseling for the students.

"What are you saying?" Fiona interrupted. "You think all Asian girls look alike?"

"What?" Gabriel said. "No. Course not." He stared at her. "Why would you even say that?"

"You just said, my face—and her face—"

"I didn't say nothing like that. You're putting words—"

"Let me just ask you," Fiona said. "How many Asian girls have you been with, anyway?"

"What?"

"Like, am I the first? Or do you always—"

"How many Puerto Rican dudes you been with?" Gabriel stood up, forcing her off his lap. "You got some sort of problem with me?" he said. "If you got something to say, say it. Let's talk about what's really going on here."

"Why don't you answer the question?" Fiona said. She was more drunk than she realized, and she uncrossed her arms and put both hands on the bed, touching something solid to steady herself.

"Look at this place," Gabriel cried, flinging his arms around.

"You got all this nice shit, gold frames for your art prints and everything. Heavy crystal glasses for drinking some fancy-ass rum."

"This isn't even my apartment," Fiona said. "What's your point?"

Fiona lived alone, a luxury she'd lucked into through a friend of a friend. The apartment in Gramercy belonged to a woman who was away for a year in Florence, conducting research for her dissertation. On what, Fiona didn't know. Renaissance art? The tall bookshelf in the corner was crammed with oversized tomes of European art history and theories of aesthetics. Framed prints of the Madonna cradling baby Jesus adorned every available wall space. When she'd first moved in, Fiona couldn't shake the feeling of being watched, that the eyes of the various Virgins were following her around the studio. Now she was used to them; sometimes she even talked to them, finding sympathy in their long-suffering glances.

"Talking about, 'My mom wants to invest in this and that.' What kind of person just ups and drops out of law school, and you can still afford to live like this?" Gabriel said. "You saw how I'm living. I'm thirty-six and I got two roommates, okay?"

"Keep my mother out of this," she said. "Who the hell— You know what? Just get out."

"Who owns this place, then? Your family, right?" He shook his head. "I get it. You're rich. It's not a problem. I got some Chinese students at my school. Only thing is, I see the way their parents look down on me. They think it should be some white dude up there, teaching literature." He crossed to the sofa, where his vest was slung over the arm.

"You don't know anything about me," Fiona said. "Nothing."

"Oh yeah?" Gabriel said. "Why don't you tell me something, then."

"I was lucky to get this sublet, after my ex robbed me for everything." She felt angry tears rising in her throat and choked them back down. "I helped him sign up for these credit cards to finance his stupid film project—he said that was how some famous indie director made his first movie—then he maxed them out on shit he could flip for cash."

Gabriel stood there, silent.

"Another time, he straight-up emptied my bank account." Fiona turned away to wipe the tears from her face. "And you know what's really fucked up? After all that, I got back together with him." She drew in a sharp breath and let it out slowly.

In Fiona's mind something suddenly shifted, and now she was the girl who lay twisted on the ground at the bottom of the empty elevator shaft, eyes wide-open, staring up at a square of cerulean far above. But how could she see the sky, smell the rusting pipes, and feel the cool concrete against her back if she was already dead?

Gabriel was shrugging his vest on. He stood with his hand on the doorknob. "Why'd you even agree to go out with me?" he said quietly. "You should probably . . ." He trailed off without finishing his sentence.

The way Gabriel looked at her now, Fiona wished she hadn't blurted out the whole pathetic Willy saga. She would do anything to get back to the way they were at the restaurant earlier tonight. How he complimented her and admired her profile in the mirror. She saw no way of retrieving her dignity now.

Her favorite Mary was the one hanging next to the front door, who wore a ruby diadem and a crimson robe trimmed in gold thread. Her right breast was exposed, and the baby in her lap suckled with pleasure at the nipple. Fiona fixed her gaze on the red Mary now, avoiding Gabriel's eyes but still holding him in her field of vision, as if preserving him in memory.

He opened the door and stepped into the hallway. The door shut behind him with a quiet click.

"I'm not rich," she said bitterly. "And you're an asshole."

At her desk the next day, Fiona opened up a browser to the Jobs section on Craigslist Los Angeles. She found a few legal research jobs, similar to what she was doing now, but the advertised salary ranges were ten grand less than what she was currently paid. For a moment she entertained the idea of returning to law school, like she kept promising her mother. That possibility depressed her even more. She closed the browser window and decided to go for a walk to clear her head.

Downstairs, she headed east toward Herald Square. The sidewalk was wet from an early-morning shower. She stepped carefully over a slick metal grate. Fiona still felt haunted by Willy's presence all over the city. Last week she thought she saw him reading a folded-up paperback on the downtown platform as her train slowed to a stop at the 14th Street station. It wasn't him. The week before, she could've sworn it was him hailing a cab in front of that fried chicken joint on West Thirty-Second. Wrong again. Just one of his doppelgängers, another East Asian dude in tight black jeans and an oversized green utility coat, sporting a growing-out fade. She recalled the way he plowed the sidewalk, fists jammed into his pockets, shoulders hunched against some invisible impending wind. Still handsome in her memory, though she hated his guts. With every false sighting, her heart dropped. She scolded herself each time for wishing, just for a second, that she'd actually seen him.

Fiona shook her head and plucked a cigarette out of the soft pack crushed in her coat pocket, stuck it between her lips, and lit up. She fished her phone out of the other pocket.

Her mother picked up on the third ring, her voice scratchy with sleep. "Ona?"

"I can't give you the money you asked for."

Her mother was silent.

"It's not because I don't want to," Fiona said. "I looked at the website, and you were right. It's legitimate."

"What did I tell you? You think Mommy is such a fool?"

"I'm the fool," Fiona said, her voice breaking. "I wish I could help you, Mom, but I'm in some trouble—I made a mistake, I trusted Willy, and he—he—" Fiona stuttered, trying to find the words to explain herself.

"Willy?" her mother said. "What happened?"

"We broke up." There was nothing to do but to come right out and say it. "He stole money from me. All my savings. Everything I had."

"Did you call the police? They have to arrest him!"

"It was my fault, Mom. I made a joint bank account, and credit cards . . ."

"Oh no," her mother moaned. "Ona. Really? Oh, dear."

"I'm going to quit smoking," Fiona said. "I'm getting the patch this week."

Her mother sighed, and the silence between them stretched long and wide.

"Everyone makes mistakes," her mother said finally. "But, Ona, this isn't your fault. Okay? I have five thousand dollars. I'll give it to you. To help you move back home." A pause. "You can rest for a while."

"That's money you were going to invest into your business," Fiona said. "I can't take that from you, Mom."

"Ona," her mother said. "Last Christmas, I could read it in your face. So much stress. Sadness. Anger. You looked so lonely." Her mother heaved another sigh. "Take the money. Come home."

Gabriel had accused her of being rich, and she'd denied it. But here was her mother, floating Fiona a lifeline. Five thousand dollars until she figured out her next move. She felt shame burning in her chest, tethered to relief. She told her mother she would think about it, but in her heart Fiona already knew her

answer. In truth, hadn't she already been leaning in this direction? She'd put most of her belongings into storage a year ago,
when she moved into the Gramercy sublet. Living among the
Virgin Marys, she seemed to have become a supplicant without
realizing it. Fiona no longer wanted restitution—from Willy,
from the difficulty of life in New York. She wanted peace.

It was Halloween, and Fiona's last weekend in New York.
She and Tish were headed downtown for a party, though
neither one had made the effort to dress up this year. On the
bench across from them sat a sexy Dorothy in a short blue pin-
afore, white fishnets, and four-inch platform heels, carrying a
stuffed Toto in her wicker basket. In front of Dorothy, seven
CrossFit types in body stockings held on to the overhead bar,
each representing a stripe of the rainbow. They swayed and
buckled with the train, attended by an eighth, a redhead wearing a green blazer over black bike shorts. He clutched a plastic
bucket filled with gold chocolate coins, which he handed out
jovially to everyone around him. Fiona accepted one and unwrapped the foil.

"I still can't believe you're doing it," Tish said. "Who actually leaves New York?"

"You'll come visit?" Fiona said. "After I get settled."

Tish sniffed. "If I ever forgive you."

Fiona hadn't seen much of Tish in the last month. She was getting serious with her latest beau, a private equities trader. He kept an apartment in Manhattan but lived in Westchester, and that was where he and Tish retired most weekends. Sisterhood of hoes or not, even Tish wasn't immune to cuffing season, after all.

They hopped off at Second Avenue. As they strolled up to the club on Chrystie Street, Fiona recognized a throaty guffaw. It was coming from the barricaded smoking area set up next to the entrance.

Gabriel was wearing a long-sleeved T-shirt that had been slashed to shreds, and his face was painted in zombie makeup. Strings of blood dripped from his mouth and down his throat, glistened over his Adam's apple, and disappeared into the neck of his shirt. He was smoking a cigarette with a woman in a kid-sized A-Rod jersey and silver hot pants.

Tish followed Fiona's gaze. "You know them?" she asked. "That bitch looks cold," she added.

"Remember the guy who freaked out on me?" Fiona glanced over again, and then she wasn't sure anymore that it was him. She shook her head and turned away. "Can we please just go somewhere else?"

"But Ari and his friends," Tish protested. "They have a table. We won't even have to wait on line."

Fiona kept her head down, chin tucked into the collar of her coat, and followed Tish up to the bouncer. She felt the cutting glances thrown their way by the three white girls waiting at the front of the line, who shifted restlessly from one leg to the other. One of them, whose breasts spilled over the top of her black satin corset like two wobbly poached eggs, sighed loudly and snapped the gum she'd been grinding in her mouth. The other two were dressed similarly in S&M-inspired costumes, vinyl thigh-highs and spiked collars and chain link bracelets. None of the three was beautiful, exactly, but all together, they stood as a kind of advertisement for the club, attracting everyone's attention who passed by. It was working, too. The line was growing longer by the minute.

Tish and Fiona made their way down a dim corridor that opened up into a large room with a sunken dance floor surrounded by low glass tables and leather ottomans. Sumptuous dark booths lined the walls. They weaved through the crowd and found Ari in one of those cavernous black booths.

"Babe!" Tish cried. Ari swatted the air, fluttering his hands in his friend's face. The friend stood awkwardly and shuffled out. Tish slid in, and Fiona sat down next to her.

"Scoot in," Tish said. To the man standing next to Fiona, she shouted, "Gil, there's room, sit!" She introduced him to Fiona, explaining his connection to Ari. Fiona didn't quite catch it, but she nodded as if she had.

"Pour you a drink?" Gil asked, tipping his head toward the bottle of Goose leaning in the bucket. He asked her where she was from.

"LA," Fiona said. "Actually I'm moving back there in a few days. Bye-bye, New York." She found the straw with her lips and sucked. It was mostly vodka. The cranberry rested on top.

"But where are you from, from?" Gil said. "Originally, I mean."

She hesitated for a moment. "I told you. Los Angeles."

"Oh, come on. You know what I mean. What's your ethnicity?"

She turned away a little. Tish and Ari were whispering to each other between kisses. The music from the speakers stacked around the dance floor thrummed. She felt the bass vibrating in her spine.

"I'm Taiwanese," Fiona said finally.

"Oh, there's this great place I order from—I love their pad see ew and tom yum soup," he said enthusiastically.

"I said Taiwan, not—"

"I can eat it all at level-five spicy." He grinned, a pleased expression on his face.

"Cool," she said. "That's amazing. Good for you."

Underneath the table Tish squeezed her hand. "Let's go on a bathroom break."

In the ladies, they pressed into an open stall together. "Here," Tish said, and handed her the bullet.

Fiona unscrewed the cap and dipped the little spoon in.

"Ready?" Tish had a foot on the flush to cover up the sound of Fiona's snuffling.

After they each took two bumps, Tish pocketed the blow and they washed their hands at the sinks.

"What do you think of Gil?"

Fiona looked at her friend in the mirror. Tish had lined her bottom lashes with a shimmery emerald pencil tonight, which made the amber flecks in her eyes pop. "I don't know," she answered. "Who cares?"

"Didn't you hear what I said earlier?"

Fiona shook her head and turned off the tap.

"He's Ari's client? Hello?" Tish said. "He's from, like, a really rich German family. Supposedly they were Nazi sympathizers or something. It's a big secret." She uncapped a lipstick. "It's fucked up, but whatever, he's making Ari rich."

"Isn't Ari already rich?"

"Flirt with him a little, why don't you? I know he's not your usual type, but . . ."

"What's that supposed to mean?"

"Nothing," Tish said. "Just that you can try something different. A guy who can take you on vacations."

Fiona turned to watch her friend apply a coat of deep red to her lips. "You mean I should be more like you, then."

Tish capped the lipstick and slid it back into her purse. "There are worse things—"

"I'm not looking for a sugar daddy," Fiona said.

Tish gave a small laugh. "But you'll sit at Ari's table, drink his alcohol, right? Do his blow." She bared her teeth at the mirror, checking for lipstick.

"I don't care about this place." Fiona tasted the bitter medicine drips at the back of her throat. She swallowed hard. Her heart was beating fast in her chest. "I just wanted to hang with you tonight," she said. "I'm leaving, and I haven't seen you at all lately."

"You didn't pick up when I called you last week," Tish said. "We could've gone anywhere tonight."

"It's not my fault," Tish said. Behind them, a woman stumbled into the bathroom and crashed into one of the stalls, banging the door shut behind her.

"It doesn't even matter. You're moving anyway," Tish said. She shook the water from her fingers and reached for the pile of brown paper towels between the two sinks. "Look. I didn't know that when I set you up with Willy—"

"Don't, Tish," Fiona said. "We don't have to get into all that—"

"Maybe then you wouldn't be leaving New York like this—"

"Have you talked to him?" Fiona couldn't help but ask. "I keep thinking I see him," she said quietly. "Walking down the street, on the L train."

"Babe." Tish turned away from the mirror and faced her. "He's gone. I didn't know if I should tell you."

"What?"

"Willy moved to Hong Kong," Tish said. "I just heard about it from one of our college friends this week."

Fiona studied the chrome taps, the dark gray marble of the sink's counter, spotted with water.

"I'm sorry," Tish said finally. "He's there for six months for some project with a pop star. It sounds stupid, but supposedly he's getting paid bank. So the money he borrowed from you—"

"Tish. Willy didn't exactly— I didn't tell you this—he stole that money from me."

"He did what?"

Gagging sounds rose from the bathroom stall. Fiona thought of the old days when she used to binge lemon soju and Hite bombs with Jane and Won. She could almost smell the fry oil that permeated the air in that hole-in-the-wall Korean place in Garden Grove. The parking lot in back where she'd vomited, then kept drinking with her friends. How small her world seemed now, suddenly.

She'd moved to New York because she believed doing so meant something, corny as it sounded: she came here with the intention of discovering herself. Eight years later, she had none of what she'd set out to achieve. Somewhere, she lost her head. Her heart. Jasper, her college boyfriend—he lived in Astoria, and beyond that she knew nothing about him anymore. Kenji, the friend she'd seen through cancer treatment, and who'd carried her through the worst of her breakup, had left the city for a teaching fellowship in London two years ago. The leave of absence she'd taken from law school, for her mental health. She'd met Tish in a women's group her therapist recommended; that was where jokes about the sisterhood of hoes had begun, all those men she'd tried out after she left Jasper. Tish introduced her to Willy. Oh, him. Willy moved to Hong Kong. Fiona let out the breath she'd been holding.

"You okay?" Tish asked. "What do you mean, Willy stole from you?"

Fiona reached out and grabbed Tish's hand. "Come on," she said. "I'll tell you later."

Back at the booth, they found Gil sitting alone. "I feel like dancing," Fiona said to him.

"Oh no," he said, looking up. "I don't do that."

"Where's Ari?" Tish asked, sinking down in the booth. Gil shrugged.

"You can dance with me," Fiona said. "I'll show you."

She led him to the crowded floor, draped her arms over his shoulders, and linked her fingers behind his neck. She felt Gil's hands, tentative at her waist. They dragged and swayed, slowly and without paying any mind to the blaring music, a deep house number with a bright trumpet melody. Everyone else was thrashing about, as if jolted alive by the thumping bass line. Fiona and Gil moved together like this for a while, gently holding each other, keeping the space of an egg between them. And then someone elbowed Gil in his back and he lurched toward her. The gap between them closed, the egg crushed. She pressed into him, and they kept dancing.

Over Gil's shoulder she caught sight of Tish, shimmying with her eyes closed. Ari grooved behind her, his arms circled around her waist. Fiona thought of all the times she and Tish had prowled the city looking for a good time. She recalled a hotel lounge in the Meatpacking high above the black cobblestone alleys, floor-to-ceiling glass, the bar in the corner pulsing white, then violet, then blue, a startling effect on the ten-foot Buddha relaxing next to the coat check. They'd told each other that rubbing the Buddha's big toe meant good luck—that you'd find excellent dick that night. She thought of the SoHo rooftop with the view of the Hudson, the West Side Highway running electric alongside it. Leaning against the stone balustrade, Fiona had watched those two columns of ghostly light in Battery Park. She remembered last summer, a windowless basement in the Bowery, the underground cave a giant sweating mass of bodies grinding to Daft Punk and Massive Attack; a rumor whispered that Q-Tip was supposed to show up for a secret set.

Fiona fixed her gaze on Tish, across the dance floor. Under the strobing light, she couldn't tell if Tish was looking back. I don't blame you for Willy, she wanted Tish to know. In fact, crazy as it sounded, Fiona was glad she had met him. With Willy, Fiona surrendered. For the first time, she chose to stop pushing so hard. She'd learned to give in. To lose—and lose big—was a new and thrilling kind of freedom, when Fiona loosened her grip on shame. All of a sudden she understood why Gabriel had said she reminded him of his student, the girl who jumped into the elevator shaft. Something about Fiona's face must have telegraphed her desire for escape.

"Want to get out of here?" Gil whispered in her ear. "Trick or treat," he mumbled drunkenly.

Fiona hesitated. She didn't want to leave yet. She wanted to stay for just a while longer. "Keep dancing with me, will you?"

She looked over Gil's shoulder. Her eyes skimmed the crowd,

and Fiona realized she was wishing, once again, to catch a glimpse of Willy, one last time. Then she remembered that was impossible now. Tish had disappeared from her spot next to the speakers near the edge of the dance floor. Ari was gone, too. There was no one Fiona recognized in the crowd.

Cold Turkey

I never agreed to it, but after Carly and I split up, Won appointed himself my life coach. His first directive: I had to swear on everything I wouldn't call Carly or try to see her; no exceptions, never again, bye girl, have a nice life.

"Remember me and Jesse?" he said.

"The go-go boy?"

"Camping trip in Joshua Tree. Fantasia's quarter-life crisis slash birthday weekend." Won narrowed his eyes at me across the table. "What go-go boy are you talking about?"

"Where was I?" I said. "Why didn't I get an invitation?"

"Somewhere with Carly, obviously," he said. "Being boring," he added. "Anyway, Jesse should've been a one-night stand. Then my stupid ass couldn't say no to him once we were back in LA."

The server brought out our food: grilled pork banh mi for me, pho tai with the raw beef on the side for Won. Any time he deigned to travel east of Fairfax, Won insisted on eating at this tiny spot tucked inside Chinatown's Central Plaza, no more than four tables here, the brown wood clock in the shape of Vietnam on the wall behind the cash register. Usually, I had to drive west to see him.

Won picked up a wedge of lime and squeezed it into his soup bowl, cupping a protective hand around it. "Then he has to tell me about his mom's dementia, how he's the only one who takes care of her, blah blah blah—"

"Don't compare me and Carly to one of your meaningless sexcapades, please."

"Point is, there's only one way you get through these things," Won said. "Cold turkey." The next step in my regimen, Won instructed, was keeping a journal. "Your first assignment is to write down all of the things you hated about her," he said.

"There's nothing," I replied. "I didn't want to break up." I shook my head. "I shouldn't have gotten so— I lost it. When she said—"

"This is a safe space. You can tell me," Won said. He leaned toward me and lowered his voice. "She had that white girl funk downstairs, didn't she."

I told him he was fired, effective immediately.

"I don't know how you do all that shit anyway. It looks so scary, all that skin, like it's about to attack you." He clawed the air with his hands in loose fists, fingers half-curled, as if defending himself against a predator.

"You're literally the stupidest person I know," I said. My mouth was half-full, and a bit of cilantro flew out and landed on the table. "I do mean literally."

"Okay, okay. Enough joking around." He reached into the canvas messenger bag that hung from the back of his chair and took out a small blue notebook, bound with a spiral ring. "You have to make a list," Won said. "When you start feeling all nostalgic, remembering the good times, you'll have this in your hands as a reality check."

I touched a finger to the blue elastic band running down the right side of the cover.

"What if I never meet anyone ever again," I said after a moment.

"Jane," he said. "We're twenty-six. What are you talking about?"

"What if Carly was the one?"

"She wasn't, though."

"How do you know?" I said. "What if she was my chance—"

"If we're both still single by the time we turn thirty, let's get married," he said. "I'm serious, Jane. Think about the registry—"

"Your mom would be so happy," I said.

"We should invite Miss King," he added.

"Obviously she'll officiate," I said.

"What about Fiona?" Then he asked if I'd talked to her lately. I mumbled something about the three-hour time difference between us.

"She broke up with Jasper. Did you hear?" he said. "I don't know how, but they're still living together."

"What?" I said. "Why?"

"You should call her," he said. "She's going through major—"

"Why doesn't she call me?" I said. "She has my number."

Won looked at me for a moment but didn't press it.

"I'm going through some shit, too." I stared back at Won, and he knew I wasn't just talking about the breakup with Carly. Suddenly the joke he made about us getting married wasn't funny at all. It made me think of my parents. My dad. Then I was angry, and I wanted lunch to end.

I made up an excuse about forgetting an appointment. Won knew I was lying, but I didn't care.

"Take the notebook," he said. I swiped it off the table before I cut out, leaving Won by himself.

Lately, it seemed anger trembled under the surface of my skin, behind my eyeballs: hot emotion lying in wait for any opportunity to erupt. It was what happened with Carly, too. Without thinking, I'd slapped her. Said things I regret now. Won was right. Cold-ass, rock-hard, freezer-burned turkey was the way it had to be. Not like I had a choice, anyway. She wasn't returning my calls or emails.

At home that afternoon, I cracked the notebook open. I wrote today's date at the top of the first page. Stared at the lined sheet for a while. I felt silly, transported to the oily-faced, gangly teenage girl writing at her desk, transcribing the daily accounts of injuries she suffered, slights perceived large and small, the general and vast unfairness of everything.

Last time I kept a diary I was still living at home. I stopped writing in it after Mah began snooping in my room. Though I'd kept it hidden inside a shoe box under my bed, Mah managed to dig it up; that was how she found out about me and Ping, my piano teacher. Baba had moved to Taipei, then to Shanghai. In those years it felt as if Mah and I were constantly tearing at each other's throats, never a moment's peace between us. We'd never been close, my mother and me; I was my father's child. Without Baba's protection—Mah had always accused him of coddling me—I was left to fend for myself, her paranoia fueled by the hearsay culture of suburban Taiwanese mothers who circulated alarmist emails on, for example, the resurgence of the 1970s party drug called Ecstasy among American teens; how pedophiles insinuated themselves into AOL chat rooms; what to do if you've been kidnapped and locked inside the trunk of a Toyota Camry.

Mah confronted me, bending my diary open to the pages where I'd sketched crude illustrations of Ping and me wrapped around each other in various configurations, hands touching, mouths kissing, tongues licking. It must've been obvious who I was drawing, from the tattoos and enormous dangling breasts, the grand piano off to the side and floating music notes every-where. Ping wasn't my piano teacher anymore when Mah found my diary, but we'd had something when I was a senior in high school. That was how I came out to Mah—I was nineteen and working four days a week at the optometrist's office on Alon-dra, just farting around—and when I knew I had to move out of her house.

Under orders from Won, a new notebook. I felt strange as I began to write.

1. Jealousy issues . . .

Carly hated it that I'd been with guys before her. Men were the enemy, even the queer ones. I didn't take her seriously, but she often ranted that eventually society would evolve to a point where men became obsolete.

"What about babies?" I asked her once.

"Cloning," she replied.

"What about straight women? Won't they be lonely?"

Carly thought for a moment. She said, "Heterosexuality is a performance. Once the stage is removed, women will be liber-ated, and—"

I kissed her to make her stop talking. She knew this trick but didn't mind.

Over and over, she pressed me for details surrounding my last boyfriend. I didn't want to talk about him, but she kept needling me. How'd you meet, why'd you break up, how often did you have sex, and the big one: Did you love him. Did you really love him? How much? Why him?

"No, baby," I said. "I thought I knew all about what love was, but I had no idea," I added. "Until now, with you." Sometimes she accepted this answer with a smile. Most of the time, she didn't buy it.

My past with men became the source of countless fights. Carly believed the more we talked about it, the closer we'd get to the truth. She thought if she could understand it, she might cure me, my attraction to men merely a bad habit to correct, as if I were one of the dogs she worked with at the obedience school.

I wondered if the reason she hated men was as simple as tracing back what Carly's dad did to her mom. Carly was four when she died. Her dad shot her with a handgun. Carly's grandparents took her younger brother, but they didn't want to raise another girl who would just end up like her mom, Carly said, so she passed through foster families and group homes until she emancipated at seventeen. She never saw her brother, those grandparents, again.

"I don't think about them," she claimed. "I stopped existing to them, so they don't exist to me."

When I asked if her dad was in jail, Carly had nodded her head grimly. After a minute, she said if he ever got parole, she would find him and kill him herself. She'd make him suffer. Feed his limbs to her dogs. Carly had a beautiful German shepherd named Xena and a golden retriever mix with corgi legs called Gabrielle. The muddy greens of her irises were suddenly clear, bright blue.

She asked about my father, but I didn't tell her the whole truth.

"He passed away a few years ago," I said.

"I'm sorry," she said. "At least you still have your mom."

I didn't tell Carly he took his own life. He was alone. Without family. My fault, because I'd outed him to Mah. He'd trusted me, his only child. My baby daughter, he used to call me. I let him down.

I didn't tell her I hadn't cried once, not since he died.

I just nodded, then changed the subject.

Carly met Won one time, when she and I first started dating last summer. The three of us got together for happy hour at the Abbey. Won complimented the blue in Carly's hair—Manic Panic, she'd replied, patting her crown self-consciously—and then he asked for her advice about Pepper, the Pomeranian he'd recently adopted. Maybe she felt defensive because I'd told her Won cuts hair at a celebrity salon in Beverly Hills; instead of answering, she cracked a joke about Asians eating dog meat. Won laughed without missing a beat, and the conversation moved on before I had a chance to react. When I confronted Carly later that night, she'd started bawling. She kept insisting she hadn't meant it "like that." Like what, I didn't know. Anyway, I forgave her; it was a mistake. A dumb joke.

Something changed, though. A shift between us, as if before then, I hadn't realized she was—really, truly—a white girl. I just didn't think of her that way. She was Carly. My girlfriend. I never talked to Won about it after. There wasn't ever a good time to bring it up.

"You have one thing on your list," Won said. I sat at his station with a black smock tied at my throat. "I think we should do a side part for you," he added. "Do you trust me?"

"I tried my best. Honest," I said. "I couldn't come up with anything else."

His hands stopped moving through my hair, and he found my eyes in the opulent salon mirror. "Did you consider writing down 'controlling'?"

"Carly wasn't controlling," I said.

"Let's see," he said. "How many times did I see you last year? One, my birthday. Then that last haircut you thought was too short but you were wrong."

"You were busy, too," I said. "You were always working— your hair shows—and Korea all summer—"

"I was in Seoul for two weeks," he said.

"Didn't realize you were keeping score," I muttered.

Won didn't answer.

"I'm back," I said. "I'm here now." I threw up my hands and jazzed them, a halfhearted joke. "You missed me?"

"Do you want to know what happened with Jesse?" His eyes were on my hair again.

"Your Joshua Tree Klingon?"

"I didn't tell you he was positive. He didn't say anything until we'd already hooked up a few times."

"What? Are you saying— Did you—"

"After that sob story about his mom losing her mind, I kind of fell for him."

"When was this?" I said. "Why didn't you call me?"

"Don't worry. I'm clean." He was still pulling and snipping locks of my hair. "I got tested right away, then again three months later. I'm good."

I tilted my head away from his hands and turned in my chair to face him. "Won. I'm sorry." I touched his arm. "I should've been there—if I knew—"

"The crazy part?" He stood back and paused a moment. The hand holding the scissors dropped to his side, and with his other hand Won pinched his left earlobe and pulled on it gently a few times. The gesture reminded me suddenly of my father. I shook my head, as if to clear it of this strange connection between Won and him. "The first thing that popped into my head wasn't even—you know, whatever—that shit is serious." Won made a grimace, still rubbing his earlobe as he talked. "My first thought was: well, Jesse and me, we could have it together."

Shame flooded through me. The first thought that had popped into *my* head was that I'd shared a straw with Won at lunch the other day—I'd wanted to taste his avocado and red bean smoothie, and I'd remembered there was a canker sore healing in my mouth. An open wound. That was the first thought I had.

"That's how much I liked him," he said. "I wasn't even mad at him for lying."

Won pulled the blow-dryer out of a drawer underneath the mirror and turned it on my head. We stopped talking for a minute. I was grateful for the break. Then ashamed, again, that I needed a break from the story Won just told me. When he finished blasting me, Won checked the length of my haircut by pulling pieces on opposite sides of my face toward my nose. Satisfied, he squirted out a dollop of hair oil and rubbed his palms together a few times, then fanned his fingers through my hair.

"Not too short, right?" He handed me a mirror and spun my chair around so I could admire the back of my new cut.

I was hardly paying attention to my reflection. Instead, I studied Won's face and tried to see beyond it, to recall his other face: the one he had when we were in high school.

Over the last five or six years, Won had undergone a few cosmetic procedures. It started out innocently enough with the eyelid surgery. First, the surgeon snipped the outer corners to lengthen his eyes, Won had explained. Then she punctured the skin over his top lashes, stitched and knotted surgical thread to generate scar tissue that forced the lid to fold externally, instead of retreating inside.

About a year after, Won found fault with his nose. Too flat at the space between his brand-new set of eyes and too broad at its base, the nostrils indelicately formed, according to him. A different doctor, someone a salon client recommended, did his rhinoplasty. With a small incision between the nostrils and cuts along the sides, the doctor lifted the skin off his nose, loosened it from the bone, and implanted a false bridge. Seven months later, another nose job, because Won was unhappy with the results from the first. This time, the doctor shaved off more cartilage along the shaft. Lately he's been talking about how his weak chin has held him back his whole life. He was researching the best chin-augmentation specialists in Seoul, Bangkok, and Singapore.

If you never knew him, back when I knew him, maybe you wouldn't notice the difference. Years ago, Won was the first person to come out to me. He didn't know it then, of course— I didn't, either—but his words granted me permission. I remembered that boyish face, his eyes at sixteen, as dearly as I recalled my first crush on a girl: the feeling of Ping's fingers hovering on top of mine over the piano keys, barely touching, the heat radiating from the palm of her hand while it covered my own. Back then, Won's gaze on me seemed to telegraph a message carried by some distant future light, one that asked me to trust in the possibility of a different road than what was offered to my father, the burden of which—my mother, me, the semblance of our lives together as a family—eventually killed him.

Won untied the smock at my throat and shook it loose with a flourish. I stood from the chair and stepped aside from his station while Won swept up the pieces of my hair on the ground with a broom. I checked out my reflection, turned my head from side to side. My bob looked great, styled in an effortless way like nothing I could duplicate at home. I thanked Won and tried to tuck some bills into his jeans pocket, but he waved me off.

"Just do me a favor, Jane?" He paused, and I waited for him to go on. "Keep writing in that notebook, will you?"

"I told you," I said. "I can't think of anything else I hated—"

He held up a hand to stop me. "Not about Carly," he said. "Write something else."

"Like what?"

"Anything," he said. "Ideas. Thoughts you have."

I frowned.

"Write a letter to Fiona," he said. "No time difference on paper."

"You're taking this life-coach thing a little too seriously."

"Write to your dad," he said.

"For what?" I said. "Got nothing to say."

"I think you do, though."

I was silent for a moment. "Maybe we should push the marriage pact to thirty-two," I said finally. "Thirty-three. Also," I added, "we need a provision for kids."

"Oh hell no," he said. "Kids? Why are you always trying to get me in bed? Hard pass—"

"Shut up, Won," I said. "I hate you so much—"

"I hate you more," he said.

"I'm leaving," I said. "Don't call me."

"Why are you still here?"

"I love you, stupid."

"You're welcome for the haircut!"

"I know you love me, too," I said.

"Stop coming on to me," he said. "I don't like you like that, Jane. I told you—"

"Stop lying," I said. "You asked me to marry you."

2. Controlling

I thought about the fight we'd had about my mother. After Mah's knee surgery, I started visiting her at home more regularly on the weekends. Up until then, Saturdays had been my standing date night with Carly, when we treated ourselves to dinner out and a movie at the ArcLight, or cooked a meal together at her place, Xena and Gabrielle underfoot. After accepting a few rain checks, Carly wanted to cash in. She said she wanted to meet my mother. I hesitated. She asked if I was out to my family, and I reassured her I was. Mah knew what was up with me, though she wasn't exactly rallying to head up her own local Asian American chapter of PFLAG. I told Carly I needed more time.

Besides my past with men, this issue became another battle she waged constantly. I told Carly I wasn't close to my mother. Still, I was her only child, and as her daughter I had certain responsibilities. When she needed help around the house, I showed up. I had to. There was no one else.

Later on, Carly started following a new thread. "She met your ex," she said.

"Baby. Don't start."

"She liked him? What was his name?"

I didn't answer. She knew his name was Danny and that he was locked up now for assault and battery, grand larceny.

"Because he's Asian?" she said.

"She's going through a lot," I said. "She's still recovering from her surgery."

"I just want to know what kind of bigot I'm dealing with," Carly said.

"What did you say?"

"You're blind to it, Jane. Your mother is ignorant. She uses her Bible—"

That was when I stood up and without thinking, I slapped her face hard.

"Don't you ever talk about my mother like that," I said.

She sat there quiet, cradling her cheek in her hand, her eyes wet.

I remembered the shock of feeling her skin beneath my hand, how soft it was. How easily her head snapped sideways, against her shoulder. The fear in her eyes, the reproach in her down-turned mouth, how much like a child she looked then.

I apologized right away—I fell to my knees—I don't know what came over me, I said. Please, baby, I said.

But I knew something had changed for her. In that moment, I'd become her father. And there was no coming back from that.

Saturday afternoon I drove out to the suburbs to visit Mah. I threw my overflowing laundry hamper in my trunk before I left my place and tossed a load into the machine in the garage before going inside.

"I'm here," I shouted. "Mah! You home?"

The Jesus painting we'd had since forever hung crooked above the sofa. I sank into the worn cushions and found the remote in the crack between the seat and the arm. The TV flickered to life on LA-18, in the middle of a Mandarin talk show. I watched for a few seconds before I flipped through the channels, settling on cartoons.

Mah poked her head out of the bedroom, blinking her eyes. Her hair was flattened against one side of her head. I must've caught her in the middle of her afternoon nap.

"Eat yet?" she said.

She headed for the kitchen before I could reply, and I jumped up and followed her.

Mah listed a number of dishes she could cook for me to eat, tapping her fingers against her thumb. "Noodles, you want? Or white rice? With braised short rib stew." She filled up a dented pot with water and set it over the flame. "You cut your hair?"

"Won did it," I replied.

"Too short," she said, dismayed. "Just like a boy."

"I like it short, Mah."

"Makes your face look big."

"Don't you know it's the style now?" I said. "Having a big face is very popular. Every girl wants a big face. Bigger the better."

Mah smiled and shook her head. When the water boiled, she tossed two bundles of clear rice noodle sticks into the pot. She stirred the strands apart with a pair of long wooden chopsticks, talked with her back to me about her plans to redo the kitchen tiles this summer. Ever since her fall and the subsequent surgery, Mah stood crooked on her feet. She favored her right hip now. When she looked over her shoulder at me, her body seemed as curved as a bell.

I skirted out during a pause in her monologue to stuff the wash into the dryer. In the garage there were boxes and boxes of my father's stuff. After all this time, Mah couldn't bear to donate it or throw it out. I didn't know what all was there, and I didn't want to find out. Tossing everything without going through it seemed wrong, though. Nothing to do but leave the boxes stacked there, gathering dust with time.

Back in the kitchen Mah pulled two bowls off the dish rack and set them down on the counter. She ladled noodles and steaming broth into each. A silence hung between Mah and me. It wasn't a bad silence. Just the same old quiet. We sat down at the counter stools. I finished the first bowl and filled another. I ate until I was full.

She asked how Won was doing. I said he was fine.

"He asked me to marry him," I said.

Mah looked up.

"He was joking," I said.

"I need your help," Mah said finally, as if making an announcement. She pushed her soup bowl away from her. "You won't like it," she added. "But my toenails grow long. I can't bend down."

I sat on the edge of the tub, waiting for the plastic basin to fill up with warm water from the faucet. While I was trimming her nails, I noticed the dirt and lint crusted between her toes, on the tops of her feet, and remarked on it. Mah had sighed and given an embarrassed smile. Six months after her surgery, Mah seemed fine, except for the slight limp. She didn't need her cane anymore. Mah was back at work, driving herself to appointments, eating out with the church ladies, just like before. Last week she told me proudly the deacons had reinstated her Sunday school role with the first and second graders, a job she enjoyed more than anything else she did the rest of the week. She was kinder to those brats and far more lenient, I was sure, than she ever was with me. Some of their crayon drawings hung taped to the wall in our living room, next to the upright piano I hadn't touched in years. One of them portrayed three crosses on a green hill, indistinct figures pinned on them with their arms outstretched—morbid, I thought—but the others were of normal kid stuff: cats and dogs, blue skies and white clouds, houses with windows, families of people wearing giant smiles. I was amazed at how fast she seemed to recover. Seeing the dirt caked on her feet, though, depressed me. How long had she waited before she felt she had to ask me for help?

I carried the basin over to the sofa where Mah sat waiting, watching TV. She'd turned it back to LA-18. I set the water down next to her, and she lifted one of her feet in the air, dipped a toe in to test the temperature.

"Too hot?"

She shook her head and submerged both her feet. I watched her face. Her eyes were soft. I asked about the soap opera. A rich family going bankrupt, she replied. It was a popular Korean miniseries, dubbed over in Mandarin. Mah pointed to the actress on-screen, a beautiful woman with disdain in her eyes and full, dark red lips. "They hire her to trick the uncle," she said. "But falling in love." Then she said, "This girl, a little bit like your friend Fiona."

I studied the actress for a few seconds. "She's pretty," I agreed.

I sat down cross-legged on the carpet in front of Mah, the white plastic tub between us. I wet a clean towel I'd found, wrapped it around the nub of soap I'd grabbed off her bathroom sink, and worked up a good lather. I cupped one of Mah's heels in my left hand under the water. The bottom of her foot was smooth, flat. Mah had no arch in her foot at all.

With the towel, I started washing her shins, her calves. Her sweatpants were rolled up to her knees. The skin on her legs was as white as tofu custard. Blue veins branched underneath the surface, from her knees to her ankles. She rested her toes on the edge while I rubbed the towel over the top of her foot, and lifted it so I could clean her toes individually, sliding the towel in the spaces between each of them. After I finished her right foot I moved on to her left. By the time I finished, the water in the basin was gray with dirty suds.

"All done," I said. Mah said thank you. I felt embarrassed all of a sudden and stood up to carry the filthy water out from sight.

I opened up the blue notebook again that night, back at my apartment.

Dear Fiona, I wrote.

I don't know what to say. Won told me to write to you.

I broke up with a girl I was dating. Her name ~~*was*~~ *is Carly.*

I'm sorry I haven't called.

How are you?

Hey, remember the time . . . you said . . . and then I

Remember how we

I was just thinking . . .

We drove everywhere in Shamu, her Civic hatchback. The 91 to the 605 to the 5. The 110 to the 10. She wore that spaghetti-strap dress, those patent leather Mary Janes. Her ponytail was tied with a strand of pink ribbon. Or, her hair was down and parted in the middle, loose and tumbling over her shoulders, caressing the small of her back. The feeling I had when Fiona was by my side: like we could do anything. Get everything we'd ever wanted—until I realized that what we wanted didn't match up anymore.

She left, of course, after high school. Me and Won stuck around. I got my license, finally. He enrolled in Vidal Sassoon Academy, and I convinced Mah I was on a gap year, which turned into two, then three.

I thought maybe she'd come back home after Berkeley, but Fiona only kept leaving. She followed her boyfriend to New York. Won and I had met Jasper when we drove up north for Fiona's graduation; on the way back down we'd dissected him in the car for hours, from Pleasanton to Kettleman City. "She likes him too much," Won had said. "And he knows it."

I missed her, but I didn't know how to say it. Fiona's life seemed serious. Grown-up. When she was in town over Christmas, she'd told Won and me that she planned to be engaged in the next six to nine months, the ring on her finger by next Christmas for sure. I still thought of her as my best friend, though more and more she was becoming a story to me, one whose plot I couldn't make sense of because either I was missing information or maybe I'd forgotten something from before—something important—and it was too late to ask about it now, because it would mean admitting I hadn't been paying attention.

Like: Why did she want to marry Jasper? Why had she gone with him to New York in the first place?

Maybe these were questions Won would want me to write down in the notebook, as part of the dumb life-coaching project I never agreed to but—I hated to say it—somehow, incredibly, was working for me. Little by little, day by day, I was getting better. I vacuumed my apartment for the first time in months even though I didn't expect company. I booked a dentist appointment when I realized it had been more than a year and a half since I last had my teeth cleaned. Carly was still the first thought in my head when I woke up every morning, but the empty space in my bed didn't feel as pathetic and lonely as before.

I visited Mah on the weekends still, but I never washed her feet again. The experience was too mortifying for both of us to repeat. The next time I went over, she showed me the long-handled body brush she'd bought at Daiso for $1.99. "I get one for you, too," she said, thrusting it at me. "Make sure you hang it after each shower," she added, "so it can dry out between use." Like me, Mah was getting better, too. Her life coach was Jesus, and their relationship, even if I didn't understand it, had kept her heart beating all this time, after everything with my father.

I gave the brush to Won when we met up for dinner at the same Vietnamese spot in Chinatown. There was a wait, and we stood outside in the plaza after putting our name down on the list. The sunset made our shadows long on the ground.

"This feels weird," he said, holding the brush. "It's new, right? You haven't—"

"Shut up," I said. "I'm trying to say thank you, okay?"

He looked at me for a moment. Then he said, "You're welcome," and after that, he never brought up life coaching me again.

"I'm not going to use this," he added. "I don't want to accidentally think about you when I'm in the shower."

"It's a gift," I said. "You can do whatever you want."

"I know," he said. "I'll wash Pepper with it."

"I just thought you could exfoliate your dry, crusty ass."

"My ass is perfect," he said. "Thank you very much!"

"Please stop coming on to me," I said. "It makes me uncomfortable."

Won laughed. "You stole my line—"

"I value our friendship, Won. Perfect ass and everything, it's not worth it to me."

"You're just going to break my heart," he said. "Leave me for another white girl."

"I won't—"

"That's what they all say." He shook his head and feigned a sigh. "At least I'll have . . . this shower brush . . ."

"I won't do that again," I said quietly.

"Do what?"

"I won't drop out on you," I said. "I swear."

"This is about me and Jesse? Jane. I'm fine. I told you, I'm healthy." I asked if he'd talked to Jesse since. "I had to go cold turkey on that situation," he said. He shook his head and looked away.

"Did you love him?" The question Carly always asked me.

"No. I thought I did. But that wasn't love," he said. "That was something else."

I touched his shoulder. "You deserved better than that, Won."

He blinked a few times. "I did, right?" He turned to me. "I'm a good person. I have a job. I give my mom money every month."

I studied his face, the pain etched in his eyes. In the fading light of dusk, Won seemed to glow. He looked beautiful, the way he always appeared to me.

"No one wants Asian guys," he said.

"I do," I said. Won scoffed. "Especially Koreans," I said. "Especially you—"

"Shut up," he said, smiling. "Rice queen."

"You're just my type," I said. "Hot. Unavailable."

"You got issues," he said.

"Can a Taiwanese girl be a rice queen?" I asked.

"I found a doctor I like," Won said. He traced a finger along his jawline. I told him, not for the first time, that he was already perfect. "Then let's call it 'enhancing perfection,'" he said.

They called my name at the restaurant door and I answered, "*Here.*"

The surgeon was based in Seoul, someone who worked on actors and runway models, Won said, excitement in his voice. I promised to give him a ride to LAX and to pick him up when he returned, polished and new, after recovery. I already missed him.

Kenji's Notebook

Tuesday evening, Fiona rode the 6 train downtown after seeing Kenji home from the hospital. She'd tucked him into bed and made sure the packet of OxyContin lay within his reach on the nightstand, next to his notebook. *He looks terrible*, Fiona had thought. Like a wilting jack-o'-lantern left out long after Halloween, a face falling into itself. She didn't want to admit that she felt afraid. Kenji was thirty-two, six years older than she was. He had cancer of the mouth and throat. On alternating Tuesdays, she and Jasper, her boyfriend—her ex-boyfriend, that is—took turns sitting with Kenji while the chemo drained into his arm. He was on his second round of six weeks, and skeletal from it. Kenji was Jasper's best friend, but Fiona had grown to love him, too. Four months ago, Kenji got the prognosis: surgery to clear out as much of the cancer as they could manage, then radiation and chemotherapy. A month and a half later, Fiona learned that Jasper had been sleeping with a woman in his writing program at Hunter. She'd read about it in Kenji's notebook, snooping around one night while he slept.

It was July now, and Fiona was biding her time. She'd survived her first year at NYU Law, on top of everything else. It had been the most punishing eight months of her life. She and Jasper had come to an agreement about living together through the end of their lease. Neither one was in a financial position to move out before then. Fiona claimed the queen bed; Jasper took up residence on the futon. He owned full access to the TV, but she had the window-unit AC in the bedroom. They exchanged information about Kenji's recovery and not much else.

The humidity hung nearly solid on her walk from the Canal Street station to her building on Mulberry and Hester. In the lobby, Fiona checked the mailbox marked LIN & CHANG. It was empty—Jasper must've picked up their mail already. She climbed the five flights up to the apartment, considering how she would tell him that Kenji needed another surgery. He'd lost too much weight. His doctors wanted to put a tube in his stomach so that Kenji could feed himself protein shakes through a plastic funnel.

She heard the TV blaring from the hallway. Fiona imagined Jasper parked on the futon, staring vacantly at the extra-wide flat-screen, that outsized monstrosity he'd insisted on buying last fall. He needed it for "research"—plus the Netflix subscription, DVDs in the mail every week—narrative structure, beats and silences. Four o'clock in the morning on Black Friday he'd camped out in front of Kmart on Astor Place to get the deal that included a free DVD player. She put her key in the deadbolt and waited a moment, gathering herself before she turned the knob.

A soccer match played on the TV, the field a million light pixels of blinding, verdant green. Jasper turned toward her, his face in profile backlit by the brilliant pitch. He asked how it went with Kenji tonight.

"Can you not get crumbs everywhere?" She cast a weary glance toward the bag of Utz chips in his lap. "I saw two roaches last week."

"Big ones?" Jasper scanned the floor around his feet, as if searching out evidence of the roaches she accused him of attracting. "I haven't seen any since the exterminator—"

"I have to tell you something, but don't freak out." She was still standing by the door with her flats on. "They said he needs to have another surgery."

"The hell?" he said. "They found another—"

"No, no," she said quickly. "You know it's hard for him to swallow anything now." Nudging her shoes off, Fiona leafed through the pile of mail on the small table next to the door. The Con Ed bill, a couple preapproved credit card offers, a reminder for a teeth-cleaning, and—what's this? A save-the-date postcard for her friend Amir's wedding in October, upstate in Woodstock.

Fiona explained what the doctor had said about the procedure Kenji needed.

"A feeding tube?" said Jasper. "Jesus."

"Are you free Friday? He's scheduled for ten in the morning," she said. "Or else I could ask to take off work—do a half day." Fiona was clerking for an appellate judge this summer, a coveted internship she'd won over other 1Ls in her cohort. The work was demanding and joyless—not that she'd expected anything different—but she was glad for the solid hours of citation research, memo drafting, and proofreading, which kept her from feeling like an object unraveling in six different directions.

"I can do it," said Jasper. "I'll go."

"Okay," she said. "Thanks."

"Yeah." He turned back to the TV.

Clutching the save-the-date in her hand, she brushed past the futon and into the bedroom. She shut the door and flipped on the AC, then sat down to study the postcard. Amir, her law school buddy, in a white shirt with the sleeves rolled up, a lavender silk tie. He grinned sheepishly, as if aware of and slightly embarrassed about his disarming handsomeness. His arm was curled around his fiancée's waist: Khadijah, a glamorous Black woman who stood half a head taller than him. She was a pediatric resident at a children's hospital. They were perfect together. Fiona crushed the postcard in her hands.

"Oh shit!" Jasper shouted from the living room, startling her. "Fuck yeah!" She realized he was yelling at the TV.

Fiona shook her head. She knew Jasper was scattering potato chip crumbs everywhere. Well, he could sleep with the roaches crawling all over him. She didn't care.

All she wanted now was to make it through the end of the lease in peace. Less than two months. Fiona didn't know where she would go, but she would find some place. She'd have to put out feelers soon to see if anyone she knew needed a roommate, to ask for leads on upcoming vacancies. By September, Kenji would be done with the chemo. She'd be back in school, her second year. Maybe she could move into Kenji's apartment, just for a while. He had a place in Harlem, a spartan bachelor's studio he's kept since his time at Teachers College. They could help each other. Both of them, in remission. The fact that Jasper would hate it made the idea more delicious.

In March, Kenji had told them the news after finally getting what he thought were swollen lymph nodes checked out. The three of them were standing outside a crappy midtown sports bar where they'd just witnessed Cal massacred in the first round of March Madness. There was a Japanese American boy on the starting five, a lanky shooting guard whose last name also happened to be Mura, and Kenji had told everyone at the bar that he was the player's cousin, spinning a story about youth league booster clubs, aunties who pounded and sold exquisite mochi back home in Gardena. Fiona and Jasper had gone along with it, because every time Mura put up points, someone sent them a round. In the end, however, Mura's offense wasn't enough to save the team from elimination. As they were saying goodbye, Kenji headed uptown and Fiona and Jasper downtown, he'd slipped in the news in a quiet, by-the-way voice.

Fiona wasn't sure she'd heard him right. "What? What did you say?"

"Throat and mouth cancer," Kenji said.

"What?" she said again. "But you don't even smoke."

Kenji shrugged. They were all quiet for a few moments.

Jasper had been the one to break the silence. "What happens now?"

Kenji told them his surgery was already scheduled for the following Thursday.

"Where? What hospital?" Fiona shoved him. "Why didn't you tell us sooner?"

"I'm sorry," Kenji said after a moment. "I didn't know how— what to say—"

"Bro." Jasper hesitated. "You scared?"

The night traffic coursed down Seventh Avenue, flashes of light in the dark. Fiona was glad for the buzz she felt from all the shots.

"Kenji, do you want to—I don't know—come over to our place?" she said. "Get another drink somewhere?"

Kenji shook his head. "I still have to finish grading some papers tonight." He glanced up the street and folded his wool beanie down over his ears, raised his arm to hail a cab. One pulled over for him. "Mura out." He bumped forearms with Jasper and then submitted to a tight hug from Fiona.

She didn't want to let him go. His long black hair, which he wore down that night, spilled over her shoulders. She breathed in his shampoo, but underneath it, behind his earlobes, she thought she smelled something murkier, darker. Even after he dropped his arms, she held on to him, and she only let go after he made a show of prying himself loose from her grip.

The subway ride back home was quiet. Fiona looped her arm into Jasper's on the walk from the station and felt him squeezing back with his elbow. They made love that night with a tenderness they hadn't shown one another for months, in bed or otherwise. She felt guilty for only having noticed its absence now. "I'm sorry," she murmured in the dark, after they'd finished. "I've been so busy, trying to keep up with all my school reading—I haven't been around for you."

Jasper's back was turned to her. Fiona pressed her breasts and stomach against him, nuzzled his neck with her nose, her lips. "How are you, baby? What's going on with your writing?" He didn't answer her—she figured he was asleep.

"I love you," she said softly. "Jasper Chang. I love you."

The soccer match over, Jasper pulled the futon out flat for the night. Lying down, he listened to the sounds coming from behind the bedroom door. The moan of the blow-dryer told him Fiona was perched on the edge of the bed—she never went to sleep with her hair wet, an old superstition she'd made him follow, too—probably wearing one of his ratty T-shirts that she'd long ago claimed for pajamas. Then, the asthmatic rubbery sound of the window being thrust open. Fiona ducking out for a smoke on the fire escape.

Jasper clicked off the local news in the middle of a report from the Bronx—a brick factory spewing orange flames from its windows—and waited for his eyes to adjust to the dark. He lay there, cramped, bitter about the unfairness of it all. So he'd made a mistake. Was she so perfect? He'd never confronted her about it, but he suspected Fiona and her Pakistani friend from law school—what was his name?—liked each other more than the normal amount. Late-night study sessions and whatnot. Had he ever said anything? No way. Wasn't his style to be so petty, register every little concern. Point being that he, Jasper, could overlook certain things. How could Fiona be so ready to toss out the whole relationship, these past six years? She didn't mean it. She couldn't mean it. It was a mistake. A big misunderstanding. They were getting back together, he knew it. She knew it. Kenji knew it, too.

Helen Park. He'd been resentful that their classmates assumed the two struck up an alliance because they were the only two Asian American fiction writers in their year. In fact, Jasper had intentionally ignored Helen's friendly glances during the orientation events. He'd also made a point to steer clear of Phuong Ly, a poet in the year above, to combat the stereotype that all Asians stuck together. Jasper wasn't going to be pigeonholed.

He thought Helen was a lesbian at first. She wore her short black hair gelled into spikes, a rotating uniform of loose chambray shirts topped by colorful fringed scarves, and always, some clown lipstick was painted on her mouth, bright tangerine, sparkly purple, and, occasionally, goth-metal black. He made it through the fall without engaging her much, but a month into the spring semester, she'd plopped down next to him at the bar where everyone congregated after workshop and called him out: "You're avoiding me, right?" Though her lips were parted in a smile, she delivered the line as if lobbing an insult, her eyes glittering. He'd noticed then that Helen had a tooth on the side of her grin shaped like a fang.

"I have a girlfriend," he blurted out.

Helen snorted. "Relax," she said. "Girlfriend. Cool. Well, what is she?"

"What do you mean, *what* is she?" he said. "She's a law student."

Helen shook her head. Her hair didn't move. "No, I mean, like—is she Asian?"

"She's Taiwanese," Jasper said. Helen raised an eyebrow. "So what?"

"Why don't you ever invite her out with us? Everyone else brings their boos and randos."

"I don't know, she's busy." He didn't want to tell her that Fiona would find their conversations—about books, writing, their professors—insufferable.

Jasper had long suspected that Fiona wasn't totally on board

with his writing ambitions. The program was designed to ac-
commodate working professionals, but Jasper had insisted on
quitting his day job to fully immerse himself in the MFA. He
had some savings and took out a student loan. He'd wanted to
chance a higher amount, max out both the subsidized and un-
subsidized federal limits, but Fiona had advised against it. What
about all your law school debt? he'd said. That's different, she
replied. After I finish I'll actually— She didn't finish the sentence, just let the words hang there. He'd been stung by her
frankness, though he knew she was only being pragmatic.

"Why'd you ask if she's Asian?" Jasper said.

"You seem like—I don't know." Helen shrugged. "Your stories in workshop—"

"What?"

She shrugged again.

Helen was only a year out of college, the same age Jasper was
when he moved to New York with Fiona. That night at the bar,
she told him to stop writing stories about white people. He'd
scoffed and then they'd argued—"Just because I don't indicate
what *race* the characters are doesn't automatically mean they're
white!" "Um, yeah, dude, it reads like that, sorry to break it to
you." "Not true. That's your own racist reading bias. Not my
problem!"—until Jasper realized their raised voices had attracted everyone else's attention. The others from their workshop stood around the bar clutching PBR cans, staring at them.

Jasper stood suddenly, knocking over his barstool. He tossed down a few bills and stormed out. Helen followed him. They shouted at each other out on the sidewalk. Frustrated, he grabbed her hard by both arms—he thought maybe he would shake her. An alarmed expression crossed Helen's widened dark eyes. Jasper remembered himself. Then, she was leading him to another bar, where they took shots and kept arguing, but there was laughter in it now, and something else; something more dangerous, Jasper recalled. Later still, when he followed her up the stairs to her apartment on Delancey—Helen was going to lend him her copy of Theresa Hak Kyung Cha's *Dictee*—Jasper thought: *Nothing's happened yet, and nothing might happen, anyway. Pull yourself together, Chang.*

When he got home that night, Jasper took a scalding shower before falling into bed with Fiona. Six years together: Fiona wasn't the first girl he'd slept with, but she was pretty close to it. Jasper promised himself it was only going to be that one time, with Helen. The sex wasn't anything spectacular, and her room smelled vaguely like cat piss. The next Monday after workshop, however, they fucked again; then another time, another day of the week, until Jasper couldn't remember why it mattered, as though he'd somehow believed that cheating on Fiona, if done on a Monday, gave him moral immunity.

When Kenji broke the news of his cancer diagnosis, Jasper had been hooking up with Helen for three months. That week, Jasper felt pulled back from some precipice he hadn't known he was standing on. Kenji was his best friend, and Fiona was his girl, still. One day, he was certain, she'd be his wife. He had to stop seeing Helen. There was no romance between them, only the intoxicating fumes of mutual derision, which each accepted for erotic intrigue. Helen made no complaints when he ended things. He returned the copy of Cha's poetry to her, unread.

The faint line of light under the bedroom door snapped black, and Jasper heard Fiona settle in, the comforter rustling. An image of Fiona's bare legs, her inner thighs brushing softly against each other, passed through his mind. He missed her, and the missing was tinged with anger and shame. The beginning of a dream cast its net over him: Fiona straddling him on the futon, the gray outline of her body in the darkness of the living room. Her fingertips on his nipples, teasing. They hadn't touched one another since somewhere near the end of April, when Fiona had found out about Helen, after everything was already over. Kenji's fault, punk ass with that notebook. But Jasper couldn't even be mad—dude was fighting cancer, right?

Jasper startled awake at four in the morning, the world still dark. The apartment was suffused with the smell of melted butter and hot sugar, as it was every morning, rising from the Italian bakery that occupied the ground floor. He rubbed his eyes and yawned, tried to float back to sleep, but felt suddenly chilled by the sensation of being watched.

"Fiona?" Jasper rubbed his eyes again. "You okay?" He sat up on the futon. A figure stood by the bedroom door.

"What if," she said, her voice barely a whisper. "What if Kenji doesn't—"

"He's doing so good," Jasper said. "You can't think like that." He patted the space next to him. She stepped toward him on silent feet and sank down. After a moment, he put an arm around her.

"Are you crying?"

She shook her head and turned her face toward him, as if to prove she wasn't, even though it was dark and he could barely see. He shifted, enough to close the small distance between their mouths. Fiona met him there.

They kissed a few times before he pulled the T-shirt over her head. Jasper cupped his right hand over her breast, found her nipple between his fingers, and pinched it, hard. She gave a small gasp. With his mouth on hers, Jasper moved his hand to her neck. Under his thumb he felt her pulse jumping. Her hands were tugging at his shorts. He pushed her down on the futon mattress. All of a sudden Jasper remembered how it was, the frenzied pleasure of sex with someone you loved and who you knew loved you back. He wanted to call her a bitch for how she'd been treating him. He fought the urge to say, I love you—

Jasper stayed silent and kept thrusting, the palm of his hand pressed against Fiona's neck. He was only doing what she liked—to be brutalized, just a little. Made to acquiesce, pinned down, her vagina slapped and bruised. And afterward, he knew she liked to be held. He tightened his grip around her throat. She whimpered and moaned, writhing underneath him.

They moved together in the dark, as one. They generated heat. The air seemed to buzz in Jasper's ears, the sound of honeybees. He held his breath. He waited for her to come. In another minute, she arrived.

Friday morning, Jasper was dressed and downstairs before nine. Kenji's surgery, scheduled for ten at Mount Sinai uptown. Outside, the vendors on Mulberry Street were setting up for the day. He strolled past a fruit stand piled high with lychees, clusters of longan, bright pink dragon fruit the size of his fist.

Earbuds in, an old DJ Shadow playlist cued up, he passed one stall after another on Canal Street selling junk souvenirs: miniature jade figurines, knotted red rope ornaments, novelty lighters and keychains, and those conical bamboo hats. Maybe they were all storefronts for illegitimate businesses. Knockoff designer handbags, miniature turtles, bootleg DVDs. Or something more sinister? Poor girls imported from China, some trained to work at massage parlors, jerking out perfunctory happy endings, others assigned to long hours crouched at the gnarled feet of hardened Manhattan women, scrubbing calluses and sawing off toenails.

He swiped through the turnstile at Lafayette, recalling the time he and Kenji had staggered into one of those shady massage parlors south of Canal with a neon-lit OPEN sign. Three in the morning, they were both faded as hell, elbowing each other forward and knocking over shit in the small front room. An older woman who reminded Jasper too much of his mother ushered them into a dim hallway behind a red beaded curtain. In the end he had backed out. He smoked several cigarettes on the sidewalk while he waited; Kenji swayed out half an hour later, the red from all the tequila shots drained from his cheeks. He'd laughed, and thrown an arm around Jasper's neck. "Goddamn. You're a pussy, you know that?" Then he ran for the gutter and vomited into it, bent over with one hand pressed on the sidewalk.

Jasper came above ground a half hour later at Ninety-Sixth and Lex. Two blocks west, and two blocks north. The surgery building was brand-new and clean-looking. Upstairs, a set of blue chairs lined the waiting room, and a yellowing philodendron relaxed in one corner. Only two of the seats were filled. An Asian man in his seventies, his face sallow and dotted with large brown spots, sat beside someone who must be his son, because the younger man had the exact same face, without the liver marks. Neither one looked up when Jasper shuffled past them up to the glass window at the back of the room. A young white nurse sat typing into a computer. Jasper asked if Kenji had arrived and checked in already.

"Last name?"

He told her, and she thumbed through a stack of papers next

to the keyboard. "Philip Mura for the gastroendoscopy?" She looked at him for confirmation over a set of seafoam-green reading glasses.

"The what?" He'd forgotten that Kenji used his English name for official records. "It's for his stomach."

The nurse told him the procedure would be done in about an hour and a half.

Jasper sat down at one of the blue chairs. He glanced over at the father and son. If they gave him an opening, Jasper would gladly explain the story.

Was it wrong? The thrill he got from telling people his best friend had cancer, and then waited for the glimmer of sympathy in their eyes as he nonchalantly elaborated that he was Kenji's primary caretaker—well, one of them, anyway.

Jasper planned to write about the whole thing: how the surgeon split open Kenji's neck to scrape off the tumors, cut out a third of his tongue, and then stitched in a circle of flesh from the inside of his left forearm. Next, the radiation treatments that burned purple scars into Kenji's chin and throat. That was when he'd stopped talking—hurt to use his tongue, hurt to swallow down spit—and started using the notebook to communicate.

The chemo bags were supposed to be the last thing, poisoning any chances of future growth. But now, while Jasper sat waiting, Kenji was on a table back there. A hole, two inches below the sternum. A plastic tube for funneling liquid food. Weird, Jasper thought. Weird, gross, and sad. A winning trifecta for a short story. Maybe he'd weave in a backstory about the Japanese American internment during World War II. A wound in the chest . . . he groped for a metaphor.

That would show Helen he wrote fiction with Asian American characters. He'd prove her wrong.

He considered calling Fiona. Jasper hadn't seen much of her after what happened early Wednesday morning. She'd made herself scarce the last couple nights.

The handsome young man in the hospital waiting room peered out the window with his intense brown eyes . . . An intentionally bad line. Jasper smiled, and then looked toward the clock on the wall.

Jasper didn't expect the wheelchair escort. Kenji had on a Team Japan jersey—the World Cup semifinals were broadcasting later tonight. The shirt hung on him like how it might look draped on a coatrack. Jasper probably had a good forty pounds on him, since the chemo. Even Kenji's head had shrunk, the most disconcerting part of the weight loss.

"You good?" Jasper asked. Kenji raised a thumb in the air.

Downstairs, Jasper hailed a cab crawling north on Madison. Kenji sat waiting in the wheelchair, squinting against the sun. The cab pulled to the curb, and Jasper took a hold of his friend's elbow to guide him into the back seat, then shut the door for him. He walked around to the other side and got in.

"Where to, chief?" the driver asked. Jasper gave him the block.

Months before, when he'd confided in Kenji about slipping up with Helen, he hadn't considered the possibility that Kenji would be angry with him. They were supposed to be boys. Homies for life. They'd been floormates in Unit 3 when Jasper was a freshman, Kenji a third-year transfer at twenty-four—he bought everyone's beers. Jasper never thought for a second that Kenji would take Fiona's side of things—he'd been the one to convince Jasper the massage parlor didn't count as cheating. It was like watching porn, or going to a strip club, Kenji had said about the place on Doyers. Strictly professional. Jasper needed a friend to talk to about the Helen situation. Kenji had scolded him, like he was some immature kid.

And then, Kenji had done the worst: he leaked the secret to Fiona. He swore it happened by accident—Fiona had opened up the notebook and read it without his permission. There was a confrontation, then retreat, which led into Jasper and Fiona's present stalemate.

Kenji said he was staying neutral; he loved them both. Still, Jasper couldn't shake the feeling that Kenji had been irretrievably lost to him. He didn't know when it happened. Kenji belonged to Fiona now.

In the back seat of the cab, Jasper glanced over at Kenji dozing. He wondered if Kenji liked the chemo days with Fiona better than the ones with him. Did they laugh? Did she tell stories to entertain him while his body swallowed up all that medicine? A maddening thought: What if, after all this, Kenji and Fiona got together? One time at the gym, Jasper caught a glimpse of Kenji's dick in the locker room—uncircumcised, and fucking huge.

The cab lurched to a stop in front of Kenji's building. Upstairs, he helped get Kenji settled into the bed. Jasper checked the fridge: nothing but a Brita pitcher and bottles of vanilla-flavored Ensure. An old stick of butter in the door. He glanced back at Kenji's sleeping figure before he slipped out quietly.

Jasper called Fiona from the sidewalk outside Kenji's building. "I want to talk," he said. He asked what time she'd be home tonight.

"About what?" she said. "Is Kenji okay?"

"About me and you." Jasper paused. "The other night—"

Fiona sighed. She said she'd be home at six.

Fiona met Jasper at the apartment after work, as she promised. She asked how it went with Kenji's gastroendoscopy this morning.

"Fine," he said.

"I'll go up there tomorrow," she said. "I'm going to ask him if I can stay with him—"

"Fiona." Jasper's voice was shredded. "I want to work things out. You know that."

"The lease ends after August," she said. "I can probably be out before then."

"What do I have to do? What do you want me to say?"

"You're not listening to me."

They sat on opposite ends of the futon. Fiona faced the giant TV screen, refusing to give Jasper her eyes.

"There's nothing to work out," she said. "We already talked about this."

"Whatever you want me to do, I'll do it. Couples therapy. Anything."

"Two months ago, we decided this was what needed to happen—"

"What about the other night?" he said. "You barely say two words to me for how long, then all of a sudden—"

"What happened to you?" Fiona examined her hands. Her voice was quiet. "You used to be different."

"I said I'm sorry about— I made a mistake. I told you, it didn't mean anything."

"I don't care about her," Fiona said. "I don't care what it did or didn't mean to you. It doesn't matter to me." She stood and paced the room, because she couldn't sit next to him any longer.

"I'm so confused." Jasper's eyes were wet. "I don't know what you want from me. I don't understand—I'm still me. I messed up. But I'm still the same—"

"I want this to end. I want to move out and be done with it," she said. "I don't know what the other morning was." She hesitated. "It wasn't . . . anything."

"You're lying," he said.

She watched him cry, the whites of his eyes turning red. Fiona felt a bitter satisfaction at his suffering, and a tinge of pain for him. She felt embarrassed that she was enjoying this. She didn't want to enjoy it. She didn't want to be cruel. But the feeling was there, all the same.

"Don't do this," he said now. "Please, baby. Don't give up on me—what we have—"

Fiona didn't answer. She stood there with her arms crossed, as still as anything.

"The other morning," he pleaded. "I know you felt something."

Fiona shook her head.

"Look at me." Jasper waited. "Please." Fiona turned toward him and met his gaze. Over the back of the futon, he reached out for her hand.

"I used to think, there had to be nothing left, for me to leave." Fiona stayed where she was, arms crossed. "And I thought there *was* nothing left between us. Only Kenji. Taking care of him. Making sure he's going to be okay."

"There's a lot left—there's us. Me and you." Jasper let his arm hang down over the back of the futon.

"Not enough," she said.

"Don't say that," he said. "That's not true."

She sat back down on the futon, next to him. They were silent for a while. She curled her legs up and hugged her shins. "Can you do me a favor?" She paused. "Can you help me shave my head?"

"What?"

"Kenji's been so down lately, I think it'll cheer him up." She paused. "Help him get through the rest of chemo."

Jasper didn't reply. He sat leaning forward, his elbows resting on his knees.

Fiona glanced over at him. The way Jasper looked at her then, like she was a wonder, something magic, Fiona knew that she would always love him. She'd forgotten that feeling, the pleasure of being seen by someone you loved and who loved you back. For a moment, before she stepped into the future on her own, and the past—their past—closed for good, she reached for him as if through a door, and she held on to his hand. How soft the skin of his palm against hers, how warm and familiar his fingers. How dear he was to her, after all. Jasper had been her first love. He would always be that.

The next morning, Fiona headed uptown to check on Kenji. When she got above ground at 125th, she reached for her cigarettes. Her knuckles brushed against a crumpled ball of paper and it fell out of her purse, landing on the sidewalk at her feet. The save-the-date for Amir and Khadijah's wedding—she didn't know why she'd been carrying it around. Fiona bent down to pick it up. She unfolded the postcard, smoothing her thumbs over the wrinkles creased in the paper. When Amir had announced his engagement in an email to their clinic last quarter, she'd replied with her congratulations, and he'd sent back: "You're next!"

In the last six years, she and Jasper had talked about marriage, and kids, in a vague way. Last year, they'd agreed to wait until after they both finished their degrees before getting engaged. Fiona had once been able to imagine the wedding with confidence. Jane, her best friend, standing up there by her side. Kenji next to Jasper, of course. Now she wasn't sure about anything anymore. A long time ago, she'd pressed Jane for her honest opinion after she'd met him at Fiona's graduation at Berkeley. "Honestly? You won't get mad?" Fiona braced herself. "Just kidding—he seems great, Fi. Is he really writing a novel? What does that even mean?" Fiona's friendship with Jane in the last four years had lapsed into something dormant—last they talked, months ago now, Jane had been dating a woman named Carly, though Fiona couldn't get a read on how serious things were between them.

She strolled in the direction of Kenji's building, the sun on the back of her neck, her newly shorn crown. She felt self-conscious and kept touching her head. Were people staring at her? Did they think she was some kind of escaped Buddhist nun? When she passed Kenji's brownstone, her feet kept moving. She was still smoking the cigarette.

Fiona thought about the notebook. When she'd leafed through the pages that night while he slept, Fiona knew it was a violation of Kenji's privacy. Still, she felt it was her duty as a friend to monitor his state of mind from week to week. The notebook was part communication tool, and part journal. Kenji had lines copied from Neruda love poems, quotes from Kant and Hume on existential meaning, a series of zen koans and his earnest attempts at answering them. A few entries of recorded dreams. A list of medications. Then she'd come upon a page, just a few lines: *Enough about me, what's up with you? Did you stop seeing that girl? How'd she take it? You okay?*

She'd touched Kenji's shoulder to wake him. Showed him the page. "I'm sorry," she said. "I shouldn't have—but what is this? Is it Jasper?" Kenji had brought his hands up to his face. He'd taken the notebook from her and then he'd thrown it across the room. It had hit the wall with a dull thud.

The Movers

The buzzer squawked twice, and Fiona pressed the button on the intercom box to unlock the gate downstairs.

"You sure this is legit?" I'd told her about the Chinese moving company I used—uncles who chain-smoked Marlboros and looked like they couldn't lift boxes for shit—but you'd be surprised, I said. Still, she insisted on hiring this charity outfit, a job-training and reentry program for former felons. Fiona had heard about it through a pro bono case at her law firm.

A soft knock on the door. Fiona opened it, and two men stood waiting. They wore matching green baseball caps embroidered with the company logo.

"Ms. Lin?" The one in charge—he carried a clipboard and an air of confidence—pumped Fiona's hand a couple times. "Sam Jones." He was somewhere in his thirties, I'd guess, lean and clean-shaven. His eyes surveyed the room, and I sensed Fiona relaxing, the way she held her smile, her shoulders going slack. Something about his gaze made me think he might be older, though his face was unlined. Age was hard to tell with Black folks, same as with Asians. Take me: I turned thirty-two this year but they still wanted ID at the liquor store, every single time.

Sam said, "This is my associate, Jackson Leong. We call him Sonny." The second mover, a stocky Chinese kid, couldn't have been more than nineteen or twenty. The company T-shirt he had on, hunter green with a pocket on the chest, still bore a vertical crease down the front. The sleeves were stretched tight over his massive shoulders and biceps.

Sonny mumbled a hello into the carpet.

"Jane," I said. Sonny dragged his gaze from the floor with difficulty, landing somewhere next to my ear. He found my outstretched palm, then Fiona's.

Sam flipped through the papers pinched to his clipboard, all business. "Now let's see. Where we taking you?"

"Griffith Park and Hyperion," said Fiona.

"You two sisters?" Sam asked. "Roommates?"

"We're dating," I replied. "She's my girlfriend."

Sonny stifled a chortle. His eyes darted between Fiona and me, then back to the carpet.

"Are you now? Pardon me," Sam said. "You look like sisters." He turned to Sonny. "Don't they look like sisters to you?"

"You guys related?" I said.

"We're not together," Fiona cut in. "She's my best friend. She makes jokes," she added.

"We're not related, either." Sam threw an arm around Sonny's shoulders. "We are family, though," he said smiling. "Ain't that right, buddy?"

"I'm just here to supervise," I said. "Make sure everything's on the up and up." I flopped down on the sofa, kicked my feet up on a box.

"All right, I see. You're the boss." Sam winked at me, and somehow it was both weird and comforting.

Sonny had been silent this whole time, but I felt him running furtive glances between Fiona and me, those long narrow eyes cut into his moony face. When I caught his gaze, Sonny startled and backed away a couple steps until he was touching the wall. His neck reddened, then his whole face.

"This will be easy," Sam said, bobbing his head up and down. "Unless you're hiding a piano in the bedroom?"

"There's a pool table, though," I said.

Fiona asked him how long the move would take.

"You got somewhere else to be today?" Sam said, which made Fiona laugh. "Let's get started." He studied the clipboard. "You requested four hours? We won't be that long, I don't think."

"I was kidding," I said. "There's no pool table."

"You're the best friend. You make jokes," he said. "Important job on moving day."

Sam removed the baseball cap from his head and followed Fiona down the hallway that led to the two bedrooms. A large circle of brown skin sat on the back of his skull, surrounded by a thin moat of graying hair. I wondered then if he might be in his forties.

"Uh—I'm going back down to—grab the—" Sonny stammered, drawing a rectangle in the air with his hands. "For clothes," he added. "The box." He lurched out the door.

Sam and Fiona came back out to the living room in a few minutes and settled down on the sofa next to me. He fumbled for a pen in his pants pocket and offered it to Fiona. The palm of his hand was cut like a road map and ridged thick with calluses.

"Sonny went downstairs?" he said. "We passed by Chinatown driving over here, his old hood. Broadway, Hill Street. He don't talk much, but that's one thing he did tell me."

"Jane lives there," Fiona said.

We all looked up as Sonny crashed through the door. A tall cardboard box tumbled in front of him.

"Oops," Sonny muttered. He set it upright, then turned around and brushed out again.

Sam started to laugh. "I better go help him," he said, getting up.

When they were both gone, Fiona leaned close to me and whispered, "That kid creeps me out."

"I gave him your number while you were in the other room," I said. "Recent divorcée, hot young moving dude—did you see his arms?"

"Ha-ha, very funny, bitch," she said with a smile. "Sam seems competent," she added. "But the other guy, Sonny, I don't know—something's off." She folded her hands together in her lap. I noticed her rubbing her ring finger absently, as if twisting an invisible gold band round and round. "What kind of name is Sonny?"

"I could call up Uncle Frankie," I said. "He'll be over here with a crew in fifteen minutes. Just say the word."

Fiona shook her head and told me to lower my voice.

Sam appeared at the door with a spool of plastic. He wrapped the things Fiona couldn't pack into boxes, the hairpin legs unscrewed from the dining table, the fiberboard slats to the IKEA bookcase she kept saying she was going to replace for something sturdier.

I helped her carry the wardrobe box into the bedroom, and we started loading her clothes onto the bar.

"I unfriended Aaron on Facebook yesterday."

"Where's he staying?" I asked. "Do you know?"

"I can't believe you used that word," she said. She hesitated a moment. "But it's true—you're right—"

"What word?"

"You called me a divorcée."

"Come on, I was joking," I said. "Fi. I didn't mean—"

"I'm meeting my lawyer next week to sign," she said quietly. "Then it'll be official."

I started apologizing. Fiona lifted a hand in the air. "Don't. It's fine," she said. She gave a hard little laugh and gazed toward the window behind me. "Fuck," she said after a moment. It felt like she was glaring at me, with only the whites of her eyes. "I went from girlfriend to wife in six months. And now, this."

I felt like an asshole. I'd meant to use the word—"divorcée"—with an ironic glamour, but the joke didn't land right.

I didn't think much of him when I first met Aaron, though I didn't say so to Fiona, of course. His dad was Malaysian, but Aaron went by his British mom's last name for auditions: he said "Aaron Johnson" sounded more like a leading man than "Aaron Liu." A pretty-boy with dimples in both cheeks, he would often talk about big-time celebrities like they were close personal friends of his. One of Aaron's favorite stories to tell involved fist-bumping LL Cool J on the set of *NCIS: Los Angeles*, the time he booked "Dead Asian Gangster #2."

I was wary of how quickly things advanced with Fiona and Aaron—moving in together after only a month of dating, married six months later—but who was I to dispute Cupid's arrow? That was how she talked in those days, like Aaron was fated into her life. Maybe I was just hating because I felt abandoned, so soon after she'd moved back to LA. She'd met him at work; Aaron was their part-time receptionist, a job that allowed him flexibility to dip out for castings. He became her work husband fast, and it was totally platonic at first. She'd been through it in

New York, she said, her entire twenties spent on losers and weirdos who wasted her time, and worse. The last one stole money from her. Fiona had said she was swearing off men. She was living with her mother, anyway, which made dating impossible. Then Aaron happened.

After he and Fiona were married for a year or so, I guess I started to accept him. When he wasn't prepping his sides and I wasn't showing vacancies or dealing with repairs, we would meet up for happy hour, killing time before Fiona clocked out. Of the three of us, she was the only one who held a job with steady hours, a paralegal at a litigation firm with the name of its partners on a high-rise downtown. Those wine-soaked afternoons eventually led into Fiona and Aaron's troubles, with me caught in the middle.

But before that happened, Aaron and I were good-time drinking buddies, then, somehow, we became friends. He was surprisingly easy to talk to, warm and charismatic in a way I didn't expect—when Fiona had first told me she was dating an actor, I'd thought: *Oh no.* But hanging with Aaron, I came to admire his ability for taking rejection day in and day out, his unflagging resolve to keep chasing his art. It made me start to think about writing again, all those pitch ideas and treatments I'd started, up on Adderall, but never finished.

One time, he and I got to analyzing my bedroom issues with Ed, the guy I was seeing. We were sitting in a booth at a naval-themed dive in Koreatown, the walls adorned with yellowing paintings of schooners and battleships, the bar lit up by Christmas lights and silver tinsel in July. "Ed" wasn't his real name, just what I called him behind his back because of the erectile dysfunction.

"Is it something that just kind of—happens?" I asked. "Is it normal in your thirties—"

"Whiskey dick?"

I told him Ed didn't drink. He asked if it happened every time, and I didn't answer.

"Jane," he said. "Seriously?"

"I mean, we do other stuff—"

"I knew there was something weird about that guy." Aaron lowered his voice. "Not that I have a problem with it, but I thought he was sort of gay."

I opened my mouth to protest. So what if Ed was a little skinny? And couldn't give an opinion about first-round draft picks? He knew things way over Aaron's head—what a diphthong was and Obama authorizing drone strikes in Iraq and the best way to open up a pomegranate without losing seeds. How I had to keep trying to talk to my dead father, even if it only felt like circles and circles back to me without any answers.

Anesthetized under the happy-hour chardonnay, though, I decided not to say anything. What was the point? I already knew he was the type of dude—this was part of my learning to accept him, for Fiona's sake—who said shit like lesbianism was natural and beautiful but the thought of two men kissing grossed him out. You had to choose your battles with family, and that was how I'd thought of Aaron back then. My best-friend-in-law.

Aaron said, "I never understood why you two— I don't see it, you and him"—and then he said Ed's real name. "I thought you liked chicks, anyway. What's so special about this guy?"

I hesitated a moment. "He writes me poems," I said, knowing how corny it must've sounded.

"'Roses are red, violets are blue,' that sort of crap?"

"No one's ever done something like that for me," I said.

Ed had books stacked on his nightstand, brick-thick tomes of Céline and Sartre, and thin spines of poetry by writers with only initials for first names. I picked one up on a morning after he'd left for work; the margins were scribbled with notes in his slanting handwriting. I didn't understand the poetry—it seemed worlds apart from those haikus on yellow stickies he'd leave in my pockets—and trying to decipher his cursive in the margins felt wrong, like reading his diary. I was afraid of what I might discover, like the time I came upon old Mrs. Chung in the basement laundry room wringing out something red and lacy at the sink.

"Poems," Aaron said. He smiled. "Huh. I didn't think you were into stuff like that."

"Shut up," I said.

"But if he can't get it up," Aaron said, "how do you—why—"

"You think sex is only about that? Man," I said, "I feel sorry for Fi—"

"Why even date a dude, if you can't, you know." He put his elbows on the table and rested his chin in his hands. "I'm asking honestly, Jane."

"Listen. I got a drawer full of dicks." Aaron leaned back in the booth, put his hands up in the air in a sign of defeat. "You asked," I said. "So I'm telling you. That's not why I—"

"Then why?"

I shook my head.

"Don't say fucking poems," Aaron said. "Poems? Come on."

"There is something," I said slowly, "about being with someone Chinese." I hesitated. "It's not everything, but—I don't know. There's a secret understanding, maybe." I wondered if saying this out loud sounded even cornier than what I'd told him about Ed's poetry. "Less explaining. You know what I mean?"

He nodded. "Fiona is very happy with me. Bedroom-wise," he added. "I'm sure she's told you—I have a huge—"

"Okay, dude," I said. "You can shut up now. For real." I was laughing. We both were. The waitress came by and we ordered another round. When she brought the drinks she said we made a beautiful couple, and that started us laughing all over again.

Fiona was in the middle of saying she might delete her Facebook account altogether when Sam popped a head in the bedroom. "We're about finished out there," he said.

I removed the last of Fiona's clothes from the closet, a section of dark blazers, and jammed the hangers onto the bar in the cardboard box. Sam carried the box out, and we followed him.

"Didn't I say it would take no time?" They'd cleared out the entire living room and adjoining eat-in kitchen, all the furniture and the boxes, in the time Fiona and I were packing up her clothes.

"Well," Fiona said. "My ex took half of it."

Sam paused, about to say something else, but seemed to change his mind. He turned to Sonny. "Let's get the bed out." He added, "Nothing in the second bedroom, so we're good to go."

They left Fiona and me standing in the bare living room. The place felt smaller somehow, with all of her and Aaron's stuff gone, the curtains off the rods. The cupboard doors in the kitchen hung open, and the ceiling fan in the dining nook spun in the bright emptiness, the only thing moving in the apartment.

"You okay?" I asked.

"I was just counting," she said, "how many apartments I've lived in, the last ten years." She was still looking at me as if with only the whites of her eyes, but the glare was gone from them. "And all the times we had to move around when I was a kid."

I thought of Mah then. She still lived in the same house in the suburbs where Fi and I grew up. My old upright Yamaha in her living room, the bench draped with the same white doily. The Jesus painting over the sofa, the cerulean of His eyes faded to gray now. Even the Lord developed cataracts in time.

"Remember that yellow apartment?" Fiona said. "Did you know we were evicted from there?"

"Your neighbor had that mean dog—"

"No, that was another place," she said. "The yellow apartment was when my brother was born."

"Why'd they evict you?"

Fiona shrugged. "Why do you think?" she said. "We didn't pay the rent."

"I didn't know—"

"You're lucky," Fiona said. "You still have the same home to go back to."

A knot grew in my throat. What she said about home made me think of my father. I couldn't stand the ceiling fan spinning around like that. Ten years ago. I'd just turned twenty-two not long before I got the call about my dad. Fiona was already in New York, or about to move there. I didn't remember her; I can't recall much of anything about that year, I realized all of a sudden.

I swallowed hard, my mouth dry. I pushed away the thoughts of my father alone by himself in the end, in some dusty apartment in Shanghai.

"Let's go down," I said. "I'll drive."

Ed and I only dated for six months. Then he flew home to Evanston for Thanksgiving and when he got back, the guy dumped me. His popo had taken him aside and told him if he kept seeing me something terrible would happen—his ED issues were an omen, she'd warned, holding up a crooked finger before his face. She's never been wrong, Ed had said when we met up to talk.

"What is she, some kind of psychic?" I asked. "How'd she know about—"

"I've been taking these Chinese medicine packets she gave me." He leaned toward me. "Maybe we can try—one last time?"

Anyway, I let him kiss me. Five minutes later, we both had our jeans off. I stuck a hand in his briefs, but his grandma's herbs weren't performing any miracles.

"Why can't you get a prescription for Cialis, like a normal person?"

Ed rattled off the list of side effects: nausea, headache, dry mouth, diarrhea. "And what if I get a boner that lasts four hours?"

"So that's it? We're breaking up?"

He didn't reply, just zipped up his pants.

The movers hoisted Fiona's sofa through the front door at the new place and set it down in a corner of the living room. While they brought in the rest of the boxes, I stripped the plastic wrap off the pilling sofa cushions and stuffed them back into place. The cushions smelled like Fiona. I wondered if she'd been sleeping on the sofa these last few months, instead of the bed.

Sonny stepped through the door with a package shrouded in a blue towel.

"Please—careful with that one." Fiona crossed the room and took it from him. She lowered it softly on the glass coffee table and unwrapped the towel.

"Haven't seen one of those in a minute," Sam said. "Does it work?"

I'd found the old typewriter at the Goodwill on Vine Street, in the electronics section next to a squat thermal paper fax machine. Immediately, I thought of buying it for Ed's Christmas gift. I knew he'd love it. He filled his apartment with all sorts of old, battered things; I didn't know if it spoke to a Chinese immigrant mentality passed down from generations who saved and salvaged everything (I'd witnessed the same compulsion in the apartments of my tenants), or if it was some eco-friendly hipster upcycling scheme. Fiona had sidled up to me in that musty aisle, and we'd stood there a moment, silently admiring the blue Remington case, the elegant black keys. She knew what I was thinking.

"It's perfect," she'd said, nodding. She reached out a finger and pushed down on a few keys, the corresponding silver pegs lifting out of the hatch.

I never got a chance to give it to Ed. I didn't want it in my apartment because it reminded me of him, but I couldn't bring myself to throw it out, either, so Fiona took it home.

"You're a writer?" Sam asked.

"A lawyer," she replied. She caught my eye across the room then quickly looked away.

"A lawyer?" Sam grinned at Sonny. "We know a few of those."

"I mean, I'm in law school," Fiona said.

That wasn't true, either. She'd dropped out years ago.

"And what does this lovely young lady do?" Sam asked.

"Nothing," I said.

"Nothing?"

"I manage an apartment building."

"All by yourself?"

"It's not too hard," I said.

"You know about our foundation? If you ever need our services." He slid a hand into his pants pocket and pulled out a business card.

"She's the writer," Fiona said.

I accepted the card from Sam, and my fingers brushed against the calluses curled in his hands. "I'll definitely use you guys next time," I told him, even though I knew I wouldn't call, because I couldn't leave Uncle Frankie's team out to dry like that.

"She writes screenplays," Fiona continued.

"No, I don't," I said. "You two always work together?"

"We can request it," Sam answered. "I'm a team leader, so sometimes I get put up on bigger jobs." He glanced over at Sonny and gave a nod. "One day Sonny will train to be team leader, too."

"You're from Chinatown?" I asked. Sonny looked blankly at

me. "Chinatown?" I said again. "Sam said earlier you lived there."

"Oh," he said. There was a silence while Fiona, Sam, and I waited.

Sonny blinked rapidly several times, then raised both hands to his face and rubbed up and down. Finally, he said, "Grew up there, yeah. Don't live there no more."

In a kind voice, Fiona asked him whether he still had family in the neighborhood.

Sonny's expression darkened. A scowl gripped his face, tightened the clench of his jaw.

"Sonny, you all right?" Sam peered at him, frowning.

Sonny leaned against the wall next to the door, looking as if he wanted to throw it open and sprint off. "I'm okay, boss," he said. He turned his gaze toward Fiona. "Thing is—I'm not supposed to set foot near—after what I did to that old lady—"

"All right," Sam interrupted. "All right, Son."

Fiona backed away from him. "Let me just— Where's my—" she stammered.

Sam opened up the front door and clasped Sonny's elbow. "Come on, let's go outside," he said. Over his shoulder, he said to Fiona, "I'll be back in just a sec, nothing doing. Be just a sec."

Fiona drew in a sharp breath and let it out slowly after they stepped out. "I should've used the movers you recommended," she said in a low voice.

"You're fine," I said. "He's harmless," I added.

"I'm living by myself now," she said. "I have to be more careful. I'm on my own."

We heard the sound of footsteps approaching. Sam hopped through the door.

"Where's that clipboard?" he said brightly. He showed Fiona the tally, and she counted out the bills from her wallet.

"Let me see if I've got some change," Sam said.

"No, it's all for you," Fiona said. "The rest is gratuity."

Sam thanked her but explained their policy was not to accept tips. "I'll write it down as a donation for the foundation," Sam said. "You know, few years ago I might've taken it without writing it down," he added, waving the wad of cash in the air. "This job changed my life. It's all about integrity now."

"I'm not in law school," Fiona blurted out. "I'm just a legal assistant—"

"Ms. Lin," Sam said. He hesitated a moment. "Wasn't going to tell you this, but today was Sonny's first day. He's gone through all the steps—I trained him personally, and I'm the best we've got—but when it comes down to it, you never can tell how things will turn out."

"What did he do?" I asked. "What was Sonny locked up for?"

"Jane, don't—"

"I mean, who's to say he won't come right back here another night?" I said. "He's seen all her stuff, he's cased the joint—"

"You're making a whole lot of assumptions right now." The smile he'd been wearing all morning was wiped from Sam's face. "Just because the foundation—"

"I'm sorry," Fiona said. "Sam, I apologize—she's my best friend—she just meant—"

Sam shook his head. "Forget it." He asked Fiona to sign on the clipboard, and then he left without saying another word.

"Why'd you do that?" Fiona said to me when it was just the two of us alone.

"I thought—you were scared, and I had to say something."

"No," she said. "You didn't have to, Jane."

The last time I saw Aaron, we were back at that same naval-themed bar in Ktown. Fiona was getting off work soon.

"She'll be here any minute," Aaron said. His eyes were on his phone while he keyed in a reply. "Jane," he said without looking up, "when she gets here, she's going to ask you if we're having an affair."

I choked on my drink. "What?"

"I told her not to ask you. I told her she was acting crazy."

"Aaron—why would Fi—"

"She says it's the only way she'll know the truth." He didn't have time to elaborate. Fiona stood at the door, glancing around the windowless room of the bar with her eyes squinted. Aaron lifted a hand and waved, and she made a jerky gesture of relief, then made her way over to the table. When she sat down on Aaron's side he nudged a glass of chardonnay toward her. She sipped and then made a face.

"I'll drink that," I said. "So I heard you want to ask me something."

"You told her," Fiona cried. She glared at Aaron. "I told you don't say anything until I get here."

"Should I leave?" he said.

"What the hell, Fiona?"

"I can't do it—Aaron, you say it."

Aaron took a breath and said in a rush: "Fiona thinks there's something going on with us. She won't believe anything I say. She wants to talk about it out in the open, like this."

"Is there something going on?" Fiona still wouldn't meet my eyes. "You tell me, Jane." She talked to the wall behind me, then to the scratches on the table. "Something doesn't feel right to me—"

"Are you serious?" I asked. "Is this some kind of joke?"

She finally looked at me. "No," she said flatly. "It's not a joke. This is my marriage."

I glanced toward Aaron for help. All the color had drained from his face. His mouth was set in a straight hard line. Mirthless dimples marked his cheeks.

I stood up. "I'm leaving. This is so wrong—you guys have issues—"

"See, babe," Aaron said. "What'd I tell you?"

"Shut up, Aaron," I said.

"Don't you understand I had to ask you?" Fiona said. "Jane. I just had to."

"Like this? You had to ask me like this?" I said. "I can't believe you would think I— How long have we—"

"Come on, sit down," Aaron said. "Let's get another round—"

"I'm sorry," Fiona said. "But you're—he's my husband, but he spends more time with you than me."

"You said you wanted me and Aaron to be friends," I said. "I thought you wanted us to get to know each other."

"I didn't know you guys would—listen, I didn't really think—"

"I'm gone."

I knew I couldn't drive, so I started walking. I didn't mean to, but I swayed toward Ed's building. He lived on Westmoreland, in an old brick job with metal spikes on the window ledges to keep the pigeons off.

"Ed! Ed!" I shouted up at his window. "Ed!"

I was so drunk by then I'd forgotten that I only called him Ed behind his back. It had been months since we broke up. Why was I still thinking about him? Every morning, I stirred awake with some idea of him clutched in my mind, sifted into consciousness from the last dream before I opened my eyes. I could never fully remember my dreams, but I always felt as if all my memories of him unfurled in those darkened hours, like some poison gas spreading through the chambers of my brain, even though in my waking life I could hardly recall the look of his face anymore. A stupid recurring thought I had: Baba would've liked Ed. I don't know how I knew it, but I did.

Standing outside his apartment, I remembered that Tuesday

nights he met with his writing group, the progressive poets of color collective. Or was it Wednesdays he met with the poets? And Tuesday he played in the adult volleyball league? I couldn't remember, and anyway maybe his schedule wasn't the same anymore.

I felt my phone vibrate in my purse. My heart leaped, hoping it was Ed somehow. Then I remembered I'd blocked his number.

It was Fiona. "Where are you?" she asked.

"Nothing's going on between Aaron and me," I said.

"I know," she said. "Come back. Please?"

I was already staggering in the direction of the bar.

When I got there, Fiona was standing by herself outside, smoking a cigarette. She looked like she'd been crying.

"Where's Aaron?"

"Jane," she said. "I'm so sorry."

"It's okay," I said. "It was a mistake."

"No it wasn't," she choked out. "He's sleeping with someone else. Some actress," she added. She dropped the cigarette on the ground and tented her hands over her face. "He said he's in love with her. He said he's in love with both of us. What does that even mean?" She shook her head. "Why does this always happen to me?"

Later, I drove us back to my apartment. We lay down to sleep side by side in my bed, something we hadn't done in years. She turned her back to me, and I slid an arm over her, found her hand in the dark, curled into a fist. I held her like that for a while. Smelling her hair, the back of her neck, I held her. I liked being Fiona's big spoon. Even after I heard her breath go steady, I kept holding on.

We started unpacking in the kitchen, unwrapping the dishes and glasses and placing them in her new cabinets. The rice cooker fit over there, under the microwave mounted to the wall. Then, the living room: we replaced the slats into the bookshelf, crammed her books in tight until there was no more space in each row. She broke the silence, said she needed to buy something made of real wood, and then we were quiet again.

We worked steadily for two hours, putting her apartment in order. It was three o'clock before we realized we were hungry. We walked to a sushi restaurant two blocks away on Hyperion, ate quickly, then returned to finish. I knew it was important for Fiona to feel at home on her first night in the new place, to get as much of the unpacking completed as she could.

After the last box was opened and put away, we uncorked a bottle of red, poured two glasses, and sank into opposite ends of the sofa.

"This shit is worn-out," she said about the sofa.

"It's comfortable," I said.

"Why did I even move it over here?"

I told her the new place looked good, that it had a good vibe.

"Jane," she said. She paused for a moment. "I'm sorry, you

know? I was a jerk to you. About Aaron. I just thought— I
don't know what I thought—"

"He's a dick," I said. "A narcissist."

"I'm sorry," she said again. She hesitated before adding, "I
was jealous. The two of you, it's like you had your own little
club, your private in-jokes."

"I was stupid," I said. "It shouldn't have been like that."

"I should've trusted you. I don't know why I didn't trust
you."

"Fiona," I said.

"You're my best friend, and I—"

"I have to tell you something." I hesitated. "I swear to God,
I was going to talk to you about it, but I was so wrapped up in
my own shit, with Ed—I know it's not an excuse—and then—"

"Wait. What are you talking about?"

"I knew," I said. I heard myself tell her that I knew about
Aaron and the actress, that he'd confessed it to me at one of our
happy hours.

"He told you," Fiona said slowly. "He talked to you about
cheating on me?"

"I didn't know he had feelings for her," I said. "He said it
only happened one time. So I thought it was a mistake—"

"And you didn't tell me?" she said. "Why didn't you tell me?"

"And then you went and accused me—"

"Don't turn this around," she said. "I knew something weird
was going on—I just didn't think—"

"I screwed up," I said. "I don't have— I'm sorry, Fi. Okay? Please—"

"I can't believe you did this to me." She crossed her arms, hugging herself. "You're supposed to be my best friend. And this is what you do—"

"I didn't know what to do," I said.

"So you helped him lie to me?" she said. "Don't say anything. Just go." She stood and turned her back to me. "I can't do this. I want you to leave."

"I wasn't helping him lie," I said. "I was trying to protect you—"

"Protect me?" she cried. "I don't need you to protect me, Jane. I need you to tell me the truth." She shook her head. "What's wrong with you?"

I didn't have an answer to that.

Fiona sighed. "Just go, okay? I can't deal with this. Not right now." Her voice was in shreds, caught in her throat. "Thank you for your help," she added. I wasn't sure if she meant for my being here with the movers today, or if she threw it out as a jab.

She walked into the bedroom and shut the door behind her. I stared at the doorknob for a minute, my heart pounding in my chest.

On one of the shelves, in front of the row of books, stood a framed photo of Fi as a kid with her mom. I remembered that girl: fresh-off-the-boat bowl cut, glasses that magnified her eyes. When she showed up in Miss King's class, she was still Ona. Only her mom called her that now. I remembered liking her right away. She was good at drawing Snoopy and Mickey Mouse, and she always traded her cheese crackers for my fruit leather. Because she was new, I taught her things: how to play hopscotch, where the extra jump ropes were stored, how many pellets to feed the class guinea pig, Annabel Lee. I translated for her sometimes, but by the next year—third grade—she didn't need my help anymore. Maybe that was the last time she really needed me, way back when.

The blue typewriter was still on the coffee table. I wrapped it back up in the towel and took it with me when I left.

I steered down Sunset from Fiona's new place, which turned into Cesar Chavez on the edge of Chinatown. The streets were jammed with cars funneling toward Dodger Stadium, blue-and-white flags waving from their windows. The late-afternoon sun tunneled through the layer of smog that seemed to steep everything, all of us, in an amber-pink haze. The typewriter rested in my passenger seat. I thought of Sonny, the mover. How he said he wasn't supposed to set foot near Chinatown. I didn't grow up here, but it felt like home to me now, after these last four years. Mah had helped me find the apartment, vouched for my ability to take over as manager when the previous owner sold the building and the new landlord needed someone on site who spoke English and Mandarin.

Maybe I shouldn't have told Fiona that I knew about Aaron. Why didn't I say anything when he'd first confessed it to me?

Did I really believe I was protecting her? Or was it something else? I gripped the steering wheel. My chest felt tight.

I thought of my father. How I'd spilled to Mah about his affair with Lee, his old college buddy, all those years ago. Baba had trusted me with his secret, and I couldn't keep my mouth shut. My telling led to everything else—our family breaking up. Baba never came back from that, no chance of recovery. All because of me. My big mouth. Ten years ago, he died. If only I hadn't told—

I turned left on Hill Street. Almost home. My nose burned. A knot formed in my throat. No tears came, though I'd been waiting for them, for years now.

Maybe he'd still be alive, if I hadn't told. Maybe we would've had a chance to reconcile. Things could've been different. If only I'd kept quiet.

The last good memory I have of Ed, when I dropped him off at LAX for his flight to Chicago last Thanksgiving: we'd stood by my car and hugged on the curb. I told him to have a safe flight, one of those things you say at the airport that doesn't mean anything.

"I can't wait to tell my popo all about you," he'd said. "She's going to be so happy I'm dating a nice Taiwanese girl."

A nice Taiwanese girl. He'd meant it as a joke, I guess.

I pulled into the driveway and idled there for a minute. I put a hand over the typewriter keys. Then I put the car in reverse, and I traced the same route I'd just traveled, back to my best friend. I practiced what I wanted to say. I'm sorry. I was wrong. We'll get through this. Talk to me. Tell me. I'm listening. Forgive me. I didn't know. I love you. Don't give up on us. I can't lose you. I love you. I love you.

Clairvoyance

Fiona hadn't been invited to Jasper's wedding, obviously. Later on, she saw pictures online, posted by old college friends they both knew. Jasper and his bride posing on the beach in Honolulu. He had on white linen slacks and a cream-colored guayabera, a lei of dark green leaves draped over his shoulders that hung in two thick vines down the front. The wife, pretty in a bookish way, with a bright smile and dark blond corkscrews. She wore a crown of gardenias and baby's breath on her head. The top and bottom halves of her body looked as if they belonged to two different women. She had narrow shoulders and arms like matchsticks but below the waist, her hips flared voluptuously. Fiona studied the pictures, trying to decide if she felt anything about them. Jasper, her college sweetheart, her first love.

She reached for the phone to call up Jane.

"Well, you're winning," Jane said. "You're on your second marriage, he's only on the first." A laugh in her voice. "What an amateur."

"He looks constipated," Fiona said. "He never knew how to smile like a real person."

"It takes practice to look like a real person," Jane agreed.

"I never thought he would get married," said Fiona. "I always had a feeling he would end up alone and weird—"

"What's her name?" Jane asked. "Who is she?"

"Kenji said she's rich."

"Rich how? What did he say?"

"Maybe now he can finally finish writing his novel," Fiona said.

It had been more than a decade since Fiona moved to New York, straight from undergrad. Back then, she and Jasper were boundless, dancing along the city's golden rhythm. Nothing and nobody could stop them.

"Fi? You still there?" Jane said.

Fiona realized she'd been silent a long while. "I'm still here," she said. "Guess what." She hesitated a moment. "I'm—well, the thing is . . . I'm pregnant."

"What?"

"I went to the doctor's yesterday. It's only eleven weeks, but—"

"You're having a baby?" Jane said. "I didn't even know you were trying to—wait a minute," Jane said, her voice suddenly serious. "You want this, right?"

"Yes," Fiona said quickly. "I do. We do."

"Oh my God. I can't believe it," Jane said. She was quiet for a moment. "A baby!" she said. "Congratulations," she added. "Did I say that already?"

Fiona felt warmth spread through her chest. She recognized then that she felt relieved. Now that she'd told Jane, the baby felt real.

"Are you having a boy or a girl?"

"Too early to tell," Fiona said. "Bobby wants a girl."

"Course he does," said Jane. "By the way, I can't believe you told him before you told me."

Fiona laughed. "I mean—he's only the dad—"

"So what?" The laughing was back in her voice. "Male privilege strikes again."

"You hate babies," Fiona said.

"I won't hate yours."

"You said babies shouldn't be allowed in public last week."

"Your baby won't be an asshole like the one sitting next to us at brunch."

"What if she is an asshole?" Fiona said. "Or he?"

"Dude, see," Jane said. "You're totally winning over Jasper. It's sealed now, with this baby."

Fiona recalled the time she and Jasper walked over the bridge into Brooklyn to cheer for Kenji in the Idiotarod: stolen Pathmark carts festooned in tin foil, silk flowers, and painted cardboard; grown men in stretch-Lycra bodysuits muffing down Bedford Avenue. Kenji was on a team with some teachers from his school. Dirty, hardened snow piled up along the sidewalk, her breath visible in the air. At the finish line, she stood with her hand tucked inside the pocket of Jasper's corduroy coat, her ears frozen, nose dripping, watching for Kenji to bend around the corner. When he finally appeared, shopping cart wheels scraping, she'd waved wildly and shouted his name but couldn't catch his eye. Kenji rushed for the long red ribbon that hung across the middle of the wet black street. She'd looked up at Jasper then. A smile creased his face. In his eyes, she glimpsed her whole future.

That was all before Kenji got sick.

He'd recovered, anyway. It took time, but he got his mouth back. His throat, his voice. His hair grew in after the chemo rounds, his eyebrows and eyelashes. His skin lost that waxy, plastic doll sheen. She'd been afraid he might die. If he had, Fiona thought, maybe she and Jasper might have worked things out, sewn together by grief. Then she felt terrible for imagining that possibility.

In her New York years, Fiona had lost touch with Jane. She wondered now if it had been on purpose, the way she let the time between returning Jane's phone calls, her emails, stretch out languorously. In truth, didn't she believe her life, the choices she made possible for herself, superior to Jane's? The odd jobs Jane worked, and often lost, carelessly, after they graduated high school. Of course, Jane didn't really have to work, did she? Her mother always floated her money anyway. Then her father died, the way he did. Fiona had left California that year.

"Did I ever tell you," Fiona said quietly into the phone, "about the time—Jasper and me, we accidentally . . ." She couldn't bring herself to say the words. Was it bad luck to bring it up now?

"What happened?" Jane said.

"Nothing," Fiona said. She touched a hand to her belly. If she hadn't done it, that child would be—how old? Almost a teenager.

"Hey. You okay?" Jane said. "I was joking. About Jasper, winning—"

"I had an abortion. Years ago," Fiona said. "Obviously, I had to. I mean, we talked about it. What if we—Jasper wanted to keep it, more than me."

Jane was quiet.

"It happened right after we moved to New York. We didn't even have a sofa yet." Fiona shook her head. "It's not like I regret it or anything." She thought of that apartment on Mulberry Street and recalled the scent of almond cookies from the Italian bakery on the ground floor. "It was the right decision."

"Of course it was," Jane replied.

"But it just makes me think," Fiona said after a moment. "And seeing his dumb wedding photos—"

"Think what?"

"I don't know," said Fiona. "That some part of me still—I remember thinking, when I took that pill to make the abortion happen—we'll get to do it for real one day, you know? Me and him."

"Part of you still, what?"

"Loves him."

"No—"

"It doesn't mean anything," Fiona said. "I'm happy." She laughed, though she didn't know why. "I'm happy, I mean it. Everything's great."

"What's going on?" Jane asked. "Seriously—is Bobby—"

"Nothing," Fiona said. "I swear. I'm fine." She laughed again, and this time it felt like she'd pressed a valve, pressure alleviated. "Janie," she said. "Don't you ever think about what other lives you could be living?"

"Hell no," said Jane. "What's the point of that? Once it's done, I'm over it. No regrets."

"You weren't always like that—"

"I learned from Won."

"Now we know where you went wrong," said Fiona, and then they both laughed. After a moment, Fiona said, "I was thinking about my mom this week."

Jane made a noise, half grunt and part moan. A comforting sound. "I know." She was quiet. "I miss her, too," she said finally. It had been two years since Auntie Wendy passed. "I think she would've liked Bobby," Jane said.

"You think so?" Fiona wanted to believe her.

"Tell him I said congrats, too," Jane said, and Fiona promised she would.

"Can I tell you something?" Fiona said suddenly. Jane waited for her to go on. "I've never told you about my dad." She paused a moment. "My biological father. Back in Taiwan." She took a breath. "I can finally talk about it, now that Mom's . . ."

Jane listened to her best friend tell the story of how her mother became a mother, at sixteen. Her father, Fiona said, was an older boy—a college student, studying under Fiona's grandfather. In all the years they'd been friends, Jane had never asked Fiona about her father. It wasn't that she hadn't been curious; some things, even between friends like they were, remained unspoken, passed over in silence. Fiona talked on. Jane could hardly imagine it; Auntie Wendy, a scandalized teenage mother, all on her own. And yet, she could see it all so clearly: Fiona as a little girl, her mother's treasure, protected at all cost. They were happy, Jane knew without Fiona saying so, mother and daughter close in a way that had always felt foreign to Jane.

Growing up, Jane preferred playing at Fiona's house, where there were no restrictions on what they could watch on TV, how long the set stayed on, or whether they'd finished their homework first; where their afternoon snacks were pepperoni Hot Pockets heated up in stiff paper sleeves, fried shrimp and teriyaki hot wings from the casino buffet in Styrofoam takeout containers; where all sorts of kids in the apartment complex dropped by to ask if Fiona wanted to go ride bikes, if they'd heard the ice-cream truck go past yet today. And when they were teenagers, Fiona's mother was more like a friend than a parent. She gossiped with the girls, told them outrageous stories about the casino regulars. Auntie Wendy never scolded, unlike Jane's mother, who was always breathing down her daughter's neck, finding fault.

"Do you ever think about finding him? Your . . . father?"

"No," said Fiona without hesitation. "And anyway, now, there's no point." She was quiet for a moment. "I don't ever want my baby to feel that way," Fiona said. "Unwanted."

"Fiona—"

"I made my mom's life so hard. And then I think about what I did—"

"You were wanted," Jane said. "What you and Jasper chose to do—it was the right thing." A pause. Then: "And this baby? She's wanted, too."

"She?"

"I have a feeling," said Jane.

They hung up the phone. In her apartment, Jane settled back into the sofa. She folded her hands in her lap. It was Saturday, and she had the rest of the afternoon ahead, nothing planned other than a couple errands: the car due for an oil change, and another thing she couldn't remember now. What was it? Something or other she'd put off all week. Still she sat there, considering what Fiona had just told her. A baby coming. Fiona and Bobby's baby. She was going to be an aunt! Jane sighed. Everything was going to change. She stood and plodded to the kitchen, opened the refrigerator door, and peered inside.

Fiona was going away, she thought. There were three cans of

Diet Coke left. A wedge of Parmigiano-Reggiano in a sandwich bag. Jane felt afraid. She thought of Bobby and despised him a little. She thought of the annoying habits he had that Fiona complained about, and then the ones she'd noticed herself but kept quiet on—analyzing Bobby was like commenting on the weather. He existed regardless, her best friend's husband, and Jane accepted this as fact. She shut the refrigerator door.

At the grocery store later, after the oil change, Jane overheard a man on the phone asking if there was enough butter, or if he should pick up another package. Do we get the salted or the unsalted? he said. Jane thought it was a lovely question. She reached for the red carton of salted butter and placed it in her basket even though it wasn't on her list.

She was happy for her best friend. She hadn't known that Fiona wanted a baby. After her mother passed, Fiona suddenly became serious about meeting a man and marrying again. For a while, after divorcing Aaron, she'd shut off that part of herself, it seemed. All their lives, Fiona had attracted attention without trying. It wasn't only that she was beautiful, smart, stylish. Jane understood now that there was something guarded about Fiona, as if she were always looking behind her, watching her back. Even while her eyes were fixed on you, Fiona was casing the room for the exits. Some alert quality about her that was unsettling, and sexy.

Jane had never felt jealous of Fiona. She didn't compete with her; she'd only ever wanted her to stay. When they were younger, she never wanted Fiona to go home at the end of the night. She could sit in Shamu, talking on, forever. The two of them shared everything, and a compliment to one was accepted equally by the other, though most often, Jane knew, it was Fiona to whom the unsolicited kind words were directed, and Jane who stood in the refracted light.

Groceries stowed in the trunk, she drove back to her apartment listlessly.

Everything seemed back on track again in Fiona's life. Last year, she'd transferred her credits to UCLA and completed the law degree she'd abandoned in New York. She passed the California bar on the first try. She met Bobby on Tinder. Now, a baby.

Jane was happy for her. Yes, she really was. But what was this other feeling, buried within it? Fiona was leaving again. She was always leaving. And this time, Jane feared there would be no coming back. A baby changed everything, more than a man ever could. She'd thought they had more time. There were still so many silences, passed over. Fiona was going away now—some other planet, where mothers lived—while Jane remained here in place. She moved through the apartment, from room to room, turning on the lamps, as though searching for something. Nothing was missing. She felt as lonely as she'd ever been.

Fiona and Jane

Fiona and Bobby were throwing a New Year's Eve party—a big deal for them since Gracie was born. Won was in Ibiza or somewhere with the gaysian mafia. I tried to tell Fi I had another commitment, but she saw right through me; she knew my only plans were with a bottle of red and watching the ball drop on TV. I don't want to be the seventeenth wheel, I said, at a party with a bunch of your straight married friends. It's not going to be like that, she snapped. It's going to be all kinds of people there. Don't you want to spend New Year's Eve with your best friend?

It wasn't all kinds of people at her party. A few of Fiona's social justice–type coworkers, whose earnest faces rang vaguely familiar from her wedding; some crunchy-looking white people who were probably Fi and Bobby's neighbors (this was Silver Lake, after all); the paunchy middle-aged Asian guys who formed Bobby's college friend group and their milfy wives, who all looked significantly more fit than their husbands, and younger by years. I'd mentioned this phenomenon once to Fiona, and she asked if I thought of her and Bobby like that. I told her the truth. She put him on a low-carb diet and now they worked out with a personal trainer twice a week.

I started drinking. Midnight was still a couple hours off. I thought about waking up Gracie for an auntie hang, but Fi said Bobby's parents were babysitting for the night. Then, in the middle of a kitchen conversation, in walked someone new. He looked no older than thirty, save for a head of graying hair that he wore brushed back on top, the sides and back cut short and neat. He was a beautiful man, dark gold skin and hawk's eyes, black and darting. He had a melancholy mouth, with full sensuous lips.

I wasn't the only one who noticed. "Who's that?" Fiona's co-worker asked. I couldn't remember her name. Sherrie, or Sheryl, I thought. She had on a cream-colored shift dress with rosebuds embroidered on the chest, the fit-and-flare skirt tight over her hips. A white mini-fascinator rested on one side of her head, a crazy thing with tulle netting and feather quills.

"He's cute," said Sheryl. "But too short for me." Just a minute ago she was complaining about how the last two guys she dated, a Viet and a Korean before that, both broke up with her because they said they couldn't get serious with a white girl.

"That's Julian. Bobby's boy from back in the day," said Elena. Her ex-husband was also a part of Bobby's old crew. Elena got full custody, the condo, and Bobby and Fi in the divorce. She was dressed like a normal person, in dark jeans and a navy blue sweater with bits of silver thread around the neck. "He just quit the Marines." Elena lowered her voice. "I heard he's screwed up in the head."

I said I've never heard Fiona mention him at all.

"He was in Afghanistan," Elena continued in a whisper. "What I heard was he got captured one time, some kind of raid—"

"I bet he's got a hottie body," Sheryl said. "Is he Mexican? Elena, you can tell."

Elena raised an eyebrow. "Not everyone brown's Mexican," she said. "Julian's Filipino," she added.

"I don't think that," Sheryl said.

"You thought I was Mexican for the longest time," Elena said.

Sheryl said that wasn't true, and Elena just smiled. I liked that Elena enjoyed teasing her. Not all of Fi's mommy-friends were funny like that.

Julian stood by the door, nudging his shoes off. He wore a plain white T-shirt and rumpled khaki pants that hung baggy around the ankles. I clocked him at about five-six, maybe five-seven, tops. His gaze seemed to fly around the room, looking for somewhere safe to land. One hand gripped the neck of a bottle wrapped in brown paper.

Bobby barreled over from the living room and swooped him
up in a back-pounding bear hug. They stood back and grinned
at each other, then performed an elaborate handshake, slapping
palms, pounding fists. At the end of it, Bobby threw an arm
around Julian's neck and dragged him over to the kitchen to
make introductions. Captain De Leon, Bobby called him, and
Julian's face flushed red.

Julian leaned over and gave Elena a kiss on the cheek. "Long
time," he said, then started to say something about the divorce.
She waved it away. "How's your brother doing out in Virginia?" she asked.

He shook hands with me and Fi's coworker. Her name, it
turned out, was Carol, not Sheryl.

Bobby tapped Julian's chest with the back of his hand. "Look
at this tough little shit. I've known this Ilocano muhfucka since
before his balls dropped." He made a move to grab Julian's junk,
which turned into a shoving match. Elena and I moved out of
the way, but somehow Carol caught an elbow in the stomach.
She stumbled back against the counter. The glass of red wine she
was holding spilled down the front of her dress.

"Oh shit. I'm sorry," said Julian. "It was an accident—"

"This is silk crepe," Carol cried. Her face turned bright pink.
"Bobby! It's ruined! What am I supposed to—"

"Whoa, whoa. Calm down," Bobby said. The entire kitchen
hushed all of a sudden. People were looking this way. "Everyone just calm down a sec," he said.

Fiona appeared out of nowhere. "What happened?" She

looked into each of our faces. "Bobby?" Her eyes flicked over to Julian quickly, then away. It was fast, but I caught it: she didn't want Julian here, and it pleased her that Carol was crying and carrying on, causing a scene.

"It wasn't nobody's fault," Bobby started. "We were horsing around—"

"I'm really sorry," said Julian. "I didn't mean—"

"Are you still here?" Fiona said. "Bobby mentioned you're moving to New York." She said it as if she wished he were already gone, three thousand miles away and not at her house now, here in LA.

"Look at me. This dress," Carol said. "It's ruined!"

"I'll pay for it," Julian said. "You can buy a new one. Just tell me how much—"

"This is vintage, from the 1960s. You can't just"—she held up her fingers to rake quotes in the air—"'buy a new a one.'" The ostrich feathers in her tiny hat shook indignantly.

"Honey, we can find something in my closet for you to change into," said Fiona. Before she led Carol and Elena down the hall, she gave Bobby a final, meaningful stare and fluttered her hands at him, as if shaking them dry.

"Dude, it was a complete accident," Julian said. He looked from Bobby to me. "You think it's going to wash out?"

"Fuck her dress," Bobby said. "Carol needs to calm her ass down."

"Bobby did it," I said. "It wasn't your fault."

"Damn, Jane. So it's like that?" Bobby said.

Julian's eyes lit up, as if he wanted to laugh. I noticed his eyelashes. Long and dark, with a soft curl at their tips. Sleepless blue shadows ringed the skin under his eyes.

I said Carol was just being drunk and dramatic.

"You saw that crazy hat?" Bobby said. "And it wasn't me, it was definitely you, bro."

"I need a drink." Julian shook his head. "Shot?"

"Yo, you better bounce," said Bobby. His voice was grave all of a sudden. "You saw how my wife was looking at me."

"It's not that serious," I said. "Come on, Bobby boy." I felt guilty, remembering Fiona's face when she saw the spilled wine on Carol, the way she'd told Bobby with her eyes to make Julian disappear. "You should definitely stay," I said to Julian. "It's New Year's Eve. Where's he going to go?" I added.

Bobby looked away. "Party's kind of lame anyway, tell you the truth." He shrugged, passing his gaze over the kitchen, into the living room. "You don't want to be here, man. There's literally no hot chicks"—Bobby caught himself, glanced over at me. "Not that I even notice these things," he added, clearing his throat.

"You're really gonna make me leave?" Julian said. "I drove up from San Diego for this party. I haven't seen you in—"

"Janie, you're a lesbian," Bobby said. "Would you bang anyone here? Back me up. Buncha cows, am I right?"

"Babe," Fiona called from across the room, her head sticking out from behind the guest bedroom door. "I need you—"

"Hey, man," Bobby said. "We'll chill next week. I'll come down there for the weekend. What do you say?"

"I fly out Thursday," Julian replied. "New York. That's it."

"Shit, I forgot," Bobby muttered. "Thursday? Already?" He put a hand on Julian's shoulder. "Hang on, I gotta see what the boss wants."

Bobby walked off, and Julian twisted the cap off a bottle of Jack. He poured it into a tumbler, downed the contents in two hard swallows. "What was your name again?" He filled the glass a second time.

"You got a cigarette?" I said.

Outside, standing among Fiona and Bobby's succulents, we smoked in silence. I broke it, finally, by apologizing for Fiona.

"She hates my brother," Julian said. "Ever since he moved to Virginia I'm sure she's real happy Bobby doesn't see him anymore."

"Carol should be the one to leave."

"When did Bobby get so whipped?" He drank from his cup. "I shouldn't say that. Sorry."

I said he wasn't lying, and Julian laughed.

After a moment, he said: "The men in my family, we're warriors. We come from a long line of military, going way back in the Philippines. It can make you a certain type."

I knew what type Julian meant—the swaggering, mansplaining dudes Fiona cycled through in our twenties. Maybe a good part of the thirties.

"My brother and Bobby?" Julian said. "You don't know the shenanigans they used to get into."

"He's still an asshole sometimes," I said. "But Bobby's a good dad."

Julian stubbed out his cigarette on the bottom of his boot. "It's why I had to get out of the Marines. You ever lived in a place near a base?" I shook my head. "There's nothing to do. I was throwing away so much cash on strippers," he said. "Getting wasted all the time. Acting a fool."

"Bobby's right about one thing," I said. "This party is dead as hell."

"You know a better one?" He buried his hands in his pockets.

"We can chill at my place," I said. "Smoke some weed."

"I better not," he said. "I might get tested for this new job in New York." Then he met my eyes and an understanding came into his face softly. He squinted, studying me. "But didn't Bobby call you a—"

"Bobby's an idiot," I said.

"Yeah, I've met him. The guy who just kicked me out of his party."

I called a car to drive us to my apartment.

Upstairs, things got going. Then something dawned on me. It had been a long time since I kept condoms stocked at my place.

"Bad news," I said, pulling back.

"I got you," Julian said. He reached into his khakis, puddled next to the bed.

There was a beautiful, strange energy between us. As if inside him there was a magnet—I'd felt its pull even at Fi and Bobby's—drawing me to him; but the closer I came, the magnet seemed to switch to its other end and began to repel me. Then it flipped again, and I rushed toward him swiftly. Still, the entire episode lasted not long after we began. I'd forgotten how fast it goes with a man. How linear the trajectory. He asked me if I—? And I almost laughed. Yes, I said, smiling. I enjoyed him very much.

The next morning, we stood in my kitchen barefoot. While we waited for the coffee to percolate, Julian talked about the time he got blown up in Afghanistan, casual like. Just another routine patrol in the desert, he said, until the Humvee rolled over an IED, and then: a deafening boom. *The hell was that?* Julian was the ranking officer in the company. He moved quickly to check out the three other Marines—dazed, but all still breathing—before he peered outside the vehicle to assess the damage. Charred metal, broken glass, halo of dust. His eyes burned. The enemy was out there. *Fucking insurgents.* He radioed for backup, doing everything to suppress the panic crushing his throat.

"All of a sudden I started to laugh," he said. Once the laughing came on he couldn't stop. The giddiness spread through the truck, passed from man to man, like a relay baton.

The sun shone bright through the kitchen windows of my apartment. I asked him what had been so funny.

"It was just so . . . ridiculous," he said after a while. "Our underwear and socks flying out there, mixed up with all the burnt mess and debris."

"Maybe you were in shock," I said.

"Maybe." After a moment, he said: "One of the guys with me that day, I saw him come back from another patrol later on. They'd gotten blown up, too. Another fucking IED."

I asked if he turned out okay. Julian shook his head, slow. "He wasn't responding at all. Bleeding, eardrums blasted. He was drooling." He made a gesture, running his fingers from the side of his mouth down his chin. "He never recovered from that," he said. His voice was quiet, matter-of-fact. "The guy's a vegetable now. Basically."

The moka gurgled on the stove. I asked Julian how he takes his coffee. I didn't know what else to say. We sat there quiet for a while. I asked him about New York. He said he had a job lined up in Manhattan. Analyst for an investment bank. I talked about my writing, the two pilots that didn't get picked up, the sci-fi script in development purgatory. He was twenty-seven: four years in the naval academy; five years active, including two tours in Afghanistan. I told him I was thirty-two, shaving five years off my real age and our ten-year difference.

I drove him back to go pick up his car, parked on Fiona and Bobby's street. We didn't talk about what either of us would say to them, if anything. I cringed a little, imagining the expression on Fi's face.

"By the way," Julian said before getting out of my car. "Can I get your number?"

The night before he left for New York, Julian drove up to LA again. He let Bobby apologize with an expensive steak dinner, and then he came over to my place. He smelled like a cigar, and I made him scrub down in the shower before getting in bed. This time I had condoms ready.

Afterward, he couldn't sleep. I put my arms around him and held him for a while. I could feel his nervous energy bouncing all around, and underneath it, a vibrating melancholy.

"I wish," he started to say.

"What?"

A short silence. Then: "I wish I could disappear," he said haltingly. "If there was a way I could go away without hurting my family. Make it look like an accident. A car crash, or—I don't know—if I fell off a cliff, something stupid like that."

I asked him quietly if he was talking about hurting himself.

"Don't worry, Jane. I'm not . . . suicidal." He gave a hollow laugh. "I just want to disappear," he said again. "I don't want to exist."

I tensed. "What does that mean?"

"I know it doesn't make any sense," he said. "That's why it's a wish."

"You can't just go around saying that," I said. "Like it's nothing. You don't know me—"

"Do me a favor?" He turned to face me in the dark and made me promise not to tell Bobby about what he'd just said. "I don't want him to tell my brother—"

"You don't understand. My dad." I hesitated a moment. "He committed—"

"Look," Julian said flatly. "That isn't what's going on with me, okay?"

I didn't say anything back.

"You don't have to worry about me. I'm good." A sharp edge had crept into his voice. "I'm sorry about your dad," he said. "But I've had my psych evals. Talked to my boss, the chaplain, my buddies who were honorably discharged, the whole thing. I didn't leave the Marines on a whim, okay? Do you know how hard they make it for you? I told you, my brother—my whole family—"

"Relax," I said. "I'm just saying, it seems like you've probably been through some shit—"

"Don't do that," he said.

"You said you want to disappear."

"Don't you dare thank me for my fucking service—"

"What?" I said. "I wasn't going to."

"Can we just drop this?"

"Fine," I said. "Forget it. It's dropped."

Then we were both silent.

After a while, he said, "I'm sorry, Jane." I stayed quiet. "I'm lonely," he said in a soft voice. "I'm so goddamn lonely. All the time. Everyday. Especially at night—and you're so—"

He moved closer and started kissing my face, my ears, my neck. Everywhere except my mouth.

"Don't," I said. "Julian."

"It's my last night here." In a whisper, he added: "I want to feel close to you."

"I'm right here," I said. "See?"

He sighed and turned to lie on his back.

"What happened?" he said, after a moment. "With your dad—"

"Nothing," I said. Now it was my turn to be cold. "We weren't close or anything."

He asked if I had anything to drink, and I told him there were probably a few beers in the fridge.

"You want one?" he said. I shook my head. "So it's okay, if I . . . ?"

"Knock yourself out."

After that, I must have fallen asleep. When I opened my eyes, early-morning sunlight flooded the room. Julian stood by the door, dressed in the long-sleeved henley and brown corduroy pants he had on from last night.

"What time is it?" I rolled out of the bed and drifted over to him. "Did you even sleep?"

He said he had to head back down to San Diego; his flight to New York was that same night.

Through the front window, I watched him carry his duffel bag to the car and stow it in the trunk. I waved to him, but he didn't wave back. Maybe he couldn't see me, though it seemed as if he were looking right at me. I felt the magnet pulling me, drawing me to him. With difficulty I turned away from the window. I didn't want to watch him drive away.

Fiona and Bobby's boring New Year's Eve party, the hookup with Julian that was supposed to have been light, meaningless fun, but had turned into something else (though what that "something" was, I couldn't tell you). In any case, he left for New York and I tried to put the whole thing out of my mind. Not a word about it to Fiona. When she asked why I'd left their place before midnight without even saying bye, I told her Carol's dress drama gave me a headache and I had to bounce, sorry.

The second week in January, I reinstalled the dating apps. I matched right away with Naima: thirty-four, a cinematographer. We chatted a bit then made a first date for happy hour downtown on a Thursday night. Naima was cute in her pictures, but in person she was striking, a real knockout. She wore a dark denim jumpsuit with a triangle cutout under her breasts, silver bangles on both wrists, and a pair of platform espadrilles with red ribbons tied around her ankles. Her hair was cut into a short Afro and dyed a reddish-brown tone, a style that revealed the elegant slope at the nape of her neck. When she came in for a hug, I caught the scent of jasmine on her throat. I felt underdressed in my black tee, ripped jeans, and black Converse high-tops, but something in the way she held my gaze, her dark brown eyes radiating warm energy, gave me a boost of confidence.

It was one of those dates that didn't feel like a date at all, none of the stilted getting-to-know-you questions that forced you to perform some gilded version of yourself; with Naima, I immediately felt as if I were catching up with an old friend I hadn't seen in a long while, someone both familiar and new. A feature she'd worked on as DP had screened in competition at Sundance last year, and the two indie music videos she'd directed had both gone viral. We discovered we knew many of the same people, other writers and producers and directors hustling to make it to the next level in the industry, like we were.

I confessed that I felt like I was running out of time, staring down the big four-oh.

"Stop it," she said. "Each of us is on our own journey," which might've sounded corny coming from anyone else in the world. Then she asked if I believed in reincarnation; I said I wasn't sure. "Let me see your hands." I showed her, and she traced a finger across my palms, left to right. A soft tingle passed through my wrists, traveled up my arms, like bells singing. "You've been here before," she said. "You know death, intimately." She tilted her head toward her shoulder and looked at me for a long moment.

Her gaze seemed to penetrate me. I held my breath. Then she smiled and said, "Can you tell I'm bullshitting? I can't read palms." I laughed, relieved—and maybe just a little bit disappointed.

We ordered a bottle of prosecco and finished it sitting there at the bar, then walked down Spring Street to a lounge with low leather sofas and dim purple lights, a three-piece band setting up in the corner. We watched them opening up their cases, hooking up cords to amps. I put my hand on the small of her back. She turned to me, and I leaned toward her mouth. I felt her stiffen. She blinked and then looked down at her feet. I kept my hand on her back and asked her what was wrong.

"I'm not used to—" she started to say. "It's not you—there was this guy sitting at the bar. Gave us a weird look when we walked in—"

"Can I kiss you?" I leaned close to her ear, my voice a whisper. "I'd like to kiss you," I said. "Fuck him," I added. "I know the bartender here."

We kissed. I felt her back relax under my hand. We pulled apart when the band kicked in, a bluegrass number with the banjo strumming, a harmonica solo near the end. It was too loud to talk now. I watched Naima in profile, her head bobbing along to the jumping bass line.

She came home with me that night—luckily I'd tidied up before our date. After another glass of wine, she began to undress slowly, drawing out the performance, as if presenting herself to me. Our energy together felt urgent but unhurried. Next to her curves I felt boyish, narrow hips and too-big feet. It wasn't a bad thing, though. It was sexy. We made love like teasing, nudging each other toward the precipice then pulling back, flying over the edge then starting over, again and again. She was a confident lover, a woman who enjoyed her body. She rode the pleasure of our sex in waves, and I felt myself caught in her wake.

"You're a troublemaker," she said, after.

"Me?" I said. "What did I do?"

"Exactly what a troublemaker would say."

"I like you," I said. "Miss Naima."

She smiled. We kissed again. I felt her shiver under my hands.

At Julian's new job, the bank's HR department paired him up with a company mentor, another former Marine. They had a program, Julian explained one night on the phone; an affinity group within the practice to ease the transition from military life into corporate America: professional-development workshops, speakers on mental health, yoga and meditation classes.

"He was fat," Julian said about his assigned mentor, his voice laced with disgust. "Huge beer gut that hung over his pants."

"He's a regular person now. A civilian," I said. "So he ate a few burgers. He's allowed."

"You can't go around introducing yourself as a Marine

Corps vet, looking like that. It's embarrassing," he said. "He probably had a lame staff job. No way any one of my guys would've ever let themselves go like that."

I thought of Julian's brown skin, the muscles that felt like fine carved stone beneath my hands. He was proud of his body, a confidence that revealed itself in how he moved, in bed and out of it. I wondered how long he'd stay like that, now that he was a civilian nobody like everyone else.

He kept in touch—mostly through texts; sometimes with phone calls, when he couldn't fall asleep. Julian drank every night of the week, downing a whole bottle of red by himself at home, or else rounds of bourbon on the company tab at some team-building happy hour. He'd call me drunk, his voice suddenly boyish, full of smiles, rinsed of the nervous energy that otherwise clung to him. Were we becoming friends? No straight guy I'd ever slept with acted like this. Maybe he didn't know this wasn't normal behavior, that you were supposed to just ghost.

One time, he sent me an old photo of himself with his Marine buddies. The five of them stood in a row, wearing the same sand-colored digital camouflage coats and cargo pants. Hard grimaces were etched on their faces, five sets of eyes squinting into the camera lens. The picture was taken somewhere in Logar province. Julian was at least two or three shades darker than he was now, or maybe it was the camera's exposure, or that he was standing next to those guys, the only brown face in the group. An automatic rifle hung in front of his chest, attached to a sling that rested on one shoulder and crossed over the front of the body, the way a woman wore a purse with the leather strap nestled between her breasts. "Everyone always thought I was the Afghan translator," he said. "They learned, though." Learned what? I asked. "Not to fuck around with the Filipino captain."

He couldn't fall asleep without the alcohol. Even so, nightmares haunted him. Julian had no peace in bed.

"You don't want to know what I dream about," he told me one night on the phone. "It's messed up." I was curious. Finally, he relented and described the scenery in his brain under moonlight. This was an especially bad one from a couple nights ago, he said. Severed body parts, a humid butcher shop, everything slick, red. A man with no face hunting him, closing in—

He was right. I wished I hadn't insisted.

The next day, I called back and begged him to make an appointment to talk to a therapist.

"The VA hospital is a joke," he replied. "I've been through all this. They made me talk to a psychologist before. I lied my ass off—"

"So don't lie this time."

He sighed. "It's not going to do anything. Trust me."

"Why'd you lie to the psychologist?" I said. "What's the point of that?"

He said that he was giving serious thought about going back into the Marines. "At least back then I was doing something meaningful," he said. "I can't believe I quit to be a paper bitch."

"Listen," I said. "I have an idea. Let's write a movie together. Your stories, everything you already told me, plus—"

"Come on," he said. "Get serious."

"I already pitched it to my agent," I lied. "He's into the idea."

"You did what?" he cried. "I never said you could do that. I told you things—"

"It's not about military training strategies or fighting in Afghanistan. No one cares about that crap," I said, even though it was the opposite of the truth. Everyone loved a feel-good American war movie. "It's about Lapu-Lapu, reincarnated as an ex–Marine officer, working on Wall Street."

"I have questions," he said cautiously, wary of taking the bait. "And I don't actually work on Wall Street—"

"One day, L-L sees a beautiful woman inside the window of Duane Reade," I said. "Turns out, she's the granddaughter of Imelda and Ferdinand—"

"What do you know about Lapu-Lapu?" he asked, amused. "Is Magellan in this?"

"It's a rom-com, Julian."

"About the Marcos family? No way."

"Haven't you heard of irony?"

"You're crazy," he said, after he realized I was joking around. "You know that? You're out of your mind."

"Sure," I said. "I'm the crazy one."

A week later, Julian called on a Friday night. It was just after eleven here in LA, so about two o'clock in the morning out there. I was propped up in bed at home, reading a comic book. I had a whole box of them. The books had belonged to my father, and I'd rescued them from the garage when I'd stopped by to water Mah's spider plants and ferns last Sunday. She was still in Taiwan for another couple weeks, gone through Chinese New Year. Mah rooms with her sister's family and keeps up relations with my father's side, too, though she still refused to visit Baba's grave. She says it's a sin, how he died. She won't ever forgive him. Passing by her room last weekend, I remembered when Baba used to read those comics in bed, the year before he'd moved to Taiwan, the absorbed expression on his face he wore while he tugged on an earlobe with his fingers.

Julian was walking home. His cell phone picked up scraps of other people's conversations as he passed them on the sidewalk. I asked where he was coming from, and he said he'd gone out for dinner with a new friend, a woman he'd met at some young Asian professionals networking event.

I asked if it was a date. Julian laughed and said no, of course not. Then he asked if I'd been going on dates.

"Not really." Naima's face floated in my mind, and I felt a stab of guilt. "A little bit. Here and there." It wasn't that I wanted to hide her from Julian—I wanted to keep her for myself, just for a while longer.

"Come to New York. Go on a date with me."

"A date," I said. "You jealous?"

"We can work on the script. Don't you want to find out what happens?"

"I already know how it's going to turn out."

"Is there a happy ending?" Then, he added, "Not like that, you pervert."

"I'll think about it," I said. "A date?"

"You're the only person in my life who makes me feel like I exist." He paused a moment. "We don't have to call it a date," he said.

When we hung up, I went online and bought a plane ticket bound for New York City in two weeks. I forwarded the itinerary to Julian, and the next day he emailed back: "Who have you been going on dates with? Guys? Girls?"

In New York, Julian and I visited the Guggenheim. We rode the elevator up to the top then strolled down, winding leisurely through the exhibit, a retrospective of a Japanese conceptual artist. Several floors of the museum featured his "Date Paintings": for a time, the artist worked on canvases with a single date in the center, simple white letters brushed over a monochromatic background of black, navy, red, or gray paint. On one of the middle levels, tall glass walls erected between the galleries displayed tourist postcards the artist had mailed to his friends throughout the 1960s and '70s. Pictures of the Statue of Liberty washed in sunset hues, the Chrysler Building gleamed silver, the World Trade Center's Twin Towers loomed above lurid blue water, and on the backs: "I got up at 7:48 A.M." "I got up at 8:15 A.M." Next to these were a series of Western Union telegrams, each of them declaring the same refrain: "I am still alive." "I am still alive." "I am still alive."

That night in bed, I told Julian about my father. Baba had moved out on Mah and me when I was fifteen. After living in Taipei for a few years, he'd landed in Shanghai. Another job, the growing economy on the mainland, better pay.

We were kissing a little, stopping every now and then to talk, me in my flannel pajamas and Julian wearing a pair of green sweatpants stamped with USMC on one leg. He didn't have any blinds over the bedroom windows yet, and a dark orange light passed through the glass, landed on the bare white wall next to Julian's bed in a long rectangle with black vertical lines cutting through its middle.

"I was twenty-two when he died," I said to Julian. Back then I had two jobs: weekdays I answered the phones at an eye doctor's office, and weekends I worked as the hostess at a sushi bar on the west side that turned into a clubby lounge scene at night. I was supposed to be taking classes at Santa Monica College toward making a transfer to a four-year, but whatever cash I had left after paying the rent I spent on partying: dropping

Ecstasy at warehouse raves in the Inland Empire, camping trips up the coast to shroom my brains out on the beach, endless shots of Crown Royal at the various Koreatown booking clubs staked along Wilshire Boulevard. Too many blackout nights, hangover days. Fiona was gone—New York, Jasper, her old law school ambitions—those were the years we'd lost touch.

I'd given up hope my father would ever return to LA, I said. Take up position as a regular part of my life again. I was angry with him, and whenever he called me up I'd send him straight to voicemail. It happened like this, every time: he'd call again a few minutes later, and again in an hour. Sometimes he left messages. Five, six, ten times he would call, always on Sundays. I never called him back.

Near the end his call volume dwindled to two or three times on a single day, then just one try, the last Sunday. I remembered declining that call, too. The next Sunday, when my phone didn't light up with his number, I felt strange. I realized I'd drawn an uncanny comfort from the routine, rejecting his incoming attempts.

The next day, on a Monday, I got a call from an unknown international number. The person spoke Mandarin, but I had a hard time understanding his mainland accent—he was a cop, I finally gathered. The rest of the conversation was a blur, or maybe I've blocked it from memory after all these years.

"My father hanged himself," I said, lying there in Julian's bed. "From a ceiling fan."

Julian was quiet for a moment. "A guy in boot camp did that," he said finally. "It was the first body I ever saw."

"He was in his forties," I said. "Just a few years older than I am now."

"The guy in boot camp left a note for his family. Did your dad . . . ?"

I shook my head.

"Wait, what'd you say?" Julian asked. "Forty—"

"Oh that," I said. In my reverie, I'd slipped up. Then I told him my real age.

He asked me why I'd lied, and I said I didn't know. I breathed, waited for him to say something else.

"Come here," he said, and held an arm up for me to lean against his chest. He smelled like a new bar of soap. "Anything else you want to confess?"

I heard myself tell him about Naima, how I'd been getting close to her.

After I finished talking Julian cleared his throat. "I'm happy for you," he said. "She sounds like a cool chick."

Did he mean it? His voice betrayed no bitterness, no sliver of regret or jealousy. I wondered then if I'd wanted him to become upset, to act like the jilted lover. Maybe things would crystallize between us, force one or both of us to make a choice, say something we couldn't come back from. Then I realized maybe I'd already said enough, telling him about my dad.

I hadn't talked to Naima about any of that at all; when she

asked about my family I'd said that my parents were divorced and left it at that. She didn't pry. Her parents, too, were split up. Both had remarried, and Naima grew up with younger siblings from the new unions, the beloved big sister to them all. I couldn't tell her Baba had been effectively ostracized from the family, that I'd been the one to out him to Mah. I'd turned my back on him when I was eighteen, after that trip to Taipei. For four years, he tried to reestablish contact. My father was a gay man, closeted and alone. I was stupid enough to think there'd always be more time with him—I should've known better.

Under the comforter Julian found my hand. "So what are you doing wasting your time with me?"

"Are you still lonely?" I asked.

"I just want you to be happy, Jane."

"I want me to be happy, too."

He laughed quietly. Then: "I'm not lonely, no. Not right now." A short silence. "Maybe I'm happy, too? I don't know," he said. "But everything will just go back to normal after you're gone."

"After I leave New York, let's never talk again," I said suddenly. "Both of us happy, no one lonely. We'll just promise to do our best to stay this way forever."

"It'll be like those paintings we saw today," he said. "One day at a time." He squeezed my hand.

"I got up today," I said.

"I am still alive," he replied.

"I am still alive," I said back, after a moment.

When Mah came back from Taiwan I went over to her place for a belated New Year's dinner. I picked up a roast duck from ABC on my way down, Mah's favorite in Chinatown. She updated me on the family gossip: Third Uncle lost a pile of money on a faulty stock tip from Cousin Ling's Singaporean girlfriend. Big Auntie Mo's youngest daughter was pregnant again by her useless, cheating husband—at least he always brought back the latest Japanese foot creams and Thai textiles from his "business trips." Mah rattled off story after story, and I listened with one ear while I stuffed myself with crispy slivers of duck skin, Mah's famous pork and shrimp paste dumplings, too many triangles of scallion pancake.

"They asked about you," she said. "'When is Jane coming to visit us next time?'"

My family used to plague Mah with questions about who I was dating, if like so many daughters of their overseas friends I'd end up marrying a kindhearted, goofy-looking white guy who ate hamburgers for breakfast, lunch, and dinner; or maybe I'd choose a handsome Black man for my husband, someone charismatic and tall like Will Smith or Barack Obama, they suggested, a good match since I was so tall myself. Just imagine it, one uncle declared: Your child could be the next Jeremy Lin! In the last few years, however, the inquiries stopped.

I stood up to clear the dishes from the table. "Mah," I said now. "Do you ever get lonely?"

She frowned slightly. Wrinkles gathered at the corners of her eyes. "What a silly question," she said. "Why would I be lonely? I have Jesus. He is walking with me all the time."

"But don't you ever wish—"

"You ate enough?" Mah said. "Still some rice left in the pot."

"All your sisters are married, and when you go visit, everyone's coupled off. You don't feel left out?"

Mah helped me carry the rest of the dishes from the dining table into the kitchen.

"Jane," she said in a quiet, steady voice. "Is that why you never married? Because I didn't . . . ?"

After Baba died, there was a gentleman from Mah's church who came around. He brought her gifts from his garden, chrysanthemum leaves and gai lan and morning glory. In exchange, Mah packed brown paper sacks with winter tangerines from her backyard tree. Then, he was gone; a job transfer to New Jersey.

"It's not too late," she said. "You can still—I pray for you."

I stayed quiet. After stacking the dirty plates and bowls in the sink, I turned the faucet on and squirted blue liquid soap to soak them.

When I turned around, Mah said, "I saw your father's grave this time."

I didn't reply. My breath was caught in my throat.

"I drove to the mountain," she said. "It's a nice place. Clean. Good air up there."

I asked if she went alone. She nodded.

"I didn't cry," she said, as if she were proud of it. "I told him some things." She paused for a long while. Finally, she said, "I told him: I forgive you, my husband. Jane's father. I let you go free, now."

"You said that to him?"

"I don't understand why he did it, but I forgive." My mother fixed her gaze on me. "You have to forgive him, too."

"Me?" I said. "Forgive Baba?"

"For leaving us," she said.

I shook my head, and Mah sighed.

It wasn't me who had to forgive my father. It was him who had to forgive me. I was the one who told his secret—I outed him to Mah. It was my fault. I was the one to blame.

"Let me show you something," she said.

Mah took out her phone and scrolled through her pictures from the trip. She stopped at a group photo of my father's side of the family and zoomed in on the man seated next to her at a large circular table laden with at least ten or twelve dishes of food.

"Remember this uncle?" I nodded, even though I didn't. "Your father's younger brother." She said his Chinese name. The middle character of the three was the same as my father's, the way my Chinese name shared the same middle character as all the cousins of my generation. "Almost like a twin, when they were kids."

I took her phone and stared at the picture of my father's brother. His hair, an elegant gray, held a wave in it, like my father's did. My uncle had a broad forehead, a pronounced eyebrow ridge above genial dark eyes, crinkled at their corners. My heart beat in my chest. My throat felt tight. There was my father's mouth. His smile.

I looked up from the phone at Mah. Tears sat in her eyes. "We never get to see him past forty-five," she said. "I think maybe, he would look something like your uncle now—if he was alive."

"Yes," I murmured. "I see it. I see his face."

I held Mah's phone in my hand a long time.

Mah packed a bag for me with a stack of Tupperware containers filled with leftovers, and a quart-sized bag of frozen dumplings. "Don't drive crazy," she said. "Call me when you get home." The same refrain every time I left her house.

"I almost forgot," I said, standing in the driveway. "I have a New Year's present for you."

"A red envelope?"

I popped the trunk and pulled out Mah's gift: a brand-new Jesus painting in a rococo gilded frame.

Mah laughed and patted me on the back as I carried it inside for her. I removed the faded Jesus from the wall and hung up the new one. The Son of God looked right at home, over the sofa. Reincarnation, I thought. A miracle made possible by Etsy. Mah beamed.

"Mah," I said suddenly. "You would be happy? If I got married."

She was silent for a moment, thinking.

"I have a new girlfriend," I said. "I want you to meet her."

Mah held my gaze. "Okay," she said. "Good," she added. "What's her name?"

I felt my stomach unclench. Somewhere between the old Jesus and the new one, Mah and I understood one another.

Late Sunday night: my phone buzzed, Julian's name flashing across the screen. Something felt off as soon as I picked up. I asked him about the weather, if it was snowing again. He answered in a dead-sounding voice.

"Are you okay?"

He said my name. He said, "I fucked up. Royally."

I asked him if he was drunk, and he said no, then yes. I waited for him to go on.

Another week at work had droned past, he said, meetings that should've been emails, a scrapped acquisition deal. He'd hit the sixty-day mark and passed the interim review with flying colors; HR officially presented him with a box of business cards. The ex-captain with the beer gut congratulated Julian with a nice bottle of rye.

"What does it mean that I hate this job," he said. "But everyone thinks I'm doing great? What a sick joke," he added. "I'll probably quit on Monday, if they don't fire me first."

Last Friday, he continued, he'd gone to happy hour with his group, where everyone clapped him on the back and bought him shots to celebrate the review. Someone suggested that they move the party to Scores—"I thought it was a sports bar!" Julian said—and the two women among the dozen or so men shouted yes the loudest. At the strip club there was Dom, and Krug, and one of those female colleagues ended up sitting next to Julian, squeezed in tight together in the middle of the velvet booth. At one point they started making out, and before he knew anything they were hailing a cab back to the office, where they polished off the rye in Julian's desk. She'd hitched up her skirt and crouched down on her knees in front of him.

"I didn't notice her wedding ring until after. Before Friday we'd barely even talked," he said. "There's cameras everywhere in the office. And I used my keycard to swipe in—"

"You're not getting fired for that," I said. I started picking up the comic books I'd been trying to read these last few weeks. One by one, I threw them back into the cardboard box. "I have to call you back," I said. "I'm on my way out—"

"I freaked out," he said. "When you told me you were seeing someone else—and all this week, you didn't call—"

"Julian," I said. "It's fine. You're going to be fine."

"I like you, okay?"

"I went all the way to New York to see you," I said. "What else do you want from me?"

"You're a real person," he said. "And when I talk to you, I feel like a real person." He hesitated. "When you told me about your dad—"

"Don't," I said. My throat constricted. "Do not—"

"I'm going to get help," he said. "I don't want to end up like that."

I hung up on him.

The phone lit up again with Julian's name on the screen. I turned the phone facedown. I was shaking.

I stood up from the bed. I took a deep breath, and then another. I lifted my hands to my face.

My cheeks were wet with tears, for the first time in a very long time.

Naima was out of town for my birthday; she got hired on a gig in Baton Rouge, an indie horror feature backed by a decent budget. Fiona took me out to dinner. Nothing fancy, just our favorite Korean barbecue joint on Eighth. They used charcoal sticks here instead of propane. The waitresses wore brown uniforms and neat white aprons, replaced the banchan dishes without you having to bug them a million times. We ordered a bottle of soju, for old times' sake.

"I slept with someone," I said after we polished off the thin-sliced chadol beef. "Not Naima, I mean."

"De Leon's little brother?" she said. "I've been waiting for you to say something about that."

"You knew? Bobby's got a big mouth—"

"I can't believe you actually went to New York," she said. "In the winter?"

"I'm working on a script," I said. "I went for research."

"You went for dick." She put down her chopsticks and gave me a look, with a smirk. "That's why you didn't tell me—"

"I'm telling you now, aren't I?"

"Bobby didn't have to say anything," she said. "I knew you left together from the party. Carol's still mad about her dress," she added.

"Why do you hate Julian's brother so much, anyway?" I poured out another shot of soju for each of us.

"Oh, he's insane," Fiona said. "He says gays are all going to hell. Poor people need to get a job and stop complaining. Don't get him started on 'illegals,' he calls them." She rolled her eyes. "Bobby wanted to ask him to be Gracie's godfather. I said hell no."

"Believe me, Julian's not that person," I said.

"How do you know?" Fiona shook her head and picked up her glass. Her lipstick left a dark red half-moon on the rim. "He got out of the military, fine. But now he's a finance bro?"

"Julian doesn't want Bobby to know," I said, "but he's pretty depressed. He used to call me when he gets panic attacks. He hides in the bathroom at work, on another floor."

"Jane," she said. Her voice was tender. I recognized it as the one she uses with Gracie, even when she was dead tired. "What's this all about?" she said. "You okay?"

"I was worried about him," I said. "I can't explain it . . ."

"What about Naima?" She lifted the bottle and poured out the next round. "When's the last time we drank this stuff?"

"It's disgusting," I agreed. We touched our glasses and threw back the shot.

"I like Naima for you," she said. I asked her why, and Fiona smiled. She picked up her chopsticks and grabbed for a piece of radish kimchi. "I just do," she said. "I can see her, in your life. It makes sense. Now, Julian—"

"He's all alone. He's got no one," I said. "Naima has everything going for her—"

"Jane," she said. "That's a good thing. Hello?" She fixed me with her gaze. "Why are you being so weird about this?"

I knew where she was going, and I wanted to turn around, change course.

"This is about your dad, isn't it?"

"What?" I said. "No."

I broke away from Fiona's eyes and surveyed the restaurant. About half the tables were filled up, young people in groups of three or four, the girls with ash highlights in their hair, boys who wore expensive-looking jeans with holes in the knees. The table closest to ours was a family; the father flipped over meat on the grill while the mother spooned steamed egg into rice bowls for the two little boys in matching striped collar shirts.

Fiona and I had never talked about my father. She knew what happened. A long time ago, I'd told her about Lee, the boyfriend of his I'd met in Taiwan. She knew that Baba died by suicide.

"No," I said. "It's not that." I studied the round banchan dishes that surrounded the grill on the table. I felt Fiona's gaze on me. "You sound like my mom," I said finally.

"You told her about Julian?"

"She said I have to forgive him," I said. "My father."

"Maybe," Fiona said slowly, "you're trying to have some sort of do-over, with this Julian situation." I looked up. For a moment I could see clearly through her eyes, all the way to the girls we used to be. "Because he's suffering—depressed—like, well." She paused a moment. "Your dad was—"

"No," I said. "That's crazy. Julian—he has nothing to do with that—"

"You're trying to save him," she said. "Why?"

"You don't understand," I said. "It was my fault—if it wasn't for me, outing him, ignoring his calls—he would still be alive—"

"Jane," she said. "No, that's not true."

"If I didn't tell my mom about what happened—about Lee—"

"What happened wasn't your fault," she said.

"Fiona," I said. "I killed him. What I did—"

"No," she said. "You didn't. You were his daughter. And what he told you about himself—it was too much for you to handle. You did the only thing you could. You told another adult." She paused again and held me in her gaze, soft as anything. I almost hated her then. I wanted to look away, but something made me stay there. Her eyes. All the years between us. I was protected, under her gaze.

"It wasn't your fault, Jane."

I shook my head slowly and glanced down at my lap. I thought of Ping, my old piano teacher, the first girl I ever liked. How I'd run from those feelings—following desperate instinct—after my father told me he was in love with a man, one evening long ago in a subway station in Taipei, on our way home. I was eighteen years old. I was still my father's daughter.

In New York last month, I'd looked for his birthday in those date paintings at the Guggenheim. I'd searched for his death date, too. Some sign from him, telegraphed to me from the ether, beaming through one of those canvases hanging on the immaculate gallery walls while I spiraled down, and down.

He wasn't there.

"I needed you," I said quietly. "I needed you when it happened. When he—"

Fiona was silent.

"You left."

"I had to leave," she said.

"Why?" I asked. "Because of Jasper?"

"I'm sorry," Fiona said. "I just had to."

"Why'd you have to leave?"

"It wasn't Jasper," she said. "Maybe at the time, I thought he was the answer." She shook her head, her brow furrowed in thought. "I needed to get away from my mom, my family." She paused. "Didn't you ever want to leave LA?"

"Sure," I said.

"Why didn't you?"

"I don't know," I said. "I guess I was waiting for you to come back."

The waitress brought the next platter of meat, the marinated strips of pork belly. Fiona used the tongs to lay a few pieces across the hot grill. She asked if I still talked to Julian, and I said no.

I didn't tell her that sometimes Julian still texted me. *I am still alive. I got up today. I am still alive.* I never answered him, but I read the texts, and I feel something loosen inside me each time. Sixteen years since my father died, and I was still alive. I got up, every morning. I lived, day by day.

I had my best friend, Fiona Lin. I had Mah, still, despite everything. Won was here, too—he was working late tonight on a magazine shoot, but Fiona and I had plans to meet up with him later, after dinner. The three of us together again. He'd probably complain that we stank like garlic crisp and charcoal smoke. We were moving fast now, everything sped up; the years seemed to fly past like nothing. I thought of Miss King, our second-grade teacher, who was probably retired by now.

"I have a new idea," I said presently. "For a thing I'm writing." I hesitated a moment. "It's about us."

Fiona shot me a suspicious look. "What are you talking about?"

"Remember your hoopty we used to ride around in?"

"Shamu!" she cried. "You still owe me gas money."

"Remember those janky fake IDs we got from the swap meet?"

Fiona lifted a finger to get the waitress's attention and ordered another soju. We waited for her to bring the green bottle.

"Is it really about us?" she asked. "What's it going to be called?"

"*Jane and Fiona*," I said. "Our stories. All the shit we got into—"

"You know what I think?" she said. "*Fiona and Jane* has a better ring to it."

Acknowledgments

Thank you to the following for grants, residencies, and other material support: The Mastheads; MacDowell; Vermont Studio Center; Yefe Nof Residency; Barbara Deming Memorial Fund; UNLV English and the Beverly Rogers, Carol C. Harter Black Mountain Institute; USC English and USC Dornsife. Thank you to the workshop spaces where parts of *Fiona and Jane* took shape: VONA/Voices; Napa Valley Writers' workshop; Kundiman; Community of Writers; Bread Loaf; Tin House.

Thank you to my agents, Ayesha Pande and Serene Hakim, for your belief in this project, and your vast patience for my tender neuroses and deranged tweets.

Thank you to my editor, Allison Lorentzen, for asking the right questions of this manuscript. Thank you for your wellspring of intellect, confidence, and enthusiasm, from which

I borrowed in order to carry on my work during the COVID-19 pandemic. Thank you also to Camille LeBlanc, and to everyone at Viking.

Thank you to my writing and literature professors, who are all so smart and also very good-looking: Jim Krusoe, Richard Wiley, Doug Unger, Maile Chapman, Jane Hafen, Vincent Perez, Dana Johnson, Viet Thanh Nguyen, Aimee Bender, Emily Hodgson Anderson, David Treuer, Danzy Senna, and Percival Everett. Thank you to Laila Lalami for kindness during an especially difficult time. Thank you, Maaza Mengiste, for introducing Edward P. Jones's *Lost in the City* into my reading life. Thank you, Vanessa Hua. Thank you, brilliant Kundiman faculty (2015, 2017, 2018): Gina Apostol, Sigrid Nunez, Peter Ho Davies, Lan Samantha Chang, Sabina Murray, Matthew Salesses, Jon Pineda, lê thi diem thúy, and Karen Tei Yamashita.

Thank you, Janalynn Bliss, for your wisdom. Thank you, Dr. Angela Liu, for teaching me how to be a person.

Shout-out to the high school besties forever and the hard-boiled editors and the 199 Orchard crew and the ceramic ladies and the SGV food club. A Charleston Chew for Julian Sambrano Jr., an angel on Earth. I stole these words from Sarah Jung, "men are like sharks, they can smell another dick on you like blood in the water"—thank you, wife. Thank you to Sunyoung Lee and Duncan Williams for letting me write in your house, and for all the food and dharma talks. Emily Yamauchi and Sarah Fuchs are two moons in my sky. Fried chicken and a pitcher of beer at the Prince to Neela Banerjee and Ky-Phong Tran. Many rounds of happy hour cocktails at the Stakeout to Brittany Bronson, Regina Ernst, Jessica Durham, and Sam Samson. Thank you, Cynthia Shaffer, a meteorite gemstone. Thank you, Lilliam Rivera and Kima Jones, for the years of encouragement. Thank you, dear Jamel Brinkley. Thank you to the many writers and colleagues I've met through USC, especially Safiya Sinclair, Muriel Leung, Vanessa Villarreal, Amy Silverberg, Lisa Lee, Mike Powers, Mary-Alice Daniel, Nikki Darling, Sam Cohen, and Chris Chien—it's an honor to pursue a doctorate among your giant, wrinkly brains. Thank you, beloved Vickie Vértiz and Kenji Liu (and Momo). Cathy Linh Che, you have my heart. Thank you, sister Monica Sok. Maurice Carlos Ruffin, thank you for bearing witness. Thank you to Angela Flournoy and Ian Blair for the apartment swap, excellent writing vibes, and taking care of my plants. For Xuan Juliana Wang: a mushroom mirror to see your teenage self again. And lastly, I bequeath $300 million each to Jade Chang and Aja Gabel (when my dogecoins hit).

Thank you to my parents, and to my family (in memory, the present, and future—).

A PENGUIN READERS GUIDE TO

FIONA AND JANE

Jean Chen Ho

An Introduction to *Fiona and Jane*

"Years later, I'd think back and remember this night, this moment, standing at the foot of the stairs outside Won's apartment. The night-blooming jasmine giving off its sweet heady scent, carried through the air on a gentle breeze. A dog barked somewhere down the street, twice. Then it was silent again, except for the steady thrum of midnight freeway traffic, the sound of fast cars cutting through the dark. A fake ID in my back pocket that would've fooled no one. Fiona's idea. Always Fiona's ideas, and me, saying yes. My best friend. We shared everything, I believed. Still, she was the one in the driver's seat. I rode shotgun."

When Jane Shen is a high school senior, she flies to Taiwan to visit her father. Over noodles on a humid night, she meets his old friend from college. She's unnerved by their playful intimacy, the wordless language they seem to speak with each other. When her father tells her that he is in love with this man, she feels betrayed, seeing with new eyes his motive for moving to Taipei and leaving her and her mother in California. This sense of abandonment intermingles with a sexual experience of her own, a fleeting relationship with her piano teacher, an older Chinese girl. When Jane returns home, she acts on a split-second impulse she will regret for decades and tells her mother about her father's relationship.

Meanwhile, Jane's beautiful and brilliant best friend, Fiona Lin, can't wait to get out of California. She follows her college boyfriend to New York in an attempt to widen the distance between the life she has known and the one she aspires to, falling out of touch with Jane in the process. Over the course of her twenties, she dates men who end up using and hurting her—one who cheats, another who drains her bank account, both, perhaps, echoes of the father she never had. Weathering heartbreak and hardship, she drops out of law school, the East Coast life she imagined for herself still out of reach.

Each story finds Fiona and Jane at some point along their two-and-a-half-decade friendship, coming together or drifting apart, grappling with the mounting resentments and everyday betrayals that mark even our closest relationships. With emotional clarity and humor, *Fiona and Jane* shines a light on the nuances of Taiwanese American identity, the parts of ourselves that we withhold from those we love the most, and the dizzying, exhilarating experience of growing up in contemporary America.

A Conversation with Jean Chen Ho

Fiona and Jane follows the evolving friendship of two Taiwanese American women over the course of two decades. Did you always know you would write about female friendship? Are there any writers or books that have made you think differently about how to tell these stories?

I've always been interested in writing female protagonists, whether in view of friendship, romance, children and family situations, sexual relationships, work dramas, etc. Asian American women's lives and thematic explorations of race, class, gender, and sexuality is fertile ground for me. Fiction, however, must always begin with compelling characters, so rather than thinking about "friendship" (or anything else) as an organizing principle, I began writing *Fiona and Jane* by simply being avidly curious about who these women were, as people. The foundational groundwork of their friendship is laid in their youth, and part of the fun of reading the stories in *Fiona and Jane*, I hope, is in seeing them find their way back to each other, as adults.

A major influence on *Fiona and Jane* is Toni Morrison's *Sula*, a masterpiece work about two childhood best friends, Sula Peace and Nel Wright. The intimacy and rivalry between them, and the delight they take in each other, is narrative energy that electrifies me every time I revisit the novel.

Why did you decide to tell the story of this friendship, and these women, from the two alternating points of view? Did you find that the story form allowed you more freedom to explore these characters?

Writing in the first person comes naturally to me, so the stories from Jane's perspective were a matter of figuring out her voice, how she sounds at different stages of her life. I chose to tell the stories about Fiona in the third person as a way to more thoroughly mine her interior depths, because this character felt more mysterious and unknown to me; the third person allowed me to take my time and really look around, to pay deep attention to her mind. A first-person story still has the quality of performance to it, because the narrator is telling you this story that's happening to her; a third-person story can take on a more direct feeling. I wanted to use these different manners of storytelling to reveal the two women throughout the book, perhaps to show that things aren't always as they seem—with distance, with time and reflection—and that form in fiction can both mimic and subvert that experience.

Fiona and Jane are both navigating the traumas they have inherited, trying to reconcile the circumstances of heritage with the lives they desire. What was it like to write about mental health as it affects different generations of Asian American immigrants?

Culturally competent mental health services are so important, and not just for Asian Americans—for everyone. I live with depression, and it's made a world of difference to work with a therapist who understands my cultural background. Mental health is a process, I've learned; it's generational and historical, and I believe that the journey to heal a part of your own story, your own person, has ripple effects throughout your community, and through time. In *Fiona and Jane*, I wanted to show that healing is nonlinear, just as I've experienced it in my own life.

Set in Los Angeles, New York, and Taipei, many of the stories in Fiona and Jane *explore the push and pull of home. You were born in Taiwan but grew up in Southern California. How has your relationship with these places changed? Do you ever feel the need to escape California, your family, or your home?*

Well, as I'm answering these questions for the purposes of the Readers Guide, I've lived in some version of quarantine/lockdown for more than a year (due to the COVID-19 pandemic), so yes, I do feel the need to escape California, my apartment in Los Angeles, sometime soon! Please! I'll go anywhere!

In all seriousness, my relationship to Taiwan has certainly changed as I've grown into adulthood (I left the island, with my parents, when I was eight years old). Most of my family still lives in Taipei, including my father, and so I'm lucky to still have people who love me there when I return for visits. My Mandarin is passable, but my Taiwanese Hokkien (the language of my maternal family) has been lost to me. When I hear my mother speak it now, her words make up a familiar song whose tune I can't sing. There's a melancholy that comes with the loss of your first language—the language you spoke with your grandparents. Still, I'm the person I am today because I grew up in California, in the U.S. I can't ever return to the Taipei I knew, as a child; quite literally, that city no longer exists. So the best I can hope for is to continue discovering Taiwan as a place in the now, each time I return. And that's pretty good.

Do you have a friend from childhood who inspired the decades-long friendship between Fiona and Jane? Has this friend read the book?

This story collection isn't inspired by one unique friendship, but rather the many different kinds of close relationships I've experienced with smart, funny, interesting women throughout my life. I do have a group of best friends who I've known since my reckless teenage years, and while none of the particulars in *Fiona and Jane* are taken from our lives, many of the feelings I've tried to excavate in these stories come from a place of reverence for those treasured friendships.

QUESTIONS AND TOPICS FOR DISCUSSION

1. Fiona and Jane betray each other over the years, but in the end, their friendship endures. They are both able to accept the past, forgive each other's mistakes, and recognize the ways the other has changed and grown over the years. Do you think they are able to forgive themselves?

2. Jane grew up solidly middle-class. Born in the United States, she is an only child with college-educated, professional parents. Fiona, on the other hand, helps support her single mother, who is a card dealer at a casino. How do you think class affects their relationship as teenagers? How does it change their relationship as they became adults?

3. Teenage Fiona is remarkably ambitious and self-sufficient. She saves up enough money to buy a car in high school, then she moves to New York and gets into law school. But after her breakup with Jasper, she seems to flounder. She drops out of law school and a dodgy boyfriend drains her bank account. What do you think causes this shift in her character or trajectory?

4. Jasper, Willy, Gabriel, Aaron, Bobby; Carly, the various Korean men, Julian, Naima. What do you think Fiona and Jane seek in romantic partners? Do you think what they look for changes over the years? How much do you think their past informs these attractions (and the relationships that ensue)?

5. When the girls are in high school, people call Jane Fiona's "bodyguard." Throughout the collection there are a number of occasions in which Jane tries to protect Fiona. Where do you think this instinct comes from? When does it succeed and when does it backfire? And where do you think the line between friend and guardian falls?

6. How do you think Jane's relationship to her father's queerness shapes her own attitudes toward identity, dating, and romance? How do you think his struggles with mental health affect her sense of self-worth?

7. Won was such an important friend to Fiona and Jane during their teenage years. What impact do you think he has on their lives? What do you make of how their relationship with him evolves? Have you had a friend like Won, someone who added a special, invaluable element to a dynamic? Are you still in touch?

8. Fiona grew up with a single mother and immigrated to the U.S. as a young girl. How do you think her childhood affects her later desire to escape her family dynamic—to move to New York and forge a new life for herself? In what ways was she successful? In what ways did she create similar, toxic patterns as an adult?

9. Before Fiona moved to New York, she stole five thousand dollars from the pastor's office at Jane's mother's church, while Jane stood guard outside. How do you think this incident changed the girls' relationship?

10. When Fiona and Jane are in their twenties and living on opposite sides of the country, they fall out of touch, the bond of their teenage years marred by unspoken distance. But when Fiona moves back to California in her thirties, they reconnect and their friendship deepens. What do you think causes the distance between them, and how do you think they are able to overcome it? Have you ever had a relationship that withstood fallow years and was able to grow stronger? Do you think there are benefits to taking friendship breaks?

11. Fiona and Jane both have complicated, often-fraught relationships with their mothers. How do you think these relationships affect the girls' sense of home and their place in society? Do their relationships with their mothers change over the years? How are the lives they seek different or similar to the lives their mothers sought?

12. While reading these stories, what surprised you about *Fiona and Jane* in regards to Asian American identity and the way it intersects with race, class, gender, and sexuality? What do you think is the role of fiction in addressing these social, political, and cultural issues in the U.S. today?